Finally Accepted:
A Freedom Lake Novel

TONI SHILOH

Scripture taken from the following versions: New King James Version®. Copyright © 1982 by Thomas Nelson. Used by permission. All rights reserved. Holy Bible, New Living Translation, copyright © 1996, 2004, 2015 by Tyndale House Foundation. Used by permission of Tyndale House Publishers, Inc., Carol Stream, Illinois 60188. All rights reserved.

Edited by Vicky Sluiter.

Cover design by Toni Shiloh.

Cover art photos © iStock.com/asiseeit used by permission.

Published in the United States of America by Toni Shiloh.

www.ToniShiloh.wordpress.com

Finally Accepted is a work of fiction. Names, characters, places, and incidents are either products of the author's imagination or used fictitiously. All characters are fictional, and any similarity to people living or dead is purely coincidental.

ISBN-13: 9781718180321

DEDICATION

To the Author and Finisher of my faith.

Prologue

"Grandma, why is my skin different than yours?" Chloe stared at her arms. They weren't white like the color in the crayon box, but they weren't dark brown like her grandma's.

"Because God made us in all different colors. It's a way for us to remember our uniqueness and how special we are to Him."

It sounded good, but… "I want to be the same color as you."

"Why?"

She frowned. Her grandma always asked a lot of questions. "So I can be Black."

She wasn't sure why people called her grandmother Black. She didn't look like the color but maybe they never heard of dark brown. The kids in her class said she wasn't Black even though her grandma was. It really didn't make any sense to her.

"Well, baby, I'm Black and your mama is Black…"

"So I'm Black?" It came out more a question than a statement as her mind tried to wrap around her grandma's words.

1

Chloe sat up straight. She didn't know what her dad looked like and right now that didn't matter.

My mom is Black. Grandma is Black. "I'm Black," she whispered.

"And loved by God, no matter how light or dark your skin is. Remember that, baby, okay?"

"I will."

Chapter One

C hloe Anne Smith stared at her reflection in the mirror with a new awareness. Her golden skin was the same as before. Her hair a little longer but otherwise the same. The only change was her knowledge—she was biracial.

Somewhere in the back of her brain, she'd often wondered if she was. She'd often been asked the "what are you?" question. No one could ever tell which ethnicity box she should check. Her black spiral curls and tawny-colored skin seemed to clue the Black community in to the fact that she was indeed one of them.

Now that her curls reached her shoulders, they seemed to take on a life of their own. She'd decided to grow them out, hoping they would make her look older, but no such luck. Entering her thirties meant nothing but on paper.

She viewed her wide-spread nose and dark eyes through the mirror's reflection. They were still her features, but not. Knowing her father was Caucasian had somehow changed her. Her identity had been shattered

3

like a precious vase meeting the floor in a kiss of death. The security of who she was ripped off like a bandage covering a seeping wound.

All the times she defended her identity as a Black woman came roaring back, deafening in its replay. Should she have been so zealous in her objection of being labeled light skinned? At the time, she had been defending her heritage as an African American. If it weren't so heartbreaking, she would laugh at life's little ironies.

Chloe winced, remembering the many soap boxes she had stood on in an effort to be seen for who she was. Yet, could a biracial person choose a side? *Should* they? All the times she'd checked Black/African American in the ethnicity box now seemed to mock her. She closed her eyes. Her mother was Black. Her grandmother was Black. She lived in a predominantly Black community.

Doesn't that make me Black?

Yet the letter she received, confirming that John Davenport was her father, informed her of a biracial heritage. It also meant she now had two half-sisters and one half-brother. Jamie, her youngest half-sister, had been sure they were related just based off their eyes and chin.

The 99.99999% accuracy rating of the DNA test overwhelmed her, staggered her in its certainty. Her father had refused all contact with her, but Jamie hadn't. Jamie wanted to know her. To be able to become true sisters, even though they only shared one parent. Chloe wasn't sure if that was possible, but having the option mattered more than she thought it would.

For the seventh time, she reread the DNA results and then carefully folded the letter, placing it back into its envelope. She was the daughter of John Davenport and Charlotte Smith. "Now you know who you are." *So what are you going to do about it, Chloe girl?*

Her ringtone halted her forage into the future. Jamie's face smiled brightly up at her from the display. She answered the call. "Hey, Jamie."

"Hey, Chloe. Do you want to go shopping today?"

"Um, sure, but you know Freedom Lake doesn't have a mall, right?" She wasn't sure Jamie was ready for small-town life, but it didn't stop the girl from constantly making plans.

Jamie's laugh danced delightfully across the lines. It reminded Chloe of a beach commercial targeted for teens. Care free and full of life. Not wilted and in despair that you were officially "in" your thirties with nothing to show for it.

"Of course I know that. I actually want to go furniture shopping, and I heard of this warehouse right outside of Kodiak City."

"Memories?" It was her favorite place to shop for pieces to use in her interior design business. How had Jamie heard of it?

"Yes. You know it?"

"I'm a regular." She straightened up at the prospect of perusing their sales. She adored Memories.

"Awesome. Then you can show me all the best things."

"Wait a moment," Chloe frowned. "Why do you need furniture?"

"I just signed a leasing agreement, so I thought it would be nice to have furniture. You know to sleep on, eat on, etc."

Suddenly she was thankful for the wall which held her slight frame up. *Jamie's moving to Freedom Lake?* Her mind couldn't wrap around the concept. What did it mean?

"Jamie, you don't even know if the test will confirm we're half-sisters." *Because you haven't told her, ninny.*

"I don't need a silly paper to tell me something I already know. But if you want me to wait until you find out, then I'll just go shopping without you."

"Don't do that. I'll go with you."

"So you got the results back then?" The squeak in Jamie's voice hinted at her excitement as subtly as a bull horn.

"Yes." She swallowed, trying to keep her composure.

"I knew it!"

Chloe moved the phone away from her ear.

"I'm so glad I made the decision to move here."

"Did you tell…did you…" she faltered. What did she call the man who supplied half her DNA but refused to acknowledge the fact?

When Jamie divulged his resistance and lack of desire to claim the title of father, her heart broke. Knowing John Davenport didn't want to be her father twisted up her words.

"Yes," Jamie replied, her voice filled with compassion. "I told him I wanted to be near you and get to know you."

"What did he say?" She gripped her cell, nerves stretched taut.

"He hung up," Jamie whispered.

Chloe closed her eyes but it was no use. The pain spread through her whole body as she tried to grasp for calm and peace. Why didn't he want her? Was it so horrible that she had an extra helping of melanin? It's not like he hadn't dated her mom. Maybe it had been a cruel joke.

She knew the pranks high school boys often pulled. The way Evan had teased her best friend, Jo, mercilessly throughout their high school years was testament to the fact. The fact that they were now engaged to be married was proof of God's work in their lives.

Surely You can work this out too?

"You still there, Chloe?"

"Yes."

"You want me to come pick you up? Or do you need time to get ready?"

"No, I'm an early riser. I'll be waiting outside."

"See you in a few."

Jamie's face blinked onto the display before it disappeared. As much as Chloe wanted her father to recognize her as his daughter, she was thankful that she had a sibling willing to call her sister. For now, it would have to be good enough.

Grabbing her stuff, she headed outside to wait. A breeze blew softly against her skin as the sun's rays peeked through the canopy of trees. It was a picturesque moment. One she would cling to while resting in God's beauty. She didn't have to make a decision about the paternity results. For now, she could enjoy the day and warmth of summer.

Jamie arrived in record time, pulling up in a bright yellow Fiat. If it weren't for the fact that Chloe needed ample trunk space for her interior design business she would have bought a similar styled vehicle. Instead, she had ended up with a bright blue Rav4 since yellow hadn't been an option. But maybe she shouldn't have everything dripping with her favorite color.

"Hey, Sis," Jamie said.

"Hey, Jamie."

Once she buckled up, Jamie grinned and stepped on the gas. Ever since they met, Jamie had been trying out different ways to greet Chloe. She said she had a nickname for her other sister and brother and needed to find one for her. Apparently, having a nickname was important to Jamie. Chloe had tried to get her to call her 'Chlo' but Jamie said it didn't sound right. Too much of an old lady. Considering she had about ten extra years on Jamie it seemed fitting, but who was she to argue?

7

Her half-sister glanced at her as they hit the highway headed toward Kodiak City. "I wanted to tell you something, but I wanted to say it face-to-face."

Chloe clutched her tote's handle. "What is it?"

"My brother and sister are coming for a visit next weekend. Or rather, your brother and sister. I mean our brother and sister." She rolled her eyes. "You get the point."

Nerves prevented her from chuckling at the awkwardness. *Would they accept her, or treat her like John Davenport had?* "Did you tell them about the DNA results?"

"I did. Called them on the way over here. Since they were so skeptical about our first meeting, I wanted to tell them right away. Even though I told them how much alike we are, they didn't want to agree until the results came in." Jamie snorted. "O ye of little faith. Anyway, now they want to meet you." Jamie looked at her again.

But she couldn't handle the look. Her mind was already churning, thinking of possible 'hello' scenarios. She let out a sigh as she stared out the window.

"Can I tell you about them now?" Jamie asked, hesitantly.

Before they mailed in the DNA samples, Jamie had been ready to spill the beans about her brother and sister and how she grew up. Only Chloe hadn't let her. *Couldn't let her.* She hadn't wanted to get attached to the idea of having three siblings if the test came back negative.

Lord, please give me peace. Putting on a brave face, she faced Jamie. "I'm ready."

The grin on Jamie's face was worth the apprehension that squeezed her gut. "So, I'm the baby even though I'm legally an adult."

Chloe laughed. "Twenty-one is barely an adult."

"Yeah, yeah, Sissy." Her nose wrinkled up.

Chloe wondered if Sissy would stick or if Jamie would continue to search for a nickname.

"JJ is two years older than me. Everyone calls him JJ even though he's technically a junior."

So her brother was John Junior. She shook her head at the surreal thought.

"Then there's Char, who's twenty-six. She'll probably be in a snit because now you're the oldest and not her. Oh, and Charlotte is her real name."

The pounding in her ears drowned out any other words Jamie had uttered after the name 'Charlotte.' She couldn't breathe. Tightness squeezed her chest as she gripped the door handle, needing an anchor. *Was this really happening?* Slowly, she turned toward Jamie. "Her name is Charlotte?" she rasped out.

Jamie gasped and pulled over. "What's wrong? Are you going to be sick? Do you need to throw up? Should we go back home? What's wrong?"

The questions swirled around her brain, making her dizzy. Heightening the panic that was threatening to ensue.

"My mother…her name is Charlotte."

∼

"You've been a champ today, Brody. You know what that means, right?" Darryl Jones asked his five-year-old patient.

"I get a sticker?"

"You got that right, buddy." He high fived Brody. "Make sure you remind Ms. Luella when you check out."

"Thanks so much, Dr. D."

"Anytime." He nodded to Brody's mother and exited the room, walking toward his office for a much needed breather.

The day was going by swiftly, and he'd been standing on his feet for the majority of it. With a quick glance at his watch, he opened his office door. He had a good 15 minutes before his next patient. It would give him time to review files and check for any urgent messages.

The desk phone had no blinking lights. Maybe he could take a moment and relax. *No.* Even though he was on break, he always took the time to complete any administrational tasks. *Ugh.* He squeezed the sides of his face and froze. Slowly, he removed his hands from his face, peering down at them.

Life had taught him at a young age the power that lay in man's hands. Unfortunately, he'd been shown their destructiveness while his father abused his mother. And then his hands had taken their own journey…had imitated his father. It was in his darkest hour when he decided to turn his life around. To use his hands for good.

The number of patients he and his business partner, Martin Simples, saw on a daily basis exhausted him, but he wouldn't have it any other way. Healing was his life's mission. Well, more like his life's atonement. He'd swore to himself he'd never use his hands to harm again. Only to heal.

And he wouldn't get much healing done if they didn't bring another doctor into the practice. He leaned back into his chair and let out a sigh. Parents had begun to murmur complaints on their wait time. Fortunately, the care they received outweighed their displeasure. Deep down, he knew he could only ask them to be patient for so long. Hopefully Jordan Kelley would accept his offer and join the practice. Except she had to okay it with her fiancé. For some reason, she hadn't brought her fiancé around for everyone to meet. She really hadn't said much about him. But who was he to judge?

He'd found that special someone and knew he'd fallen short.

There would be no falling in love. The one he admired would never look at him with adoration. Not with what he lied about in his past. Still, he wanted what Jordan had. What his friends Evan and Jo had. What Guy and Michelle had. Everyone from their Bible study group was pairing off, and he was the lone man out. His deepest wish was to be able to have the same thing.

With Chloe.

She was the most beautiful woman he had ever met, inside and out. She embodied perfection from the top of her curly hair to the bottom of her dainty feet. He longed to care for her. When he thought of the American dream, he pictured her by his side. There was nothing more that he wanted than to shower her with love and cherish her for the rest of his life.

Except he wasn't good enough to breathe the same air. He grabbed a fistful of hair, wishing he could give his brain a jolt instead. He grimaced at the feeling of hair on his ears. His curls were getting longer and entering the unruly phase. If he got a haircut, would Chloe like it?

He groaned and placed his face in his hands. Why couldn't he get her out of his head? He stared at his hands, knowing where'd they'd been. The things they'd touched. The harm they had inflicted on others. They weren't worthy to touch her. He would only ruin the best thing he'd ever known.

No, there was no way he could ever have Chloe as a girlfriend let alone as a life mate. He would just have to continue going through life alone. Or at least until he made up for every past sin he'd ever committed. He knew God was working on him. Trying to show him who He really was. Hopefully the Lord looked on and knew how much he wanted to atone for his sins.

His sports watch beeped. Time was up. He shook his

head at his negligence. He hadn't looked at the next patient's file yet. He pulled Brianna's file up, quickly scrolling through it. Assured that he remembered her history, he headed for the Barney-themed exam room, as the kids and staff referred to it.

Per usual, he knocked twice before walking into the exam room. "Good morning, Brianna, how are you?"

Her bottom lip poked out and the damp curls around her face showed signs of an illness. Her mom had called in early for a sick appointment, concerned Brianna had food poisoning.

"My tummy hurts really bad, Dr. D."

"I'm sorry to hear that. I'm going to do my best to get you well." He looked at her mother. "You told Stacy this has been going on since last night?"

"Yes. We went out to a new restaurant that just opened. About an hour after we got home, she started throwing up nonstop. She didn't keep anything down, not even water."

After examining Brianna, he had to agree with the mother. A food poisoning prognosis looked like an accurate fit. Most parents didn't realize how accurate they were in their diagnosis. Often, they let the lack of degree intimidate them into silence. Or worse, a doctor with a bad bedside manner had silenced them with his ego and pride.

"Mom, you made the right decision bringing her in." He made eye contact with Brianna's mom. "We're going to need to take her to the hospital so we can get some fluids in her. They'll also be able to run some tests. If it's a viral infection, we'll have to let it run its course. If it's bacterial, antibiotics will get her on the mend much quicker. I'll also check with the restaurant to see if there were any other complaints. Do you want to drive her to the hospital?"

"Yes, I can do that."

He offered a smile. "Great, I'll stop by once they've admitted her and check on her. You can head straight there. Stacy will give them a call to let them know you're on the way."

"Thanks, Dr. Jones."

"My pleasure."

With a sense of urgency, he headed to the nurse's station to let Stacy know of the latest development. He sighed. Days like this had he and Martin scrambling. Although Freedom Lake wasn't a huge town, it still had lots of traffic in the pediatric department. More and more city folk were moving to the town for the simple kind of life. He really hoped Jordan accepted his offer. The practice couldn't go on like this much longer.

"Stacy, notify Freedom Lake Hospital that Brianna is arriving for possible food poisoning."

"On it. By the way, you have a message from a Jordan Kelly."

"Yes!" He did a fist pump and turned around in the hallway, toward his office. With any luck he could get her on the schedule before the week was over. Her yes would be a spark of hope. Assuming she called to confirm her spot. Her answer could turn his Monday around or drag it down into the gutter.

Darryl hated Mondays. The hustle and bustle of kids that came in sick was immense. He wanted to offer a Saturday clinic for a few hours, but he and Simples were already swamped. *Lord, there's got to be a way to bring relief. I know I'm hoping Jordan will say yes, but it's just as likely she'll want to go into her own practice, or that her fiancé will want her to take a hiatus before jumping back to work. Please, please help me, if You're listening.*

Only time would tell if God heard his prayers. Evan and Guy had encouraged him to pray and try God, but it felt weird. Did God listen to non-Christians' prayers? He wouldn't be surprised if He didn't. It wasn't as if he was on the good list. Or was that Santa he was thinking of?

He smoothed his curly hair from his face. Other patients awaited, but first things first. A voicemail and a returned phone call were a must.

Chapter Two

The appeal of Memories Furniture Warehouse did nothing to penetrate the shock of hearing she had a half-sister with her mother's name. What were the odds? It was obvious John Davenport—she couldn't bring herself to think of him as her father—had feelings for her mother, even though he refused to admit it.

Then again, his wife could have picked the name and he, in the same stoic manner he shunned her mother with, refused to argue the atrocity of naming his daughter after an ex-girlfriend. One he'd fathered a child with. Then again, knowing he denied Chloe's mother's claim could explain his actions. The whole story made her want to curl up into a ball and never leave her bed.

A few months ago, one of her good friends had tried to find her biological father at Chloe's request. Michelle ended up finding one of her mother's old classmates who knew the story of how her mother became pregnant. And how John Davenport cast aside her mother as well as the life brimming inside her belly. Some thirty plus years later, he still didn't want to claim Chloe.

She sighed, staring at the black dresser.

"What's wrong, Big Sis?"

"Uh…" her mind went blank. Jamie didn't need an inside look at her thoughts. "What kind of look are you after?" She faced Jamie, thankful for the distraction of furniture shopping. Maybe if she focused solely on her little sister it would help.

Little sister. She gave a mental shake of the head. It was still too new. Would she ever get used to it?

"I want something grown up, yet…whimsical."

Chloe chuckled. That sounded exactly like something she would go for. Interesting how similar their taste was. "Whimsical, whimsical, whimsical," she mumbled, tapping her finger against her chin.

Chloe knew Memories inside and out. Of course, she had been here more times than she could count, thanks to her clients, but she would have frequented the shop for herself alone. The store was just that fantastic. Plus, the manager happily gave her a discount for all the business she brought his way. Her gaze traveled the length of the store. "I've got it!"

"What?" Jamie exclaimed.

Motioning to Jamie, she headed toward the back of the warehouse toward the left corner. The store separated everything by color, which made it easy if you were shopping by color, not so easy if you were shopping for a specific piece. If Jamie did have similar taste to Chloe, then white would give her the whimsical look she hoped for.

The white furniture section loomed ahead. "You want whimsical. Nothing states that like soft colors. I know a lot of people think white is harsh, but you can grab neutral colors or muted colors to accent and soften the palate. When I think whimsical, I think a blend of fantasy and romance. Candlelight or string lights, perhaps some drapes over the bed."

Pausing for breath, she turned to catch her little sister's gaze. She smiled at the look of shock on Jamie's face.

"That's perfect," her sister breathed out. "My room back home is similar, but it's more girly. The colors are all pinks and purple. I want to show I'm an adult, but I don't want to lose the tranquility or peaceful feel of it. I want my room to speak to my style now, not my teenage years."

"We can do that."

Jamie squealed. "Thank you so much, CeeCee." Jamie pumped a fist in the air. "Yes, that's it! That's what I'll call you. CeeCee." Jamie wrapped her thin arms around her, squeezing her tight.

It had been a while since she had been hugged by anyone in her family. She closed her eyes, touched by the hug. It squeezed her heart and raised her emotions. It felt like hope. Like love. Better yet, like acceptance.

I'm not alone.

Jamie ended the hug, her exuberance still flying high.

The rest of the shopping expedition took off since they had the mood of the room pinned down. Chloe loved the process of creating a vision and bringing it to life. It was why she had become an interior designer. That, and she loved to play around with color. Her grandmother had always teased her for using odd colors in her coloring book, but she'd like to think it was her artistic eye developing.

On the way back to Freedom Lake, silence filled the small vehicle. Chloe wanted to ask Jamie questions, to get to know her, but she was at a loss. What did you ask someone who was related to you, but who you've only known a month?

"Jamie, do you guys ever visit your grandmother? I couldn't help but wonder why I've never run into you before?"

Her father's mother stilled lived in Freedom Lake. Shouldn't he and his family have visited before?

"Dad had a falling out with Grandmother." Jamie curled her lip. "At least, that's what he said. We've never visited, talked on the phone...you get the drift."

So she wasn't the only one Mrs. Davenport wasn't acknowledging.

"Does it bother you?"

"No," Jamie answered with a shrug. "Mom's grandparents are great, so I never felt like I was missing something."

"Makes sense."

"So, what about you Chloe? Are you dating? Seeing anyone special? Interested in anyone?" The stream of questions flew from Jamie's mouth.

"Uh, no. I'm not dating or seeing anyone."

"Then there's someone you're interested in?"

A picture of Darryl flashed in her mind. Interested wasn't a word she would use. Captivated. Mesmerized. In awe of...well, that was more phrase than words.

"Well..." Jamie nudged her with her elbow.

"I, uh...yes, there's someone I'm interested in." She looked at her hands, staring at the brown lines on the palm of her hand. Did brown lines mean she was more black than white? She blinked. "I don't think he's interested."

"Why not? Do you talk to him?"

"Sort of. He's in my Bible study group."

Jamie looked at her then faced the road, zipping down the highway.

"Jamie, the speed limit is fifty-five."

"I know."

She frowned. "You're going sixty-five."

"You drive the speed limit?" The skepticism tinging her little sister's voice was almost hilarious.

"I do. Not only that, I know the sheriff. He has no problem giving you a ticket."

"Oh fine."

Chloe sighed in relief as the car slowed to the appropriate speed.

"How do you know the sheriff?" Jamie waved her hand. "Never mind. Freedom Lake is small."

"That and he goes to my Bible study."

"What?" Jamie squinted at her. She bit her lip and looked forward. "So you and religion…that's like a big thing for you?"

"Yes. You?" Finally, a conversation starter to get to know her.

"Um, not so much."

Okay, maybe she needed an easier conversation starter. Please give me the words, Lord. "May I ask why?"

"No real big reason. My mother believes in Him, but Dad…" her voice trailed off as her fingers tapped the steering wheel. "I just don't see any evidence that He makes a difference in people's lives. That's what He's supposed to do, right?"

"Definitely. Would you like to come to Bible study with me? My friends are a real testament to how He changes lives."

A puff of air escaped Jamie's lips. "I don't know. Couldn't you just tell me about the changes?"

"Sure." Chloe settled back into the seat. "Let's start with my friend, Evan. He lost his leg over a year ago in a car accident."

"Oh my word!"

"I know. He was full of anger when he moved back to Freedom Lake. He had to live with his mom and dad. Depend on them. But you should see him now." She smiled thinking of how happy he and Jo were.

They lit up whenever the other would walk into a

room. Always seeking each other, wanting to be with one another. "The light of God's love shines through him now. It's rare to see him *not* smiling."

"Wow." Jamie looked at her again. "How do you feel about God now that you know who your father is? Do you think knowing God helps you any?"

And wasn't that the question that kept her up at night?

∽

"This is the Looney Tunes room." Darryl motioned to one of the exam rooms. He watched Jordan, searching for any clue as to what she was thinking.

"Uh-huh."

He frowned. She'd had the same noncommittal response to all the rooms he showed her. "What do you think?"

"I think the clinic definitely has enough patients to warrant a third doctor. I'm just not sold on the décor of the whole place." Her hands motioned around as if she didn't know what to make of it.

The creases on his head deepened, or at least they felt like they did. "I think the kids like it."

"Really? Has anyone ever said they do or do they complain?"

Darryl folded his arms across his chest. Some of the older kids complained, but the younger ones really didn't say anything. Sighing, he relayed his thoughts to Jordan.

"Exactly. You need to either appeal to the masses, or create rooms based on age groups. The sick rooms can also be jazzed up a bit so that kids are comforted while miserably waiting around for the doctor."

"Okay, we can have a meeting with Simples and discuss the changes you're recommending."

"Great," she clapped her hands together. "You wouldn't happen to know an interior designer, would you?"

Did he ever. He cleared his throat. "Yeah, you remember Chloe from Bible study?" At her nod, he continued. "She's an interior designer. Her shop is right across the street from the Sheriff's department."

"Fantastic! I could get a quote from her so we know how much it will cost."

The idea of Chloe in his workplace was mind numbing. How would he act? What could he say? After seeing him at work, would she think he was a good doctor? Would he be able to work closely with her for the decorating? He let out a sigh.

He had no business hanging around Chloe.

It was best that he stayed away from her. He could let Jordan or Simples lead that project. "If you could get a quote that would be great. I'll double check with Simples, but I think Thursday evening would be the perfect time to sit down and discuss it."

"Say five?"

"Better make it five thirty. It'll ensure the last patients have been taken care of."

"Thank you so much for giving me this opportunity, Darryl. I look forward to working with you and Martin."

He flashed a smile. "Believe me, we couldn't be happier. We've needed the extra hands, and your last practice had wonderful things to say about you."

Her grin widened, brightening her latte colored skin. She had an engaging grin the kids were sure to love. He patted her arm. "I'll see you soon."

"Thanks again."

With a nod, he walked toward his office. Running a hand down his face, his mind swirled, thoughts running rampant. He had no idea if he could manage to stay away from Chloe while she decorated the office. Then again, Simples could nix the whole idea.

"No need to stress out now," he whispered to himself.

The sound of a ringing phone penetrated his reverie. He stopped in the doorway of his office, noticing the flashing light on his personal line. He reached for it before it could ring again. "Dr. Jones, how may I help you?"

"Darryl?"

His heart stopped. "Mama?" he whispered.

A sniffle greeted his ears.

"How did you get this number?" Caution underlined his words.

"Your grandmother gave it to me."

What? She had talked to his grandmother? He sank into his chair, squeezing his eyes shut. "Where are you?"

"I'm living in Ohio now."

He nodded, then shook his head in derision. She wouldn't be able to see the movement. "Are you well?"

"I am. I'm…I'm remarried."

And the hits kept rolling. "Is he…" He couldn't make his lips form the question in his heart.

"He's a good man, Darryl. I think you'd like him. I'd like it if you'd come and visit."

His mouth dropped open in shock. She wanted him to visit? To act like the past sixteen plus years had never happened? He squeezed the phone. "Well as you know, I'm a doctor. My schedule isn't free like that."

"Oh, I understand." Yet her sad tone told another tale.

He sat up straight, determined not to be swayed. "I'll talk to you another time. I have to go; patients are waiting."

"Sure, I understand. Think about what I said. It's an open invitation."

"Sure thing. Good-bye." *Mama* went unspoken, and he hung up the phone.

Darryl gripped the edge of his desk. What had just happened? Why would she call now? He hadn't seen his mother since she'd walked out of the house without a backward glance, leaving him to live with his grandmother.

As much as he appreciated the life his grandmother had given him, she had been unable to give him the one thing he wanted most...a mother. Ruby Jones was a fierce woman and highly respected, but she didn't always show her love. Darryl knew she loved him as sure as his next breath, but to be hugged more, to be praised more, would have been nice.

Without thinking, he grabbed the phone and called his grandmother.

"Hello?" Her strong voice filled his ears.

"Hello, Grandmother."

"Darryl, what are you up to? Shouldn't you be working?"

He chuckled. She was probably frowning at the grandfather clock in her apartment, wondering why he wasted his work hours calling her. "I'm on break. Listen, I had an interesting phone call just now."

"Ah, so she called."

She wasn't even going to deny it? Who was she and what had she done with his grandmother? "Yes, she did."

"I imagine you're surprised." It came out more statement then question.

"I am."

"I thought so. Didn't think you'd waste your break on me, but I knew I'd be hearing from you." The stern manner of her voice seemed hard, but it was familiar. She'd always talked that way.

It was the voice that had lectured, reprimanded, and barked out orders throughout his high school life. Listening to her talk had been a shock for the first few months. After living with a woman who seemed to speak timidly about everything, even something as simple as how hot or cold it was outside, his grandmother's voice had seemed to pummel him. He exhaled, pulling himself back to the present. "She said you gave her my number."

"Well, of course I did, Darryl. She's your mother after all."

"Hmm, seems she forgot that some years ago."

"A mother never forgets, no matter how much time has passed."

He shook his head. Since when did she have anything nice to say about the woman who had birthed him? "Don't you think she should have called a long time ago?"

"Perhaps she wasn't ready."

What did that mean?

A knock on the door interrupted him. He let out a heavy sigh. "Grandmother, I have to go, but I *will* talk to you later."

"You know where to find me."

He hung up. "Come in."

Martin poked his head through the door. "Brianna took a turn for the worse. They want you at the hospital."

"Got it. I'll call in as soon as I can." He took off his lab coat and grabbed his keys.

"I'll be praying," Simples said.

With a nod, he hustled out the door. *Lord, please let her be okay.*

Chapter Three

*T*he door chime trilled, the sound echoing in the shop. Chloe looked up, a smile prepared to greet the visitor, but it froze in place as Jordan Kelley walked in. *What is* she *doing here?*

The woman had recently joined the Bible study group she attended. The group started off with her, Jo, Michelle, Evan, Darryl, and Guy. Then Jordan and Claire had joined. For some reason, Darryl and Jordan seemed to hit it off. Was it because they were both doctors? And if not, why did she care so much?

"Hi, Chloe. Are you busy?" Jordan stared at her, a look of anticipation on her face.

She froze, surprised at the emotions rising inside. She did *not* want to help her. "Uh, no I'm not busy." *But I wish I was.*

The snarky tone echoed in her head. Where was all this animosity coming from? She wanted to dismiss the reason behind her irritation, but all she could think about was how much Darryl had talked to Jordan at their last Bible study. Like no one else existed. Like *she didn't* exist.

Not to mention, the absence of a ring on Jordan's finger bothered her immensely. Wasn't she supposedly engaged?

"Fantastic," Jordan exclaimed, bypassing the yellow sofa. She headed straight for the yellow-and-gray chevron chair placed in front of Chloe's design board. Jordan sat her purse in her lap. "I wanted to get a quote for your services."

Great. Chloe eyed her warily. "I take it you've found a place to move into?"

"Oh, no," Jordan said with a wave of her hand. "I want my office space redecorated. I'll be working with Darryl."

Her heart stopped.

Jordan would be working with Darryl? She'd see him every day? Well at least eight hours' worth? She swallowed, trying to get the lump in her throat to go down. It was high school all over again. The pretty, popular girl with the jock. Only now Darryl was a doctor. *Both of them are doctors.*

"I see," she said carefully.

"Of course, the other partners have to agree on the changes. Do you have time now, or should I make an appointment?" Jordan's brown eyes twinkled. Her long, wavy, black hair was pulled into a classic ponytail. She screamed class and sophistication. And friendliness.

Why did she have to be so friendly? Chloe looked down, trying to stop a frown from showing on her face. It was the friendliness that made her put forth the effort of shoving down her emotions. But they wanted to rise up, be noticed.

She felt so inadequate in the other woman's presence. Suddenly her maxi dress and curly hair screamed disheveled instead of the cool sophistication Jordan oozed. Did she look professional? Did Darryl prefer women like Jordan?

"So," Jordan said slowly. "Do I need to come back?"

Shaking her head, Chloe pulled herself together. "No, sorry. I was just in the middle of my current project, so it took me a little bit to switch gears." *Lord, please forgive that lie. I don't want her to know how much she unnerves me.* "Right now is fine. Give me a moment to get some blank paper. I'll listen to your thoughts and vision for the place."

"Perfect." Jordan flashed another grin.

She tried to answer in like manner, but knew her smile was forced. She didn't know if she would ever like Jordan...not as much as Darryl appeared to. Chloe placed her sketchpad and notebook on the desk and moved her design board over. "So you're redecorating the clinic?"

"Yes. The rooms' themes are severely outdated."

"Themes? What do you mean?"

"Darryl has one for each room. There's Barney, Sesame Street, Looney Tunes...you get the drift. Unfortunately, kids don't watch those shows anymore. Well maybe Sesame Street." Jordan flicked her wrist. "Plus, the teenagers probably cringe every time they have to be in one of those rooms."

Yikes. She could only imagine. "Okay, I'm tracking. Tell me what your vision is."

Jordan clamored on excitedly. Her hands moved to the rhythm of her speech. At first it distracted Chloe, but little by little the fervor of a new space claimed her thoughts and attention. She jotted down notes as Jordan explained her ideas. Would Darryl go for the changes?

Finally, Jordan paused for a breath. "Can you make that a reality?"

She nodded distractedly. "Let me sketch out some preliminary designs. Hold on." The draft pencils beckoned to her as her thoughts began to form.

She sketched, she looked, and sketched some more. When she was done, she showed it to Jordan.

"Here's a theme room for the younger crowd." She pointed to the yellow room. "This could appeal to the boys. The ones in love with Paw Patrol. I'm thinking it'll be the toddlers to about seven." She pointed to another sketch with the same background color. "Or you can go neutral and nix themes related to TV shows." The T-Rex taking up wall space on the exam room sketch roared. "This way you don't have to worry about redecorating every time a TV show becomes old news."

Flipping the page, she showed Jordan another sketch. "This could be for the teenagers. They want cool and hip, or whatever terms they're using these days. The abstract art is distracting so they won't feel awkward about their visit and cool enough they may even snapchat or tweet the inside."

"Wow," Jordan exclaimed. "I love it. This is exactly what I'm going for."

For the first time since Jordan had walked in, a genuine smile stretched across Chloe's face. She loved it when she turned the vision to reality. "Great. I can work up a quote, if you can tell me approximately how many rooms and the size of them. If you don't have that information with you now," she turned and opened her drawer, pulling out a card. "Here's my card with my contact info. Email it and I'll be sure to get the quote to you within a few hours."

Jordan beamed. "Thank you so much, Chloe. This will definitely win the guys over."

"Sure." She watched as Jordan stood, her navy dress showcasing her figure, but with pizazz.

The doctor walked out with pep to her step. She seemed nice enough, but Chloe wasn't sure how much Jordan faked and how much was real. For all she knew, Jordan wanted to be more than coworkers with Darryl. A couple of Bible studies here or there had yet to reveal her true character. Of course, there was always the horrible thought that Jordan truly was a nice person. That would mean Chloe's imagination had blown the whole thing out of proportion.

Help!

Chloe grabbed her keys and blindly headed for the door. The tumult of emotions rolling around her mind threatened to upend her balanced state. She needed to talk to someone to keep from feeling like a hamster. Locking her shop door, she walked a few feet over to Michelle's law office.

When her friend first moved back to Freedom Lake, she had been apprehensive. They had stopped talking 13 years' prior because her zeal for Scripture had hurt Michelle when she needed her the most. Thankfully, they had patched up their relationship.

It had been great hanging out with Michelle and Jo again. It reminded her of their high-school days with the added bonus of age and wisdom. She didn't know how she would manage life if she didn't have her girlfriends to help her get through its ups and downs.

She walked in and greeted Michelle's paralegal, Tanya. "Hey, Tanya, is Chelle in?"

"Yes, she is. She's having lunch with Guy."

"Oh." *Drat.* She needed to talk to someone.

"Should I let her know you're here?"

"No, please don't bother her. I know how hard it is for them to have time alone."

Tanya chuckled. "Twins make the perfect chaperones."

She laughed in agreement. Since their engagement, Guy's twin girls made it hard for the couple to find alone time without precious kids vying for attention. She stilled as Michelle popped her head out of her office.

"Hey, Chlo. I thought I heard your voice." Michelle walked over, and they exchanged a hug.

"Yeah, Tanya was just telling me about your lunch date."

"I was just leaving."

She turned at the smooth baritone. Guy walked forward, his sheriff's uniform crisp. He kissed Michelle softly. "See you later, Chelle Belle."

"Bye, handsome."

With a wink, he headed for the front door.

"You guys are so cute." She wanted that…with Darryl.

Michelle snorted. "I'm more than cute, girlfriend."

"You're a nut."

"Someone has to be the life of the party." Michelle grinned, wiggling her eyebrows. At her lack of laughter, Michelle's face became serious. "What's wrong?"

"Everything." She glanced down at her hands. "You have time to talk?"

"Always, my friend."

She followed Michelle back to her office, settling down into the wingback chair. Michelle sat in the seat next to her instead of at her desk.

"So what's going on, Chlo?"

Finally, a moment to unburden herself. Hopefully her friend would be able to sort out her emotions. She angled the chair and met Michelle's gaze. "Okay, Jordan came in and asked for a quote on my services. Apparently, she'll be working with Darryl. On the one hand I'm excited about a new project, on the other hand…" she paused, staring off into space as an image of Darryl occupied her mind. "On the other hand, it's Darryl's office."

Silence met her ears. Frowning, she looked at Michelle. "Aren't you going to say anything?"

"Do you want me to help you or do you just want to vent, girl?"

"What kind of question is that?" *Lord, I thought friends were supposed to help.*

"I have a lot I could say, but I don't know if you want me to help you with your problem or just listen in sympathy."

Her mouth dropped open. "I... both? I don't know."

Michelle leaned forward, resting a palm on her leg. "You like Darryl, don't you?"

Suddenly, she felt trapped. She'd been dancing around her feelings for what felt like forever. She'd assumed Michelle and Jo knew, but never came out and said it aloud. If she said yes it would make it real, but if she said no, she'd be lying. "Yes," she rasped out.

"Then let him know. I sincerely doubt you have anything to worry about with Jordan. I think she's just one of those women who are nice to everyone they meet."

"But what if Darryl likes her?"

"Then let him know you like him. Don't be shy. Don't hesitate. Just lay all the cards out on the table."

Her mind shouted at the impossibility of it all. How could she tell him she liked him? How could she convey how much her heart tripped over itself when he walked in the room? That she wanted to run her hands through his mop of curls and kiss him until her toes curled? He would think she was crazy. A stalker even.

"I don't know, Chelle. He's never hinted at any romantic interest."

Michelle snorted. "That's because you're too scared to see what's right in front of you. Believe me, he likes you. And if you doubt me, go ask Jo. She'll agree in a heartbeat."

Chloe stared at Michelle, seeing sincerity and truth shine in her hazel eyes. "Okay, I can try."

"Don't try, just tell him, Chlo. The world will be a happier place. Then there won't be such tension at Bible study."

She gaped at her friend. "There isn't tension."

"You and Darryl may be blind, but the rest of us aren't." Michelle arched an eyebrow as if daring Chloe to argue.

"Okay," she huffed out and came to a stand. "I should probably get back to work, but I appreciate you listening."

"Anytime. Be sure to call as soon as you tell him. Better yet, make it at Bible study so I can see his face."

She laughed. "Whatever, Chelle. You leading this Friday?"

"First time for everything."

"Don't worry, God will guide you." With a wave she left.

She could only pray that God would guide her as well, because it was time to let Darryl know how she felt. Even if the thought rolled her stomach.

❧

Darryl stepped out the back door onto his deck. Today had started off well but crashed and burned in the final hours of his shift. It didn't look too good for Brianna. Nothing had prepared him for it. Every doctor tried to work with the information they were given, but sometimes it wasn't good enough.

He ran a hand over his curls. Why couldn't he leave the trauma of the day at work? Instead it weighed on him like an albatross, reminding him he was only human and didn't have the final say in life or death. The look on Brianna's mother's face would haunt him for a while, especially if Brianna didn't make it. What he assumed was a simple food poisoning case had turned to much more.

Her pancreas seemed to be shutting down. If this last round of treatment didn't work, Brianna was looking at surgery. It was still touch and go. "Don't think like that," he whispered to himself.

He looked around his yard in hopes for a distraction. His little charcoal grill sat off to the side. Jo had recently finished redoing Guy's deck. Maybe he should ask her to turn his into an outside living space. He squeezed his eyes shut.

He didn't really care about the deck, but he needed to change his thoughts. Needed to think about anything other than the young girl battling for her life. A picture of Chloe filled his senses, and he inhaled a ragged breath.

Chloe.

How she haunted him, day and night. She was perfection in every way, but too perfect for him. "Lord, will I ever be good enough for her? Ever?"

The words seemed to echo in the night air, but there was no one to receive them. No one to come home to and share the burdens that weighed heavily upon him. He was alone in the world. Sure, he had his friends, but they each had their own lives. Evan and Guy were on their way to making their own families. He wanted to belong to a family, to be accepted for who he was, and wanted regardless of his faults.

Darryl stared at his hands, memories pushing toward the surface. *No.* He'd never be accepted entirely. Not if others knew his secrets, knew his sins. They'd bounce quicker than a rubber ball from a gumball machine. *Maybe one day someone will accept me. Maybe.*

Walking back inside, he tried to ignore the downward turn of his thoughts. It wasn't going to help him. It wasn't going to ease the ache of knowing he'd never be with Chloe. Instead, it would just widen the depression and the black abyss ready to swallow him whole. He stopped, the Bible on his coffee table staring up at him. Calling to him.

Could it really contain all the answers? Chloe lived by it. She seemed to devote every minute and every day to the God it talked about. He'd started reading it and going to church in the hopes that he would become good enough for her. He wanted her acceptance badly, badly enough to go to church and hear about a God he didn't believe existed.

Then Bible study had begun to chip away at his beliefs. Now the possibility of God had become real enough that he'd opened the lines of communication. Yet, silence met him at every turn. He swallowed, staring at the book. It could all be a hoax, but he was desperate enough for the salvation God seemed to offer. If what he had learned in Bible study was true, God's grace covered his sins. It was possible to be forgiven for what he'd done. He just didn't think it would make him welcome in the religious circles if they knew his past. They were too perfect. Had lived the Christian life too long.

Odd how the one woman he wanted was unattainable thanks to the tragedies of his childhood. "Lord, if I can't have her, please bring her someone worthy." He winced at the thought, but swallowed it down anyway.

Perhaps a good night's sleep would bring peace and keep his thoughts and what-ifs from piling on him.

"Here's your dinner, Hank." His mother watched her husband as he cut his steak.

He made a nod of approval as a thin line of pink showed.

Darryl held his breath as his father took the first bite. Would he find it to his satisfaction? He wanted to glance at his mother, but knew his father disliked sudden movements.

His father grunted. "'Bout time you fix a steak right."

Darryl watched his mother's shoulders sag in relief.

"Eat up, boy."

"Yes, sir." He cut his steak, thankful he could eat now. He'd been hungry since the moment he walked through the front door. But the old man never allowed snacking in-between meals. 'I don't work for you to eat up all the food,' was his father's favorite saying.

Before he could take a bite of his dinner, the sound of a shattering plate pierced the air. He dropped his fork, nerves and worry meeting to form a ball of dread in the pit of his stomach. Turning slowly, he looked in horror as his father gripped his mother's arm, his knuckles white from the force of his hold.

"You trying to kill me, woman? I don't eat cold green beans. How difficult is it to serve me a hot plate of food? Restaurants do it all the time, yet you haven't been able to since the day we married."

"I'm sorry, Hank," his mother stammered out, eyes welling with tears.

Whether they were from fright or pain, Darryl couldn't tell.

"I'll make sure you're sorry. Fixin' me a friggin' mess of cold vegetables. Like I slave away at work all day long to come home to some cold food. You've got to be kidding me."

His mother dropped to her knees, the pain too much, unbearable. Darryl could see it in her eyes. The way they glazed over, making the brown color lose life. Just a haze of pain.

Anger welled up, hot and fast, unfurling through him so *fast he thought steam would surely pour from his pores. His hands balled into fist as he watched tears slip down his mother's face. "Leave her alone!"*

Darryl stood, chest heaving with rage. He was sick and tired of his father bullying his way around the house. They couldn't breathe loudly for fear his father would pummel them into silence.

His father's eyes squinted at him, words flying from his mouth that weren't fit for general audiences. "Who do you think you're talking to, boy?"

Bravely, he took a step closer to his father's seat. "You." He tried to match the ferocious tone but the anger blinded him, rendered him deaf to where he could no longer hear his own voice.

"Darryl, sweetie, you need to sit down and eat your food."

"You better listen to your mother. You may think you're a man, but one round with me would show you otherwise."

"I'm more of a man then you'll ever be. I'd never place my hands on my wife."

The slam of the dining room chair against the wall increased the tension in the room. His mother sagged onto the floor. His father had flung her aside, a new target now in his focus. The old man took a few menacing steps toward him, but he refused to back down.

"Hank, no!"

He watched as his mother grabbed his father's arm to stop his movement. A look of disgust darkened his father's eyes to black coals, a soul nowhere in sight. With little effort, his father snatched his arm from his mother's grasp and swung his arm backward.

The slap rang loudly in his ears.

His mother crumpled to the floor.

"Don't touch her!" Rage turned into something darker. Thought had fled. There were only raw emotions coursing through Darryl's body. With a yell, he charged his father, legs pumping with action that only the best running backs seemed able to do. He jumped, ramming into his father with his shoulder. The force of his body knocked his father down.

His hands found their way to the old man's neck. Began squeezing, crushing the air from his father's body. Hands reached up to pull his away, but his rage had made him strong. Stronger than the six-feet-two-inch man that was trapped under the force of his frenzy filled teenage body.

Darryl sat up in bed, his heart pounding, his shirt clinging to his damp torso. He hadn't had the dream in years, but it was still the same, as if it hadn't missed a day. He inhaled, trying to slow his heart and breaths, but it didn't work. Swinging his legs off the bed, he laid his head in his hands.

In. Out.

He took a longer breath.

In. Out.

Finally, his heart slowed, the pulse pounding in his ears no longer drummed with the force of a taiko drummer. He stood up, noting the time. 3:00 am. Hopefully a cup of warm milk would do the trick.

To erase the nightmare. The reality of his memories. To soothe him back into a dreamless sleep.

Hopefully.

Chapter Four

*W*ednesday evening, Chloe locked the back door to The Space. With a sigh, she headed for her car. The day had been utterly draining. A new couple had moved to town and wanted their entire home decorated. They had sold all their old furniture and wanted to give her carte blanche.

She shuddered.

A customer who had no design in mind equaled a living nightmare. Some interior designers would love to put their creative stamp on a blank project, but it gave her a headache. Instead, she'd be forced to come up with tons of solutions knowing full well the customer would shoot them all down because it wasn't what they 'envisioned.' Whether people realized it or not, they had their own personal style and taste in décor.

Unfortunately, some people just weren't sure what they wanted. Or how to figure it out. It was always after they shot down hundreds of style boards that they figured out what their tastes were. Thankfully, she had created a home décor quiz a long time ago to help those types of clients narrow down their specifics.

Still, the day had been trying. The couple were opposite in all their questions. *Ugh.*

Chloe couldn't wait to get to her place and soak in the tub. Maybe then the pounding at the top of her head would cease. The fact she hadn't eaten yet only exacerbated the pain. She glanced at the dashboard. *Seven o'clock. Too late to cook.*

She wrinkled her nose. The thought of takeout didn't appeal. It was always full of preservatives and unidentifiable ingredients that she was sure would cause cancer. If not today, years later.

"Guess I'm going to the store," she murmured.

Minutes later, Chloe pulled into Freedom Lake's only organic store. The town didn't house the big chains, but fortunately there were some health-conscious citizens willing to open a mom-and-pop shop. The majority of their items came from local farms. The store had only been open a couple of years but it stayed busy. If Chloe had her way, everyone in Freedom Lake would shop there.

Grabbing a cart, Chloe set her purse on the baby seat. *What do I want to eat?* She went through her mental rolodex, checking to make sure something from all the food groups would be present. Greens. Protein. Fruit. Maybe even some grains since she was really hungry.

With that in mind, she headed for the meat section in the back of the store. Staring at the selections, she hummed softly to herself. A song from Hillsong United had been playing in the car and the tune had remained in her head.

She tilted her head sideways to check the price on the ground chicken. *Mmm, lettuce wraps.* She grinned and grabbed the package. With the main dish decided, the rest of the trip went quickly. Afterward she thanked Rodney, the cashier, then made her way outside, stuffing her receipt into the paper sack. The impact of hitting a solid body had her jerking up to check her surroundings.

A squeak eked out, oddly resembling a dog's chew toy. Her mind in hyper drive, Chloe braced herself for a fall, clutching her groceries tightly as her cheeks heated with embarrassment.

Only it never came.

Hands held onto her arms and steadied her while she got her bearings. The scent of fresh linens enveloped her, and her arms tingled from the grip of the stranger. Feeling stable, she looked up and met the startled gaze of Darryl.

Had his eyes always been such a rich brown? It reminded her of the vibrant finish of a cherry dresser she had recently bought for a client.

"Sorry about that," he stammered out.

She nodded, unable to formulate words. Why did she have to run into him now? Her words never cooperated when he was near. Either she couldn't speak or she couldn't shut up. What was it about him that had her so befuddled?

"Are you okay?" His brow furrowed in concern and a curl flopped onto his forehead.

The urge to brush it away was overwhelming. Did he realize how adorable he looked? She coughed, trying to rattle her brain into speech mode. "I'm okay." *Whew, at least she got that out.* Only, the words kept coming. "I'm sorry I wasn't paying attention to where I was going. You see, I put my receipt in my bag and when I looked up, obviously I ran into you. And so it's really me who should apologize and not you."

She bit her lip, hoping to curtail the flow of words. Why, oh why, did she have a motor mouth?

"No problem." He squeezed her arms and let go.

The rest of her words flew out the window. Her heart beat so fast her head became a little lightheaded. She drew in a ragged breath. What should she say next? What should she do? Chloe watched him in confusion, noting the way his muscles grew taught as he folded his arms. She never realized how wonderful his skin looked.

A darker shade than hers. Were both of his parents black? Was anyone one single ethnicity? She blinked as he continued to meet her gaze. He made her feel so small. How was that possible? He wasn't exactly tall. For a man, he was pretty short in the height department. But there was something about him that made her feel petite and delicate.

Good grief. Now she couldn't even stop thinking.

"Well, I guess I'll be going," Darryl said.

"Okay, yes. I should get home and make my dinner. I don't want it to warm up standing right here. Plus, I'm sure you have things to do."

"Well unless you're having hot flashes I don't think your food will warm up."

Her mouth dropped open. Did she look old enough for that to happen? A look of mortification displayed across his face. She blinked and then fell into peals of laughter.

"Sorry." He ducked his head sheepishly, chuckling softly. "I definitely put my foot into that one."

"Yeah, you did, but it was funny."

"What are you planning on making, anyway?" He stared at her expectantly.

"Lettuce wraps."

"Really? That's what I was going to make. I use shrimp, you?"

She wrinkled her nose. "Ew, I don't like seafood. Ground chicken for me."

"I've never tried that. Maybe I'll find a recipe for that."

Invite him over! "I can email you mine." She grimaced inwardly. *Coward!*

"Sure, that'll be great." He put a hand in his pocket and pulled out a business card. "Here's my email address."

She took it, trying to hide the blush that flamed onto her face as her fingers grazed his.

"It has my email."

"You said that already."

"Right." He cleared his throat.

"Okay, then. Night." She waved and walked out the store.

Chloe got in her car and sat there. Her head dropped onto the staring wheel. *You're such a goony bird. Why did you talk so much? And why did you laugh at that comment? You know you snort when you laugh too much. Plus, you should have invited him over. Instead, all you have is a card. Crazy, crazy, crazy, Chloe.*

Her thoughts replayed over and over as each remembrance of the encounter flashed through her mind, adding alternate scenarios each time. Ones that would make her more confident. Or more mysterious. Or desirable so he'd have to ask her out.

"Never going to happen," she whispered.

Putting the car in reverse, she continued berating herself as she backed up. No other man made her as tongue-tied or loose-lipped as Darryl Jones did. She didn't know what it was about him, or how she would ever be able to speak coherently in his presence. It was a wonder she didn't stumble the whole time she led Bible study. *Oh yeah*, she'd focused entirely on Michelle and Jo, despite being fully aware of his presence.

Even now, tingles lingered along her arms where he had touched her. When the scent of his clothes enveloped them, her knees had turned to Jell-O as her stomach fluttered with a thousand butterflies. It hadn't been an embrace, but her body reacted like it was. Who knew how she'd react if he ever did hug her.

I'd cry from happiness. She snorted. *Or pass out.* She nodded her head. That was more likely to happen than the tears.

The sound of her cell interrupted her thoughts. Jamie's face popped up on the screen. Chloe bit her lip. She'd call her back as soon as she got home. God didn't grace her with the gift of coordination, so she didn't even attempt to press talk and continue driving. Someone would get hurt if she did.

Moments later, she arrived safely at her apartment. She'd been so thankful when Jo let her assume the lease a couple of years ago when she moved back home to help her mom. Now, the gratitude had worn away and discontentment started to sprout. She wanted her own place. Somewhere she could have her own garden and relax after a long day. One to call home.

Funny how a picture of Darryl's place shined in her mind. When he hosted Bible study, she'd noticed how much the décor and color scheme in his home matched hers. The bright sunny yellow was her favorite. It had always appealed to her. How could one be sad when it let in light?

She needed to redirect her thoughts. One little run in didn't mean she had to let Darryl invade every thought. Pressing the speaker phone option, Chloe dialed Jamie's number and sat the phone on the counter so she could put her groceries away.

"Hey, CeeCee, what are you up to?"

She smiled at the nickname. It felt normal. "I just got home. I'm about to make dinner."

"Whatcha' making?"

"Chicken lettuce wraps."

"Yum. Hey, I was wondering if we could plan something for when Char and JJ get here?"

She straightened up, staring at the phone. Why was she so nervous? *Because there's no guarantee they'll like you as well as Jamie does.* "What do you have in mind?"

"I was thinking of dinner. Maybe at your place?"

"I don't know." She glanced around her apartment. "My place is pretty small."

"Well, do you think Mrs. Carter would host something at the B&B? I don't move into my place until the beginning of next month."

"No, we don't want to put her out. Besides, you're not the only paying guest."

What to do? She tapped her chin, trying to focus. "What time are they arriving?"

"Char thinks they'll be here by five."

Guess she would miss Bible study for the first time ever.

Invite them. She shook her head. "Why don't we go to Kodiak for dinner?"

"They may not want to get back in the car after their drive here."

"True."

"Don't worry, I'll think of something. I'm usually the brains of the family."

Chloe chuckled. "Great, just let me know what time and where to go."

"Will do. Enjoy dinner, CeeCee. Are we still hanging out tomorrow?"

Great. She'd completely forgotten their plans to buy Jamie living room furniture. "We are. Um…do you mind if we also do some shopping for some clients of mine?"

"Oh, new clients? Sounds great. Can I help?"

"Definitely." She smiled. Jamie was such a blessing.

Lord, please let Charlotte and John Jr. like me too. Amen.

Slowly she began dinner preparations, but for the first time doubts plagued her after a praying.

～～

Darryl grabbed his notepad and a bottle of water as he headed for the conference room. Jordan was ready to go over the plans to give the clinic a face lift. He sighed. Could he handle seeing Chloe every day? Running into her—literally—had thrown him for a loop. What would it be like having her in the office every day?

He sighed. The same questions were always repeating in his mind like a broken record. He walked into the room and paused. He was the first one there. Hopefully Jordan and Martin were having a good day. His thoughts drifted toward Brianna.

She had finally taken a turn for the better. Her skin was less pale and yesterday was the first time she had asked for food. A pediatric surgeon had removed half of her pancreas to save her life. Brianna would now be dependent on insulin for the rest of her life, but at least she would have one. He'd been afraid to break the news to her mother, but it turned out he didn't need to worry. She was so grateful her daughter was getting better that the new diagnosis, and the way it would impact their lives, didn't concern her at the moment.

How had she put it? "Dr. D as long as she is alive, we can handle anything that comes our way."

If only he could look at life through that lens. In his mind, there were things worse than death. *Like living with the guilt of your sins?*

"Hey, Darryl. I'm surprised you made it in here first." Jordan shot him a wide smile, her white teeth gleaming against her tan complexion.

"Me too, but it helped me wind down and change mental gears."

She crossed her legs as she swiveled in the chair. "I hear you. I'm tired, but in a good way. The kids were all pretty nice, but I had a few who didn't appreciate having a girl for a doctor."

Although she laughed, he had to wonder if she was offended. Kids could be brutal with their truth. But if they liked you, you were golden.

Martin walked in and sighed as he flopped down into a chair. "Thank God this day is over. I'm beyond exhausted. Was it me or did it seem like everyone was extra whiny today?"

"They're ready for summer," he replied.

"June's right around the corner." Jordan looked at them. "Speaking of which, do you guys have anything planned for Memorial Day?"

"I always attend the annual festival," Martin replied.

Darryl nodded in agreement with his colleague.

"What festival?" Jordan rested her chin in her hand. She almost looked like a little kid.

"Freedom Lake has a long tradition of starting the summer off with a Memorial Day celebration." He cleared his throat and continued. "It's a little different than most. We honor the fallen soldiers who were minorities. It starts with a parade of vets or descendants of vets. The parade leads right to the carnival which is held at the county grounds past the lake."

"Wow, that sounds amazing." She turned a quizzical look toward him then glanced at Martin. "I don't mean to sound ignorant, but don't the white citizens of Freedom Lake take offense?"

Martin busted out laughing. His face turned red with laughter matching his hair. Finally, his laugh subsided, and he cleared his throat. "Sorry, I wasn't laughing at you Jordan. But the only people in Freedom Lake who would ever take offense are the Davenports. Most of us knew the significance of this town before moving here.

And those of us who grew up here find it normal."

He stared at Martin. He'd never ever thought that his white friends or in this case, colleague, would take offense to the Memorial festival. It did make sense that some could be offended. He was just so used to the parade that he never gave it another thought.

Darryl stared at Martin with new eyes, taking in his colleague's reddish hair and five o'clock stubble. He'd always known Martin was white, but today was the first day it seemed to go deeper than surface level.

"Well, gentlemen, let's talk about the space and how we can make it better." Jordan smiled at them.

"I don't see what's wrong with it now," replied Martin.

"That's because you're a man. You guys aren't known for your observation powers." Jordan chuckled.

"Why do we want to update it?" Darryl asked.

"Because, the way it's decorated now does not appeal to today's kids. I'm guessing you guys listed cartoons you enjoyed and went in that direction for the décor, am I right?"

The men nodded.

"Problem is," Jordan continued. "None of today's kids know who any of those characters are unless their parents happens to share old TV shows with them."

"What do they watch then?" Simples asked, his brows furrowed.

"Paw Patrol, Dora the Explorer, Ninja Turtles. You get the idea."

"Wait, Ninja Turtles was out when I was a kid." He sat up straight in his chair. That much he knew.

Jordan laughed. "Yes it was, but it's not the same show. Trust me. You guys have done great, but all the rooms appeal to one age and one demographic: young boys. You do realize we treat teenagers and girls who would rather die than be caught in these rooms?"

"Okay, we get your point." He sighed. "How much will it cost us?"

"Chloe gave me three choices and what those all included." She passed some sheets to Martin and then to him.

Darryl picked them up, noting all the detail and sketches Chloe had included. "Wow," he whispered.

"Great, aren't they?" Jordan asked.

He nodded absentmindedly as he looked over Chloe's information. The girl had talent. He'd always known that, but seeing the evidence in person was another thing all together. It was going to be rough seeing her every day and keeping his hands in his pockets. Because he would want to touch her. To feel one of her dark, black curls against his fingers.

Remember what your hands are capable of.

He swallowed. *I remember.* But it wouldn't stop him from using them for good. Like healing sick kids. How else could he atone for his sins?

"Okay," Martin started. "I can tell these are really good. When can she start and how long will it take for her to finish? We don't want to disrupt the clinic's patient flow."

Point one for Martin.

"That's listed on page three."

The sound of paper rattled through the air. His heart stopped. Chloe was planning on starting Monday? That wasn't enough time to prepare himself. Tomorrow was already Friday, and he knew how fast the weekend passed. Before he knew it, she would be in his clinic. He wiped his hands down his jeans.

"She plans on having the rooms painted one at a time so that we only have one room out of commission. It'll need two days to air out and get rid of the fumes. All asthma patients will need to be at the farthest room away to avoid fumes. She also said she could buy industrial size fans to dry the room faster and keep the room closed during the day. At the end of day, we can leave the door open to air out any remaining fumes."

"Sounds like she thought of everything," he stated. "How long will she be here each day?" He hoped his voice sounded nonchalant.

"From my understanding not the whole day. She's hiring the painters and will be overseeing the work when necessary."

Disappointment cloaked him.

Jordan stared at him then Simples. "The only question is which plan can we handle monetary wise?"

They sorted through the rest of the details and decided on a plan. He got up, thankful the workday was now over. After bidding them goodbye, he left the building and walked to his car. But where should he go? He didn't want to be at home alone with his thoughts.

Who could he bug? He smiled and headed for Evan's house. Hopefully Jo wouldn't be there, and he could shoot the breeze before his friend kicked him out. Plus, Evan lived right behind his house. They had thought about making a door in their connecting fences, but Jo was busy lately with her construction business.

Darryl knocked on Evan's door. He tried not to be impatient and knock again. He knew it took his friend a little longer to get to the door considering he was missing a leg. Just when he thought the acceptable amount of time had passed, the door wrenched open.

"D, man," Evan said with a cagey grin. "What brings you by?"

"Didn't feel like going home, so I thought I'd hang out with you for a bit." He crossed the threshold and closed the door. Evan was already making his way to the kitchen with his forearm crutch.

"I was just making some dinner."

He raised an eyebrow. How did his friend do it? Didn't he feel off balance? "What are you making?"

"Steak kabobs. Now that it's summer, I do all my cooking outside." Evan hooked a thumb over his shoulder as he stopped at the kitchen counter. "I heard your knock when I came inside for some more food."

Darryl grabbed the platter and followed Evan outside. Over the past year, his friend had become a pro at using crutches to get around. Unfortunately, he was allergic to some of the prosthetic material and decided to forgo the use of a prosthesis.

The breeze brushed against Darryl's face, wafting the scent of the grilled steaks across his path.

"How's work going, man?" Evan asked.

"Not bad. Busy today, but a good one overall."

"Anything new with you?"

"Jordan started working at the clinic. Martin and I were drowning so it's nice not to be at that frantic pace any longer."

"Awesome." Evan squinted at him. "What's with you and Jordan anyway?"

"What? Nothing. Besides she's engaged."

"So her engagement is why there's nothing going on?"

"Not likely. She's not my type."

"Oh yeah, I forgot how much you like petite females with curly hair."

His neck warmed under the teasing of his friend. "Yeah, well…" he sighed. "Chloe's going to be redecorating the clinic starting Monday."

"Word?" Evan paused at the grill and met his gaze. "How do you feel about that?"

"Confused." He flopped into one of the deck chairs. "You know I don't know how to act around her."

"Man, why don't you just tell her you like her?"

"I'm not good enough, Ev, you know that."

"No, I don't. You're a doctor, for crying out loud. You know how many women, mamas included, want to marry a doctor?"

He chuckled, rubbing his chin. "I know, but still. My past."

"Is that. The past. Keep it there and move on with the grace God is offering you."

"Yeah, I feel you, man." He looked away, hoping Evan wouldn't see the lie in his eyes. Evan didn't have the sins he did. He was more a victim than anything. Evan had never physically hurt anyone, not like he had.

Chapter Five

F riday. Chloe sat at the desk in her bedroom, trepidation spreading through her insides like poison. Usually she greeted all the days with joy. Her morning time with God always steadied her. Now, Fridays had begun to hold a special place in her heart with Bible studies. Almost as good as Sundays.

Almost.

She stood and headed for her closet. Her outfit needed to be comfortable enough to get her through the day since summer was ramping up, yet nice enough for her meeting with JJ and Charlotte. *Charlotte.* She grimaced inwardly. Would Jamie tell her the significance of the name or had she chalked it up to coincidence?

The clothes in her closet hung there, unappealing. Gnawing her bottom lip, she flipped through the hangers. What could transition nicely from work to dinner with…*family.* Would they like her?

Please, Lord, let them like me.

"Oh," she murmured. A button-down aqua cardigan caught her interest. It would look great with her white sundress. The dress had the same color flowers as the sweater. With a smile, she laid her ensemble out on her bed.

Her friends would be meeting at Michelle and Jo's tonight for Bible study. It was the first time the bungalow would be used for the group and the first time Michelle would lead. She had taken the plunge and devoted her life to Christ and wanted a chance to share insights from her Bible reading.

I can't believe I'm going to miss it.

Chloe flopped down onto the edge of her bed. Maybe she should have invited her half-siblings to Bible study. She wanted to be there to support Michelle. *And see Darryl.* She couldn't deny it even if she wanted to.

Dressing quickly, she headed for the kitchen to grab her overnight oatmeal and probiotic smoothie. Knowing she had a busy day ahead of her, Chloe decided to bring the food with her instead of eating at home. She'd added two new clients in a week's span, and both were anxious for her to finish quickly.

Lord, could You help me do my best work to glorify You and to please my clients? I want them to find the decorations to their liking, fitting their personality. Of course, it wouldn't hurt if it garnered me some referrals. With an "Amen," she hopped in her SUV, turning it toward downtown Freedom Lake.

The morning flew by, and before she knew it the out-to-lunch sign was displayed on the door of The Space. She'd agreed to meet Jamie for lunch at LeeAnn's Bakery. She loved their grilled spinach panini, and she really needed the nourishment after such a busy morning.

Her new clients, the Millers, had changed their mind on every design idea, forcing her to redo every sketch for the rooms in their massive home. Her décor quiz had failed her.

Of course, she could always use her software program instead of a sketch pad, but her thoughts flowed much better when she sketched.

She hated starting over. It pushed her timeline back, running the risk of busting the date she'd given them. *Why did they have to be so...so scatterbrained?* Her cell chirped. She pulled it out of her purse. It was from Jamie.

CALL ME!

Hitting speed dial, she listened to the music as she waited for Jamie to answer her phone.

"Hey, CeeCee. Char and JJ showed up early so I was wondering if you could come over to the B&B for lunch? Mrs. Carter has already made a great spread and said the more the merrier."

Chloe's stomach clenched as if it had a jaw and teeth of its own. Her mouth watered in preparation of a full-out stomach revolt.

They were here? Already?

She wasn't ready. Wasn't prepared. *Lord, why so soon?* She gulped. "I'll be there shortly." Hopefully, Jamie didn't hear her unsteady tone.

"Great, see you soon."

She squeezed her eyes shut. "No, no, no," she murmured. This wasn't how it was supposed to happen. She'd planned on praying before the meeting to center herself. Now she would have to pray in the car. It was fine for a quick prayer here or there, but being still in complete quiet was her preference.

It took about five minutes to go anywhere in Freedom Lake, but if she went the long way, maybe she could add to her time so she could get a prayer in, because she desperately needed one. Pressing the off button on her radio, she began to pray aloud.

"Lord, I can't believe how nervous I am. It wasn't like this when I met Jamie. Then again, she just dropped by out of the blue." She thought back to the day Jamie showed up in Freedom Lake asking Guy if he knew how to contact her. "Lord, for some reason this feels worse. Is it because there are two of them? Or are You trying to prepare me for the worst?"

She sighed and turned onto the street that would lead straight to the B&B. "Lord, please be with me. Please let them like me. And please, let me know what to say. How to act. What to do. *Please.*"

Grimacing, Chloe shifted to Park and stared out the window. *Just go in.* But her body remained rooted to the driver's seat. The parking lot was on the side of the house, so no one would know she was here unless they happened to look out through a window on this side. Yet she didn't want to play coward and sit there until it was time to go back to work. She had to get out of the car. Needed to.

You can do this.

With a nod of agreement, she opened her door and headed for the beautiful front porch that overlooked the lake. Before she could even knock, the door opened and Jamie stepped out.

"Yay," she squealed. "I'm so glad you're here. I can't wait to introduce you. You're going to love them."

Jamie chatted happily away as she pulled Chloe down the hallway toward the kitchen.

Would Mrs. Carter be there or had she made herself scarce? She was one of the sweetest women Chloe had ever met. Plus, she was Evan's mom so that seemed to help in some way. It was nice knowing her friend's family. Sometimes she would pretend they were her own, and Mrs. Carter had usually been front and center of those day dreams. But having Evan for a brother had always put a wrinkle in her plans. Although, now that he had changed and found Jesus, it wouldn't be such a bad thing.

Jamie slowed as they entered the kitchen. Chloe forced her feet to move forward as a guy and young woman rose from the breakfast table.

"Guys, this is Chloe." Jamie announced.

The guy...well her brother...looked at her warily, his dark hair hanging slightly over his forehead. His five o'clock shadow made him look a little bit older than his twenty-three years. He had the same nose as Charlotte. No, she would have to think of her as Char. Chloe didn't think she could call her half-sister by her mother's name.

"Chloe, this is John, but we all call him JJ."

He nodded. "Nice to meet you."

"You too," she replied softly.

"And Chloe this is Char. The oldest...well, I mean former oldest," Jamie said with a grin, her dimple flashing and her dark eyes dancing.

Char rolled her brown eyes and tucked her short black hair behind her ear. "I'm still the oldest. *She* doesn't change a thing."

Chloe froze. It was like her nightmare became reality. Char hated her on sight? Why? Licking her lips, she gathered her courage. "It's nice to meet you."

"Yeah, whatever."

"Char," Jamie exclaimed. "Don't be like that. You're such a brat."

"Whatever. You may believe she's related to us, but I don't."

Jamie huffed, crossing her slender arms across her chest. "We have DNA *proof*. Unless *you're* adopted, she's our sister."

"Half," Char snapped.

"Char, cut it out," JJ responded. "If Jamie has proof, then that's that." He looked at Chloe. "Sorry, she can be an attention hog. It's just a little strange to find out we've had a half-sister all this time."

Chloe nodded, too numb to speak.

"So, um…" JJ walked a little closer. "What do you do for fun around here?"

Chloe offered him a smile. He was trying and for that she was grateful. "Hang out at the lake or drive to the city. My friends and I also do Bible studies together."

"Huh, you're religious? Go figure. Dad's anti-religion."

The sinking feeling widened. *Right now would be a really good time to sound the trumpet, Lord.* The 'anti-religion' comment explained Jamie's avoidance of the subject. How did JJ feel? "And you? Are you anti-religion?"

He ran a hand over his gelled hair. "Not anti, more like indifferent."

"Well, you should come to Bible study and see what God's about."

JJ nodded and slid his hands into his khaki pockets. "Maybe. We're here until Monday and then, who knows."

She hated the awkwardness. How was she supposed to sit down and eat? The thought of food had Darth Vader's theme song rising in her mind.

"Let's sit down and eat," Jamie encouraged.

Char and JJ slid into the bench seat against the wall. She and Jamie took up the chairs facing them. Mrs. Carter had filled the table with fried chicken, baked macaroni and cheese, and green beans with bacon bits in it. Images of her panini from LeeAnn's danced in her mind. *One bad meal won't hurt.*

Silence descended as they put food on their plate.

"Why is everyone so quiet?" Jamie asked.

"It's just a little much to take in, Ames." JJ grabbed another piece of chicken. He looked at Chloe. "So, sister dear, what do you do for a living?"

Somehow, the endearment sounded anything but. "I'm an interior designer."

Char looked at her sharply, then turned her head as she met her gaze.

What now?

"Wow, that sounds cool. What company do you work for?"

"She owns her own business." Jamie beamed at them. "It's totally chic and cool. We went shopping for her new clients. She let me help."

She smiled at Jamie thankful for her support and affection. "It was fun."

"Definitely. Maybe you could come next time, Char." Jamie stared at her older sister.

Chloe watched as silent communication seemed to pass back and forth. For a moment, she was envious of their connection. How would her life had turned out if she had been raised with them?

"I'd rather not." Char stood up and huffed as she stomped out of the kitchen.

"Well, that was just peachy," JJ stated to the quiet room.

∽

Darryl pulled up to the gray bungalow and stopped at the curb. The driveway was already filled with cars. His shoulders dropped as he realized Chloe's SUV wasn't in sight. She was rarely late. What could have kept her?

He hustled up the sidewalk, eager to hang out with his friends. The work week had been draining and the promised relaxation was like a drop of water in the desert. Every Bible study meeting had him asking the same question: would he finally know that God would accept him, flaws and all? Or more accurately, sins and all?

Sure, they had discussed grace and forgiveness, but it didn't help him any. Although he was ashamed of his actions, wasn't he just a product of his environment? Life had dealt harshly with him and it only made logical sense that he would react in a way that showcased how he grew up.

Yet he was old enough to realize that those actions, his way of life, could isolate him from those he wanted to be around. Like Chloe. He sighed and knocked on the door. Stalling outside hadn't given him an opportunity to see her drive up, so he might as well go in.

"Hey, Darryl," Jo said with a smile.

"Hey, JoJo." He walked in and inhaled the smell of burgers. "Who's doing the cooking?"

"Guy is. Evan's just yapping his ear off."

He chuckled, then glanced around. "So, um…"

"Chloe's not coming. She had some family business."

Since when?

His mind floundered, having trouble grasping the information. As far as he was aware, Chloe didn't have any family. Her grandmother had passed, which he knew because his grandmother had been one of her closest friends. He'd never seen any other family come around.

Curiosity clawed at him, but instead of asking questions he simply nodded and headed for the back. He waved at Michelle and Claire on the way to the porch. The sight of Michelle and Jo's backyard looked like some backyard oasis. Trees wrapped it in shade and various shrubbery closed it in, giving it a secluded feeling. The abundance of flowers sprinkled amount the greenery gave it a feminine feel.

"D, man!" Evan cried out.

He clapped Evan's back, then Guy's. "What's up fellas?"

"Just trying to finish cooking the food." Guy waved a spatula at him.

Darryl gestured around him. "What's with their yard? I feel like I have a chance of losing my man card standing out here."

Guy let out a bark of laughter. "You should have seen it in the spring time. My kids kept calling it the Princess garden."

He shuddered. "Next time, let's have it at your house. Unless the girls' have turned the whole place girly."

Guy laughed, rubbing at the stubble on his chin. "No. Jo just finished the deck. Maybe we could do it there next time."

"Deal."

"So what's up with you?" Evan asked.

"Not much." He flopped into the chair. "Hey, what's going on with Chloe?"

Guy and Evan exchanged glances and then looked at him.

"Oh, man, that's no fair. Your fiancées told you, but you can't tell me?"

Again, they exchanged glances.

He scoffed. Why was he the only one clueless about what was going on?

"Word of advice," Evan stated. "Ask her out. Be her friend. Then maybe you'll be the one she comes running to when life gets tough."

Not that again. No one seemed to understand why he couldn't ask her out. As much as he wanted to…as much as he needed to…he just couldn't take the plunge. When it came down to it, he couldn't reconcile himself and equate it to the kind of man she deserved.

She was everything he wasn't, and the pain ran deep. Like barbed wire wrapped around his wrist and ankles. He couldn't move, couldn't plead for help. His hands were tied.

"Take his advice, man," Guy added.

"I'll think about it." Who was he kidding? It was all he thought about.

Fortunately, they changed the topic and the tension let up. Once the burgers were done, they headed inside to the dining room. He was glad Guy's secretary, Claire, was comfortable enough to come without Jordan, but it felt weird that Jordan wasn't there. He'd gotten used to seeing her at work every day. She was like the kid sister he never had.

Jordan was meeting with her fiancé to finalize their housing and wedding plans. Apparently, he was going to be the new principal at the junior high in town. Darryl hadn't met him yet, but she was considering bringing him to the Memorial Day Festival. For some reason, she didn't want to include him in the Bible studies.

A knock at the door brought him from his thoughts.

"Who in the world?" Michelle muttered. She got up and marched toward the front door.

Unfortunately, the dining room didn't give an open view. Part of him hoped it was Chloe, the other part knew he'd be better off if it wasn't. But the melodic female voice floating their way proved it was.

She came.

He tried to sit there looking nonchalant, but he couldn't quite pull it off when his collar felt too tight and his heart pounded loud enough to echo his pulse points. When she walked into the dining room, it was all he could do to keep the grin off his face. He felt like the male counterpart of Fantasia's song, "When I See You."

There was something about her black curls against her golden complexion that made his heart skip a beat. And when she smiled…he was a goner. He cleared his throat and stared at the Bible, hoping his rejoicing didn't come off of him like heat waves.

"Sorry I'm late, guys," Chloe said softly.

"No problem, Chlo. I thought—" Jo let her sentence hang in the air.

"It did *not* go well at all." Her nose scrunched up.

She was cute even when she was obviously irritated. What had her so riled up? He looked around the room and everyone seemed to be nodding in understanding. How could they all know?

Ask her. He licked his lips. "What happened?"

Chloe met his gaze. Her eyes were like liquid pools of dark chocolate. He wanted to melt in them. Get lost in them. Tell her all his secrets. Maybe they'd actually be safe with her.

Her shoulders rose, and then she exhaled. "I met my half-brother and sister today."

If a record had been playing, the sound of a scratch would have roared in the room. Yet no one appeared to be surprised. He really was the last to know. "I'm sorry it didn't go well."

She nodded, then looked down at her hands. "Me too," she replied softly.

Michelle patted her back. "Do you want to talk about it?"

"No," she answered with a shake of her head. "I'm just ready to get into the Word. I definitely need it right now."

"Okay, let's get started then." Michelle bowed her head and led them in prayer.

Her voice sounded shaky, as if she was nervous. Leading the study took guts, in his book. He didn't know if he could do it. So far, he was the only one who hadn't. Well, Claire too, but she had just started coming.

Practicing medicine was the only thing he could trust. And even that had its bad days, where you questioned every decision and prognosis or diagnosis.

Michelle held up her cell phone as she swiped her finger on the screen. "I want us to go to Ephesians chapter one."

He flipped his Bible open. The one Chloe had given him the first day he went to church. He'd even filled out the front of it with the date. Not that he'd ever forget it or show anyone else.

"We're going to read from verse three to the end of six." Michelle's clear voice rang out as she read the Scripture. "Blessed *be* the God and Father of our Lord Jesus Christ, Who has blessed us with every spiritual blessing in the heavenly *places* in Christ, just as He chose us in Him before the foundation of the world, that we should be holy and without blame before Him in love, having predestined us to adoption as sons by Jesus Christ to Himself, according to the good pleasure of His will, to the praise of the glory of His grace, by which He made us accepted in the Beloved."

Quickly, he reread the words, letting them sink in. He looked up. "It says predestined. Are you saying God already picked us out of the lineup?"

Michelle grinned. "When I read this passage that's exactly the word that caught my attention. Predestined. We were all predestined. He knew us, knew we would be followers of Christ, and He has been waiting for us to catch up. That last bit is my opinion," she said with a chuckle.

Once again, he reread the verses. Could it be true? Could he really belong to God? Already? Was he merely catching up to God's plans? He reread the verses one more time.

"In the New Living Translation, verse five reads: "God decided in advance to adopt us into His own family by bringing us to Himself through Jesus Christ." She looked up from her phone.

"We're adopted by God. As an orphan, I can't tell you how much this means to me. Being alone is all I knew for so long. Even though I had my dear friends, I had this overwhelming sense of isolation. I wanted to belong to someone. To be loved by someone. And the best thing about this is that God will never leave. Nothing will separate us. Death won't end our relationship." Michelle smiled in satisfaction. "In fact, it advances us to the next level, the real level where we can be free from all the hurt and suffering we've been through or even caused in some cases."

Darryl sat back, overwhelmed. Everything word she said spoke to his heart. He wanted to belong and be accepted for who he was. According to this passage in the Bible, God had adopted him in advance.

Me. Darryl Jones.

He was accepted. He gulped, his Adam's apple moving up and down sluggishly, trying to pass the ball of emotion in his throat. *He was accepted.* Looking at the words weren't enough for him. Slowly, he traced them with his finger as if he could engrave them on his body through osmosis.

"I want to belong," he said.

Silence descended, and he looked up to see a surprised expression on a few of their faces and a smile on Chloe's. Darryl hadn't been aware that he'd spoke out loud, but he wasn't surprised. The words needed to be said aloud. Belonging is all he ever wanted. Acceptance from family was what he craved, and God had set it in motion before time began.

"Would you like me to lead you in prayer?" Chloe asked.

He nodded, too thankful that she had offered.

"Repeat after me."

"Father, thank You for adopting me as Your son."

He repeated, word for word, emotion for emotion.

"I know how desperately I need You, and I'm thankful for the salvation You so freely offer. I believe in Your Son, and I commit myself to follow Him. In Your Son's mighty name, Amen."

"Amen," he echoed. He closed his eyes, letting out a breath. It was done. He belonged. He was accepted. He smiled as the feeling of freedom soared through his being.

Chapter Six

C hloe sat out on her apartment deck with a cup of herbal tea and her Bible. She was supposed to be reading the book of Isaiah, but she couldn't stop thinking about Darryl. The look of peace that had come over him after praying at last night's Bible study filled her mind. Filled her emotions.

She had wanted to congratulate him, but the others swarmed him and gave him hugs after the prayer. Every fiber of her being had yearned to welcome him into God's family. Yet she held back. Her nerves had kept her rooted to her seat.

No. It wasn't just nerves, it was longing. She wanted to hug him, but it hadn't been as a fellow member of the body. No, she wanted to hug him the way a woman would hug the man she loved.

She closed her eyes. *You do not love him. It's just an infatuation.*

Which was true. Only her feelings for him had lingered over the past decade. Would she ever be the type of woman he'd be interested in? She'd seen the girls he dated in high school.

He didn't necessarily have a playboy reputation, but the number of girls he had dated hinted at it.

He'd always picked the ultra-pretty or popular types. Not a bookworm or intellectual in sight. She stared down at her hands. Looking at them used to help her center herself. But now, they were a part of her inner turmoil. They signified the chink in her identity. How could she be the calm Christian whose faith sustained her when she questioned what He was doing in her life?

Why did being half-white plague her so? Did it really matter what color she was? She wanted to say no, but couldn't. But God created people a certain way for a specific reason, right? Her life seemed to be a constant dichotomy. Wanted by one sister and despised by the other. Ignored by her father and acknowledged by a brother. Who was she really? All these years she had clung to the knowledge that she belonged to the body of Christ. That God had adopted her. In fact, the verse Michelle had used last night had been her favorite. Only now it didn't bring her comfort because her earthly family didn't want to have anything to do with her.

Why was God no longer enough?

A tear slipped down her cheek and landed on her Bible. Grabbing a napkin, she blotted at the tear, praying it wouldn't cause a stain. She treasured her Bible. It had been a gift from her grandmother and had its own shelf on her bookcase. She even used notepads to make notes instead of marking in the beloved book. Her hands stilled as she realized where her tear had landed.

Isaiah 61:3 stared up at her. Her tear had landed on *joy*. She read the verse: *"To console those who mourn in Zion, to give them beauty for ashes, the oil of joy for mourning, the garment of praise for the spirit of heaviness; That they may be called trees of righteousness, the planting of the Lord, that He may be glorified."*

She stared up into the sky, wondering if God was trying to send her a message. Was she just going through the stages of grief? Would He truly turn her mourning into joy?

Lord, please put the pieces of my heart back together. I want my father and siblings to truly like me. To want me in their lives. I want a relationship with them. They're the only family I have left on this earth.

The word 'mother' flashed in her mind. She rubbed the ache that took up the space in her heart. Was her mother still alive? She hadn't seen her since middle school. It had been quite obvious then that she was strung out on drugs.

Should I try to find her?

The decision to find her biological father had been much easier than looking for her mother. Sure, she knew her mother's name and birthdate, all the facts that could aid in the search, but her hope was gone. The only way she could find her mother was if she got her life together or ended up in jail. A drug addict could truly disappear if they wanted.

And what kind of choices were those? Did she need someone like that in her life?

Can't be much worse than your father.

She shook her head at the sad thought. When had her life become so depressing? She breathed in and reread Isaiah, focusing on the verse where her tear had landed. *Lord, I will hold on to these words. Please turn my mourning into joy. And please guide me on what to do about my family. I'm lost and confused and filled with hopelessness.* She bit her lip. *But I know you're a God who makes anything possible, so I will hold on to that truth. Thank You. Amen.*

Chloe gathered her things and laid them on the kitchen counter. Her morning devotional time didn't go like she expected, but at least it had led to a conversation with the Lord. Her grandmother had always told her as long as she was still talking it was okay to be frustrated.

A knock at the door alerted her to a visitor. She glanced at the microwave clock, wondering who could be visiting so early in the morning. *Thank goodness I'm presentable.* Flannel pants and a t-shirt weren't indecent even if she had slept in them.

The peep hole was too high for her to glance through, so she opened the door, praying for the best.

Really, Lord?

Char stood in front of her apartment, arms folded across her chest. "Chloe."

"Good morning, Charlotte."

"Do *not* call me that," she snapped out.

Her back stiffened and her face burned as if she'd been slapped. *Lord, please help me.* She wanted to slam the door in Char's face but that would never lead to a relationship. She drew in a ragged breath and moved aside to let her in. "Do you want to come in?"

Hopefully the look on her face was one of interest instead of unease. Only, the way her stomach rolled, she couldn't believe the former was the case.

"I want to talk to you."

Chloe gestured for her to come in. "Okay, do you want some tea? Want to sit on the couch?"

"The couch is fine."

Judging by the look of disdain on her face, it was Char's turn at trying to be nice. Chloe took the La-Z-Boy recliner and watched as Char—because she refused to call her by her mother's name—inspected the couch cushion before sitting down.

Her bobbed cut was wavy and her makeup flawless. She almost seemed older than her twenty-six years. Char clasped her hands together and laid them on her lap. Then her brown eyes met her gaze. "Jamie showed me the copy of the DNA results."

Silence descended in the room like carbon monoxide, silent but no less deadly. Was she supposed to say something?

"I'm sorry for the way I behaved yesterday." She sounded like a mulish child.

Chloe's mouth dropped open at the lack of sincerity.

"Oh close your mouth. You can't be too surprised I'm here today."

"Actually, I am. It's quite obvious you don't want to be here, so why even come?"

"Jamie made me."

A laugh escaped before she could censure it. "You're telling me Jamie put you up to this."

Char glanced away and then turned back, facing her. "You don't know this, but Jamie can be very persuasive when she wants to be."

"I have learned that much."

"We love her. And as the baby of the family's she gotten away with a lot."

"But you're older than her. If you don't like me, don't lie about it. I'd hate that more than the obvious disdain you have for me."

Char huffed. "Look. I have difficulties meeting new people. It's not an excuse, it is what it is. However, my *attitude*, if you would even call it that, has nothing to do with you and everything to do with your mother."

Chloe pointed a finger at her own chest. "My mom? What do you mean?"

"Jamie told me your mother's name." Char tossed her head, her hair swinging backward.

Oh.

At first glance, Chloe thought her half-sister was going to let another string of insults fly. But then, she looked closely. A water-like substance had taken residence in Char's eyes, and Chloe wondered if she was trying to keep tears at bay. *That's why she doesn't want me to call her Charlotte.*

"It could be a coincidence." She didn't know why she offered the olive branch, but suddenly she hated the thought that Char was hurting. How would she feel if her father had named her after an ex-girlfriend, coincidence or not?

A snort erupted. "Please, you don't believe that." Char picked imaginary lint from her skirt. "Anyway, I wanted to say I'm sorry for ruining our first meeting. Let's just say learning about the "coincidence" put me in a sour mood."

Chloe nodded. "It's all right. I was already prepared for the worst," she ended her sentence with a shrug.

"Both JJ and Jamie thought I was a bit harsh." Char shrugged. "I suppose they're right. I probably should have stayed home." Char let out an audible sigh. "I would like to try and make it right. Would you like to hang out with us today? Jamie mentioned some furniture warehouse in…Kodiak, is it?"

"Memories," she said with a nod. "It's a great place. Jamie already picked out some bedroom furniture from them. I think she wanted to go back to get items for a guest room."

"Yeah, that's what she said. I'm on orders to come back with you or go back home to Ohio."

Laughing, Chloe stood up. "Don't worry. I'll come. Let me go change."

Char nodded. As she passed her, Char reached out and touched her arm. "Maybe you can just call me Char."

A look passed between them. No words were necessary, but Chloe said them aloud regardless. "No problem, *Char.*"

Her sister nodded, a brief smile lighting her face.

As she walked back to her room, Chloe couldn't help but breathe a sigh of relief. Maybe God had heard her prayers. *Thank You, Lord.*

෴

Darryl stared at his reflection in his bathroom mirror. Unfortunately, the bathroom light did nothing to change the reflection staring back at him.

What did I do?

His long curls, which had been hanging over his ears, were now regulated to the top of his head. He'd woke this morning with the desire for a new look to go with a new self. He'd convinced the only barber in town to give him a cropped look. The curls were still there, only shorter. Now he could see his sideburns and his head felt lighter. This would take some time getting used to.

He ruffled his head, trying to get a glimpse of normalcy, but even that felt different.

"Oh well," he murmured.

It couldn't be changed back. He would have to embrace it and wait for it to grow. Hopefully none of his patients would freak out. It was amazing how many kids didn't recognize a person with a new haircut.

With a flick of the switch, the room darkened and he walked out. He gulped down the remainder of his lukewarm coffee. The clinic would be opening in an hour, but he needed to be there in ten minutes for their weekly meeting.

Every Monday, he and Martin went over their scheduled appointments and a game plan for last minute appointments. Plus, this would be Jordan's first full week of work.

And Chloe.

He swallowed, telling himself that the nerves were due to his hair and not the thought of seeing Chloe. He was only fooling himself. The thought of seeing her in his space had invaded his senses. No matter where he was in the office, his heart would know she was in his building. Thankfully, Jordan had said Chloe wouldn't be there constantly.

"Okay, Darryl," he rubbed a hand down his face. "Time to shape up and get to work."

When he arrived at Freedom Lake Pediatric Clinic, Darryl parked his car in the back alley and grabbed the box of muffins. He'd had the foresight to pick them up yesterday from LeeAnn's, otherwise he'd be extra late.

With quick steps, he walked into the conference room with the food and notepad in hand. "Good morning."

Martin looked up and his eyes widened in shock. Jordan's mouth dropped open. He glanced over his shoulder then back to them. "Did I grow a second head?"

Jordan's shock turned to laughter. "Where's your hair?"

"In the garbage by now." He smiled, setting the muffins down. "I grabbed some blueberry and some lemon poppy seed muffins."

"Oh," Jordan stated.

Martin grabbed a blueberry one.

"I smell LeeAnn's muffins." Luella walked in through the door.

"Hey, Ms. Luella. Got the lemon poppy seeds."

"Bless your heart." She grabbed a muffin then froze, the muffin posed halfway to her mouth. "Your hair!"

He laughed. "I know, I know. I needed a new look to go with a new me, Ms. Luella."

"'Bout time you joined the family." She rubbed his back and took a bite of the muffin all at the same time.

"Let's get this meeting started."

After everyone had a rundown of the patient lists and expectations, he headed for his office. His footsteps slowed as the musical laughter carried down the hall.

Chloe's here.

Making a quick decision, he dropped his things on the desk and headed toward her voice. He would be on pins and needles if he didn't say hello now. Quietly, he made his way to the Sesame Street room. The closer he got, the harder his heart beat. He could only pray he wouldn't have a heart attack.

Tapping on the door, he smiled as Jordan and Chloe turned his way. He leaned against the door frame, hoping for a casual stance. Of course the folded arms served to cover his heart in case it really was beating out of his chest.

A light gasp greeted his ears. Chloe's eyes widened and her mouth parted. Slowly she walked toward him, her gaze fixated on his head. He straightened up, the pulse in his neck picking up speed.

"Your hair," she whispered.

He stood, mesmerized as her hand stretched out and touched a curl. Darryl couldn't breathe. The sweet scent of honey invaded his senses. It was all he could do to stand still. He couldn't believe it.

"Why did you cut it?" Her voice hadn't raised above a whisper.

He answered in like matter. "New me."

Her dark chocolate eyes met his gaze. If she were to ask him for anything, he would give it, no questions asked.

"I liked the old you." She licked her lips and his eyes followed the motion. "But I think I like this one even more."

"Do you?" His voice edged toward raspy. He literally hadn't taken a breath since she touched him.

"Yes."

A cough cleared the air.

Chloe stepped back, as if suddenly realizing she had invaded his personal space. Not that he minded. A draft moved in where she had stood, and he longed to pull her back. He wanted to kiss her and tell her how much he cared about her.

Instead, he stepped back. "I have a patient. I'll see you later."

Blindly, he staggered down the hall. He had no idea if his patient had arrived, but he needed a breather, or better yet cold water on his face. Never in a million years had he imagined she'd have that type of reaction to his haircut. He wanted to go back in the exam room and ask her out.

Lord, I don't know if it's possible, but if belonging to You has somehow made me good enough, please tell me. I would love to go out with that woman. Actually, be with her forever.

Silence greeted his ears. Praying still felt awkward, but hopefully he was doing it correctly. This was one prayer he would love an answer to. Still, silence prevailed. Maybe he had done it wrong. Next time he saw Evan or Guy he'd ask them the rules.

He entered the bathroom, splashing water on his face and taking deep breaths. Finally, his heart rate slowed and he ripped off a paper towel to dry his face. The cold had jolted him a little, enough to pass for lucid. Hopefully his patients wouldn't notice anything amiss, or Chloe if he ran into her again.

Chapter Seven

*D*arryl had cut off all his hair.

Chloe just stood there. Stunned. Confused. Why did she care so much? His new look had shocked her. She loved his old look, the curls that would drape over his ears begging to be tousled, but the new look was powerful.

More like breathtaking.

She wasn't sure if that was a word you could attribute to a man, but Darryl had taken her breath away. The close-cropped curls begged to be touched and so she had. She swallowed, feeling her face heat up once again, remembering the way a curl had wrapped around her finger. Thankfully, Jordan had ignored the whole encounter and continued her spiel on the room.

The painters were due to arrive in a few minutes, but Chloe couldn't focus. All she could picture was Darryl. With his new look his light brown skin had glowed, making his chocolate eyes appear more caramel in color. The five o'clock shadow had given him an edgy look that made her want to get closer.

I can't believe I touched his hair.

The warmth that had wrapped around her when she stood in front of him had dazed her. It called to the deepest parts of her heart. Who knew what would have happened if Jordan hadn't coughed. Of course, it could all be a figment of her imagination, but for a moment, just a teeny speck of time, interest seemed to gleam in Darryl's eyes. Were Jo and Michelle right? Did he really like her?

Find out.

Shaking her head, her curls bounced in her face. As much as she wanted to know, she was petrified that he would and petrified that he wouldn't. Which was the lesser of two evils? Her mind swirled in confusion. *Lord, I don't know what to do with these emotions, but I know I have to work. So please help me focus.*

"Knock, knock."

With a whispered, "Amen," she turned and saw the painters walk in. With a deep breath, she got to work.

The morning flew by. While Chloe did administrative work outside the room, the men had managed to prime the room. The color and wallpaper trim would be added tomorrow. Everything was on schedule and she couldn't be happier. All she had to do was grab some lunch and then meet the Millers for their afternoon consult. Hopefully they had at least settled on a look for their master bedroom.

She grabbed her design sketchbook and purse. There was no reason for her to hang around any longer since she had written down the other exam rooms' dimensions. Quietly, she turned the knob and waved goodbye to the painters.

"Oof!"

A weird sense of déjà vu passed as she flailed, trying to catch herself. A warm arm wrapped around her waist, stilling her movements, and the comforting smell of fresh laundry assaulted her senses. Somehow she had ended up in Darryl's arm. Again. She looked up and met his gaze. His smile widened, cheeks pushing upward, lines appeared at the corner of his eyes. A sigh escaped her lips, and she had a fleeting sense of raw masculinity.

"We have got to stop running into each other."

The husky tone of his voice sent chill bumps up her arms. She shivered then found herself closer. Did he pull her closer or did she move of her own accord? How was there even still room to get closer? "I guess I should pay better attention."

"Then I may never get the chance to hold you again."

"All you have to do is ask." She blinked. *Did I really just say that?*

His eyes darkened and heat flamed around her. "Have lunch with me?"

"Yes," she breathed out.

Darryl let go and she reached out, grabbing the door handle to steady her movements. Suddenly she felt cold and alone.

"I'm going to LeeAnn's. Would that be okay?"

Wordlessly, she nodded.

"Would you like to take my car?"

"Um…" *Think, Chloe.* "I actually have some meetings this afternoon. It would be better if I could just meet you there."

He slid his hands in his pockets. "Fair enough. However, I'd like to pay for your lunch."

"Okay." Suddenly, she felt self-conscious. Was this a date? The need to check her hair and clothes was overwhelming. No wonder women primped and ogled mirrors when dating. It was some innate sense of desire to appeal to the opposite sex.

"Great, let's go."

Darryl's hand cupped her elbow as he led her out back to their cars. She couldn't believe they were going to eat lunch, just the two of them.

Will wonders never cease?

～

Darryl parked his car in front of LeeAnn's. On the drive over he tried to calm down, but it wasn't happening. His pulse was jittery and nerves were coursing through him like the waves during a hurricane.

A bottle of Pepto-Bismol or Tums would come in handy right about now. How was he supposed to choke down lunch when he was out with the woman of his dreams? *Help, please!* Chloe deserved his best.

Lord, I don't know if this is an answer to my prayer. Sure feels like one. Please don't let me mess this up.

He straightened his tie and headed for the door. Chloe paused on the sidewalk, having just gotten out of her SUV. He grabbed the bakery doors and opened it.

"Thank you."

"My pleasure." He grinned at her and saw her cheeks turn pink. His grin widened. He couldn't help himself. Blushing was a good thing, wasn't it? "Where do you want to sit?"

"How about a booth?"

That would work just fine. "I can place the orders if you wouldn't mind grabbing us a booth."

"Sure. I'll take the spinach panini and hot green tea."

"That's my favorite."

Her eyes sparkled as the corners of her mouth turned upward.

She's beautiful.

Darryl didn't realize it would be so hard to keep his cool around her. He reached up to run his hand over his hair. He paused momentarily when he realized that the length was missing. His short curls would take some getting used to. He glanced at Chloe as she grabbed a booth in the back.

The sun shined on her, showing brown highlights in her black curls. Her skin glowed, reminding him of warm honey.

"Dr. D, you ready to order?"

He turned, surprised to see the patrons before him gone and LeeAnn staring at him expectantly. He stepped forward. "Sorry, I was thinking."

"Sure you were," she said with a smirk. "Two spinach paninis and green tea?" Her eyebrows rose in question.

All he could do was laugh. "You know us well, LeeAnn."

"Sure do. Wondered how long it would take the two people who ordered the same thing every day to get together and actually share a meal."

He ducked his head, embarrassment heating his face. Did everyone know how much he liked Chloe?

Everyone but her.

"Thanks, LeeAnn."

"No problem. I'll call you when it's ready."

He paid and then walked toward the booth. He needed a conversation starter. Something to ask Chloe to help him skip over small talk. Isn't that how dates went, even if it was for lunch?

He slid into the booth, his hands resting on the tabletop. Chloe stared at him, her face an unreadable mask. Before he could ask her for her thoughts, she began speaking.

"I need to tell you something."

"All right, I'm listening." *Please don't let her say she only likes me as a friend.*

She stared down at her hands, visibly gathering her composure. Dread filled his heart. It was never good when a woman had to tell a guy something, and it looked like this conversation was about to go into that category.

"Look, whatever it is, just tell me." He softened his tone, hoping to put her at ease and get the conversation over with.

She nodded. "I like you."

"Uh…" He blinked.

She held up a hand. "No, let me get it out. I've liked you ever since high school, but you were popular and always surrounded by other girls. So I never said anything. When you started coming to Bible study, I thought about telling you then. Only you seemed interested in Jordan. But this morning…" She stopped, the rush of words leaving silence in their wake. "This morning," she started again, slower, calmer. "I thought I saw a sign of interest."

She liked him. Since high school. "Wow."

A shy smile appeared. "Is that wow good or bad?"

"Good. Definitely good. I'm actually pretty stunned; otherwise, I promise I'm much more articulate than this." He ducked his head then met her gaze head on. "Since you were honest, it's my turn. I've liked you since high school as well."

He chuckled as her mouth dropped open, but continued on. "I just didn't think I had a chance. You're smart, funny, and incredibly beautiful. I figured you would go for someone that fit you better. It wasn't until recently that I wished…no, prayed, I could be good enough for you. So yes. It's a good wow."

Her eyes searched his and he prayed his were showing his sincerity. He didn't ever want her to doubt his feelings.

"Well, you'll be happy to know that I did go for someone that fit me. This incredibly smart, funny, and handsome man finally asked me out and I said yes."

He knew he had a goofy grin on his face, but he couldn't help it. She really liked him. If they gave out awards for this, his acceptance speech was already formed. "So now what?"

"Here you two go." LeeAnn placed their food in front of them.

"Thanks, LeeAnn, but you could have called me up there."

She smiled at him. "You looked like you were having an important conversation. Enjoy."

The smell of the panini invaded his senses and his stomach gave an answering growl. Chloe laughed. It was light and airy and sounded better than wind chimes.

"Obviously you know I'm hungry." Darryl smiled at her. "Shall I say grace?"

"Yes, but make it quick for your stomach's sake."

With a grin, he reached for her hands. He stared at them, petite and soft. Her touch went straight to his soul. Right now, right here, he knew he would do anything to protect her. To make sure his hands would protect and love her and keep her from harm. He cleared his throat. "Thank you for this food you've blessed us with. Amen."

"Perfect." Chloe reached for her sandwich and took a huge bite.

Grinning, he followed her example.

Chapter Eight

*C*hloe was on cloud nine. Lunch had been wonderful. Darryl had kept the mood light by sharing jokes and funny antidotes from doctoring kids. She hadn't felt so relaxed and happy since...since...who knew when. When her grandmother passed away, the shine of life had faded. Became dimmer. Now it seemed bright and sunny again.

She could only pray that God would bless her with more dates with Darryl. They had exchanged phone numbers, and he promised to call that night. She glanced at her watch. *Still a ways to go.* Her phone rang, and she smiled in anticipation. But it dimmed when Jo's smiling face showed on the screen.

"Hello?"

"Hey, Chlo. Michelle wants to have a wedding planning session tonight. Can you come over after work, or are you hanging with the sibs?"

"I can make it tonight. We're supposed to go to dinner tomorrow. Kind of a redo, since the first one was so horrible."

"Then they're coming around?"

Chloe paused, thinking about Jo's question. Shopping with Jamie and Char had been interesting. "We're finding our way."

"I'm glad. I was a little worried."

"Likewise." She wasn't a hundred percent sure it would work out for the better, so she'd keep hoping.

"Well, I'm praying for you, girl. We'll talk more when you come over tonight, 'kay?"

"See you then."

She grabbed her sketch pad and notebook. The Millers would end up waiting if she didn't hurry.

～

Chloe parked her SUV in Jo and Michelle's driveway. She was mentally exhausted, but cancelling had never been an option. Since Michelle had moved back to Freedom Lake, the three tried to get together regularly. She couldn't believe both Jo and Michelle would be married soon.

Life changes always stressed her out, but more so lately.

Her brow furrowed as she thought of the changes their upcoming nuptials would bring. Would her friends still be willing to get together? Would she feel like an outsider if they did? Somehow, she didn't think it would be as easy as it was now. With a heavy heart, she rang the doorbell. *Lord, please help me put on a brave face. I want to celebrate with them, not feel like I'm attending a funeral.*

The door opened and Jo answered with a huge grin. "Hey, Chlo."

She hugged her friend. "Hey, JoJo." She sniffed. "Something smells good."

"Chelle's trying a new recipe."

Chloe followed Jo toward the kitchen. Exotic scents permeated the air. As she crossed the doorway into the kitchen, a mixture of spices, chicken, couscous, and bread had her stomach dancing in anticipation. "Yum."

Michelle looked up. "Hey, Chlo. I'm trying a Moroccan dish. Guy and the girls have a very limited palate. I'm trying to expand it."

She chuckled. "Good luck. Some kids are very picky."

"Nah, not Rachel and Rebekah."

Guy's twins were adorable. She couldn't believe Michelle was going to be a stepmom. She sat on the barstool. "Anything I can do to help?"

"Nope." Michelle glanced at Jo who met her gaze with a small shrug.

"Okay, spill it. I can tell something's up."

Michelle laid her hands on the counter and leaned closer. "Rumor has it that a certain beloved pediatrician and the local interior designer were eating at LeeAnn's today in what seemed to be a cozy manner." Michelle wiggled her eyebrows. "Is it true?"

The blush that heated her face seemed answer enough.

Michelle squealed while Jo's mouth dropped open.

"Wait a minute, calm down you two. It was just lunch." She bit her lip, trying to contain her smile.

"Just lunch? Girl, you two have been living some tortured mental love affair for over a year now. This was more than lunch."

"True." With that, she let her grin come out. Her cheeks hurt from its weight but it felt heavenly. "Guys, he was so sweet and funny."

Jo sat down next to her. "I want to hear every detail."

So Chloe told her everything. Of course, she left out a few things like her touching his hair and him preventing her fall, but it didn't matter.

Michelle and Jo ate up every word. She was definitely going to miss this when they married.

After dinner, they gathered into the living room with tons of bridal magazines. Chloe stared at her friends. "So did you guys set a date?"

Michelle nodded. "We want to marry in July."

"Wow, I thought you'd marry this year."

"We are. July is only a couple of months away."

Her mouth dropped. "Wait. You mean this July, not next year?" *Why so fast?* But the cry remained silent, echoing loudly in her heart.

Jo snorted. "You know those two have history. It's probably better they don't wait so long."

"Whatever." Michelle playfully hit Jo on the arm, and then turned to Chloe. "We don't want a long engagement. Just a simple wedding with our friends and family."

Chloe stared at her friend. She thought Michelle would want all the pomp and circumstance for her wedding. It looked like being with Guy had mellowed her out. "Sounds great."

"It will be. We agreed to have it at the lake, and we've already reserved the date."

"Wow, Chelle." She sniffed, trying to keep the tears at bay. Time was going too fast.

"What about you, JoJo?" Michelle asked.

"We decided on September. The idea of a fall wedding appeals to me."

"Oh, Jo," Chloe breathed. "You're going to be a beautiful bride."

Jo wrinkled her nose. "If only I didn't have to wear a wedding dress."

"You have to," Michelle practically shouted.

Jo looked shocked, but it was all Chloe could do not to laugh. She really couldn't picture Jo in a wedding dress either. A dressed up pair of overalls, yes, wedding dress no. "What about if you mixed denim and wedding dress together?" She watched for Jo's reaction to her suggestion.

Jo's eyes widened and Chloe could see the spokes turning in her mind. She clapped her hands with glee. "That's perfect!" With that proclamation, they sat down to plan the weddings.

∽

Darryl glanced at the dashboard, checking the time. As much as he wanted to go home right away and call Chloe, he knew he had to bide his time. She may not even be home. Instead, he headed down a familiar street. It had been a few weeks since he visited. Work was always a viable excuse. Plus, Ruby Jones didn't expect constant company. She preferred their once a month visit.

He found a close parking spot and headed inside the senior community room.

"Hey, Dr. D." Stephanie smiled from behind the receptionist's desk.

"Hi, Stephanie. Is my grandmother in her room?"

"Yes, she just came back from an aerobics class."

"Thanks."

He headed down the residential hall, waving hello whenever he passed a resident. Finally, he stopped in front of room 115 and knocked. What would he say to her? Usually he just checked on her and asked about her life at the senior home. *Not today.* He wanted to know what had possessed her to give his mother his phone number. His private line at that.

The door opened and his grandmother stood in the doorway. All five feet five inches of her, although age had subtracted from her stature.

"Darryl," she said with a nod.

"Hello, Grandmother."

She moved back and motioned him inside. A towel hung from her neck and draped across her track suit top. "I just came back from aerobics. Have a seat. Do you want some water? Tea?"

He ran a hand down his face. "Water is fine, Grandmother."

"Good. It's the best thing to drink."

She handed him a cold bottle of water and sat down on the red wingback chair opposite from his recliner. "It's about time you went for a more mature look." She pointed toward his hair. "What prompted you to cut it?"

He resisted the urge to rub his hand over the short curls. "I've accepted Christ as my Savior." He shrugged his shoulders. "So I cut it."

"Hmm, 'bout time." Her nails clicked on the armrest of the rocking chair. "I suppose you've come to talk about Alice?"

Lord, give me strength. "Yes, Grandmother."

Her steely gaze met his, her hair pulled back in the bun, showcasing her silver head of hair. It emphasized her rigid nature. "She's your mother, no matter what's transpired."

"I understand that. Really I do. But she hasn't been one for about sixteen years now." *Sixteen years, four months, and twenty days, but who was counting?*

His grandmother watched him, her gaze giving nothing away. Of all the people he expected to side with him, Ruby Jones had been one. Since when had she grown a heart and desired a family reunion?

"You know, Darryl, time waits for no one. Once it's passed you can't get it back. It does something to a person, being filled with regrets, sorrow, anger...dare I even add bitterness."

Her owlish gaze watched him, and he tried not to squirm in his seat. If he had been a teenager again, he would have already capitulated and called his mother without so much as a sign of his discontentment. Except he was no longer a teenager that bowed to Ruby Jones' rules. "Next you'll be telling me I need to talk to my father as well."

"Humph. It's long overdue if you ask me."

His jaw dropped. *She couldn't be serious?* No way was he going to see his father.

"Oh, close your mouth," his grandmother snapped out with a wave of her hand. "I probably didn't help things when you were younger. I never encouraged you to visit. I thought it was much too soon."

For the first time, he saw a hint of regret on her face. It bowled him over. Thank goodness he was already sitting down. He'd never thought his grandmother would ever regret her actions. Not even when her son was hauled away to jail after a 'guilty' plea.

"You need to bury the hatchet so that you can get on with your life."

"I can't believe what I'm hearing. I thought you hated my father."

Her eyes welled up with tears and she turned her head, staring at the wall. "Even if there is a reason to, a mother can never hate their child. Like I said, living with regrets, sorrow, anger…it's not something you want to carry over into eternity."

Was she saying she believed in heaven and hell? As far as he knew, she had never stepped foot into a church. He sighed. Apparently he wasn't as prepared for this conversation as he thought. She was turning his world upside down. "I don't understand where this is all coming from."

"You're not the only one who's been talking to God. I've seen the error of my ways." She sat forward. "In fact, I'm going to see him this Saturday."

He raised an eyebrow. "God?"

"Your father."

The words fell from her lips and silence descended. The roar in his ears was deafening. She couldn't be serious. Could she?

She inhaled, her body shaking from the weight of it. "Come with me, Darryl. Then we can enjoy the freedom Christ so mercifully offers."

His head was shaking before she finished her sentence. "I can't. I don't ever, *ever*, want to see him again. And I can't believe you would."

A look of resignation fell upon her face. "I understand. If you change your mind, I'm leaving at nine so I can get there in time for visiting hours."

He rose. This visit wasn't going like he imagined and the only way to make it stop was to leave. "I'll see you, Grandmother."

"I'll be here" she whispered. "I'll be here."

Chapter Nine

C hloe placed her keys on the key hook by the front door. Never had she been so happy to be home. Hanging out with Jo and Michelle had been fun, but her emotions had been threatening to surface all evening long. As happy as she was for them, she couldn't help but feel sad for herself. It was like she was losing her best friends. Logically, she knew that wasn't the case, but their friendship was bound to change. How could it not? Michelle would be an instant mom and Jo would be wrapped up in Evan.

And there was nothing she could do about it. *Not that I would.*

Shaking off the melancholy, Chloe meandered into the kitchen. Maybe some tea would help her settle down. She opened her pantry, looking at her selections of tea. The dark gray box of Oolong beckoned to her. It was just what the doctor ordered.

Her cell rang, pausing her preparations. It seemed to be ringing a lot lately. Couldn't she just have silence? She looked over her shoulder, glancing to where she'd placed it on the counter, and froze.

Darryl was calling her. She wanted to be excited but nerves warped her emotions. What would she say?

Answer the phone!

With the swipe of a finger, the ringing stopped and she placed it up to her ear. "Hello?"

"Hey, Chloe, it's Darryl."

The grin on her face couldn't be stopped. His voice sounded even better over the phone then it did in person. "Hi, there. What are you up to?" She wanted to congratulate herself on the small talk, thankful she remembered how to use it.

"Just got home from a visit with my grandmother."

"She lives at the senior center, right? How does she like it?"

"She loves it. I caught her right after aerobics class."

She nodded, but then realized he couldn't see her. "Sounds good." *Now what?* Her mind was short on words, but she didn't want to get off the phone. What did you say to a guy that you had a secret crush on forever?

"What are you up to?"

"Making tea. Long evening."

His sigh reached her ears.

"Are you okay?"

"Long evening as well."

She grabbed her tea and headed for her overstuffed chair.

"Will you go out with me tomorrow night?"

Of all the times for her to have plans. "I'd love to. But I already have plans."

"Oh."

Her heart ached at his rejected tone. "My new family and I are going to retry dinner." She bit her lip, on the verge of asking him to join them. "How about Saturday?"

"Perfect."

They made plans to go out Saturday and slowly but surely, the conversation turned. Once again, he filled the space with jokes and laughter. Part of her wanted to tell him about Jamie and the others, but she didn't want to have that conversation over the phone. She didn't know why, but she felt the need to tell him they were white. That *she* was half-white. Would it make a difference in their relationship? Did they even have a relationship?

She sighed, hating how often her thoughts spun off one another like an intricate web. Hopefully God would lead her when they went out Saturday.

And with any luck, Darryl would take the news well.

Friday sped past and before Chloe knew it, she was headed out the door to pick up the Davenport clan. This time, it seemed obvious that she would miss Bible study. Char and JJ planned on going back to Ohio tomorrow, which worked out well since she would be going out with Darryl.

Jamie, however, was intent on settling in Freedom Lake and looking forward to Indiana living. She'd been hanging out more at The Space and Chloe had to admit her half-sister had a wonderful eye for design. She had never imagined herself working with someone. It was a pleasant surprise.

She turned down the street leading to the Carter's B&B. *Lord, please let this dinner go better than the last.* They had decided to go to Emilio's, the Italian place in downtown Freedom Lake, so they wouldn't have to make the drive to the city.

The summer weather was a little better now that the sun wasn't perched high in the sky. She wasn't a fan of high heat but loved the sunny skies. She buzzed the doorbell, nerves suddenly rearing their ugly heads.

Her hands felt damp and her stomach did the Polka. The door opened and JJ smiled at her. "Hey, Chloe. Mrs. Carter figured it was you." He shuffled backward. "The girls are making last minute touchups to their faces. Not that it'll help them any," he said with a laugh.

She didn't know what else to do but laugh. Her thoughts were going a million miles a minute as she stepped through the door. Words failed her as she searched for something to say. *Will I ever be completely comfortable around them?*

JJ stood there with his hands in his pockets, and suddenly she wondered if he looked like their father. Did she?

"I'm sorry about our first meeting," JJ said, his voice unsteady.

"It's okay. I'm sure you were in just as much shock as I was."

"More upset with my father than anything." He ran a hand over his hair and sighed.

"Why?" She had been afraid to ask Jamie about him or her grandparents, but she was curious. How could she not be?

"Jamie says he won't even admit you're his." He swallowed and his Adam's apple bobbed up and down. "It makes me ashamed. I never..." his voice trailed off and the click of heels carried through.

"CeeCee!" Jamie beamed and enveloped her in a hug.

Jamie had broken through every barrier she had ever erected. She hugged her back, genuinely happy to see her. "Hey, Jamie."

"I'm so excited about dinner. A little sad that Char and JJ are leaving, but glad we get to hang out." She hooked her arm through Chloe's. "Okay, people, let's go."

Jamie led the way. Her exuberance was adorable. JJ and Char smiled at her as they passed. She ducked her head. Maybe she would eventually belong.

∽

The phone light flashed, notifying Darryl of an incoming call. "Dr. Jones, how may I help you?"

"Hello, Darryl. It's your grandmother."

He chuckled to himself. Her voice identified her, but he'd let her get out her formalities. "Hello, Grandmother."

"Would you please come by after work?"

Twice in one week? His eyebrow rose. "Is everything okay?"

"Yes, I just need to see you."

"All right. I'll be there."

"Thank you."

He placed the phone in the receiver. His grandmother never called him to ask for a visit. *Never.* He ran a hand across his jaw. *I need to shave.* His brain switched gears back to his grandmother.

Was she sick? He knew that elderly patients started acting differently the older they got. It was often worse if their loved ones began dying. Some of the seniors at the community center joked that they were simply trying to get into heaven.

He drew in a breath, his shoulders shuddering. He didn't know what he would do if Ruby Jones had some incurable disease or only a few months to live. She was unshakeable. At least, she'd always been rock steady in his eyes. Even when his world fell apart, his grandmother had remained a stable force. Some would consider her behavior stoic or unfeeling. He always assumed she had feelings; he just never had a chance to see them.

The end of the work day came quickly but ended on a good note. Since adding Jordan, they had finally found their rhythm and the practice now thrived. Jordan had a way with kids and the teenagers loved her. The new dinosaur room had been completed and the younger boys loved it. Patients who had been shy were suddenly eager to talk.

Jordan was a genius.

Or rather, Chloe was. Her design skills were pure magic.

He smiled as an image of her face came to mind. Tomorrow couldn't come soon enough. He could only pray that his grandmother didn't have bad news to deliver. He'd hate his good mood to be brought down. Nevertheless, he drove to the senior center.

Darryl winced. That sounded so selfish. It was just that he was riding on a high and wanted to end the day on it. None of that would matter if his grandmother was ill. *Lord, please let her be okay. She's the only family I have left.*

Okay, so that wasn't entirely true. He did have a mother and father, but they had long since ceased to be a family in a sense that mattered. When his mother had walked away after his father's sentence to prison, a portion of him had become closed off. He had filled the space with anger and distanced himself from the female population.

Except for Chloe.

Chloe made him want to hand his heart over on a silver platter. He had a feeling it would be safe in her hands. He just wasn't too sure if she deserved to be saddled with him and his baggage. He gave a mental shake of the head, trying to regain the high he had earlier.

"Leave it alone for now," he murmured to himself.

He waved hello to the receptionist at the senior center and headed straight for his grandmother's room. His jaw tightened as he drew closer to her room. Drawing in a deep breath, Darryl sent another prayer up to God. He still wasn't sure if he was praying correctly, but at least he tried.

He knocked, holding his breath in anticipation.

The door opened and his grandmother nodded at him. "Darryl. Thank you for coming."

"Of course, Grandmother. Is everything all right?" Why wouldn't she open the door all the way?

"Yes." She stared at him.

Stared at him so long, the hairs on the nape of his neck stood at attention.

"Come in, Darryl."

He stepped over the threshold cautiously. It was like he was in some Alfred Hitchcock film. His senses were on alert, waiting for an unseen force to pop out. He looked at his grandmother, ready to beg her to share her news.

"Hello, Darryl."

He froze. He peered over his grandmother's shoulder and saw his mother rising from the couch.

Her hair is longer.

Why that was the first thought? Maybe his mind needed something to cling to in the midst of the confusion.

"What are you doing here?" He stepped back.

"I wanted to see you." She took a step forward.

After sixteen years of absence?

It was then his brain picked up on the other differences. She had put on some weight. Her forehead no longer bore stress lines although he could tell she was nervous. She no longer carried the weight of oppression on her. Still, she had abandoned him when he'd already lost his father.

"I told you—"

She held a hand up. "I know, you're not ready. And I know it's my fault. After much thought and prayer, I realized I should be the one making the first move...so here I am."

She held her hands up like an offering.

If she thought he would run into her arms, she was in for a world of heartache. Part of him, the one who used to wonder if he could earn his mother's forgiveness, wanted to talk to her. To sit and find out how life had treated her.

The other part, the one who watched his mother drive away without a backward glance, didn't even want to be in the same room with her. He turned toward his grandmother.

"It's time, Darryl," she said softly.

"No." He shook his head. "I'm afraid it's too late." He pivoted on his heel, trying to keep his composure.

"Darryl, get back here and talk to your mother."

He stopped, staring at the door that would get him out of this mess. The steel in his grandmother's voice warned him that if he left she would be seriously bent out of shape ...but the voice whispering in his ear reminded him that he was an adult.

Without a sound, he opened the door and walked out.

He didn't say hello to anyone in the hall. Didn't say goodbye to Stephanie. He didn't stop moving until he unlocked his car door. With one push of the button it unarmed, allowing him to flee inside in search for sanctuary.

He needed to go somewhere. Talk to someone. *Anyone.*

In a haze he drove by memory, turning left and right, going up the winding road. It wasn't until he was parked in the driveway that he realized he had arrived at Guy's house. He sighed in relief. Michelle's car was absent, meaning he wouldn't interrupt any visit between the engaged couple. It was only a matter of weeks before they would tie the knot.

But for now, he needed to disrupt his friend's life. He needed to unleash the fury that was swirling around in his midsection like the eye of the storm. He was quiet now, but it was only a matter of time before a trigger unleashed the anger.

It'd been awhile since he'd been this angry.

He knocked on the door, foot bouncing up and down.

"Yo, D...what's wrong?" Guy asked, his voice deepening with concern.

"My grandmother just ambushed me." He followed Guy into the living room, pacing back and forth. "My mother was there."

"Whoa, what?"

He turned and looked at his friend, taking in the look of disbelief on Guy's face. In the back of his mind he wondered if that's how he appeared when he first saw her. Did she see his shock or only care about herself like usual?

"She called about a week ago, asking to see me. I said no. So she showed up, enlisting my grandmother's help."

"Ms. Ruby actually helped?"

He snorted. "Exactly my thoughts." He stopped his pacing and stared at Guy. "What in the world makes her think she can just waltz back in my life after being absent for sixteen years? *Sixteen years!* Not a letter, a birthday card, a phone call, e-mail, text...you name it, I didn't get it. I have heard nothing from this woman, I mean *nothing!*"

He resumed his pacing, wishing he could do something with his hands. "I can't believe this mess. Just when life was finally looking up, she shows up and ruins it."

"Have you prayed, man?"

The question stopped him dead in his tracks. "I didn't even think to do it." The guilt pressed upon his shoulders. How could he forget that he was a different person now? That he had someone who would listen?

"It's okay, D. You're still new to this. It'll take a lot of practice before it becomes second nature."

Darryl nodded, still feeling horrible.

"I'll pray with you."

"Thanks, G."

He bowed his head as Guy lifted him up in prayer.

He was thankful that he had someone around who would remind him that he could pray and talk to God about anything. He added a silent prayer not to forget to pray the next time rage came his way. Because he knew as certain as his next breath that he'd be angry again.

Chapter Ten

C hloe laughed as JJ did an impression of Jamie. Everything was spot on except his voice. So far, the dinner was going far better than the first one. She wasn't completely comfortable, but it was only a matter of time.

She took a sip of her water, trying to soothe her throat. Jamie rolled her eyes but laughed good naturedly.

"Fine, so I get a little hyper."

"A little?" JJ asked incredulously. "You're like the energizer bunny after drinking a red bull."

Chloe snorted and her drink dribbled down her chin. "Stop, stop." She wiped her face. "I can't take any more. I'm already stuffed and now you're trying to get it to reverse track."

Char's nose scrunched up. "JJ, stop before Chloe runs the other direction."

"Thanks," she said softly. This was probably the nicest thing Char had said. She offered a shy smile and received one in return.

She blinked as the server appeared at their table. *Where did he come from?* All night he had performed disappearing acts.

"Excuse me. There is someone here who wishes to speak to you."

"Girl? Boy? Which one of us?" Jamie's voice rose an octave as she stared at the server in bewilderment.

"A woman and all of you."

"Okay," Char said slowly. "We'll talk to her."

The server bowed and vanished. He returned a couple of minutes later, with the visitor in tow. He bowed and vanished again.

Chloe stared at the woman, wondering who she was and what she could possibly have to say. She looked familiar. Did she live in Freedom Lake? Her blonde hair fell to her chin in a sleek bob. Her green eyes shined bright but the way she bit her lip and clutched her purse spoke of an inner agitation. She seemed timid, which was odd because she looked to be in her late thirties, early forties. Wasn't age supposed to bring confidence?

"How can we help you?" Char asked, her arms folded across her chest.

Chloe wanted to smile. Finally, she was picking up on different nuances of her siblings. Char seemed to fold her arms in preparation for something she was unsure of.

"Um, yes. I'm Hannah Blakely. I'm Mrs. Davenport's personal assistant."

Chloe swallowed. She drew in a deep breath, trying to keep the panic at bay. She'd seen this woman before around town. There was only one guess as to which Mrs. Davenport she was referring to.

Char frowned in confusion. JJ looked annoyed and Jamie looked wary.

Chloe spoke up. "Are you referring to Geraldine Davenport?"

Jamie gasped.

"Wait a minute," JJ looked between her and Ms. Blakely. "Are you talking about our grandmother?"

"Yes, sir. She requests your attendance tomorrow at five p.m." Her gaze flitted nervously between them all.

"*All* of us?" Jamie asked.

"Yes," she looked at Chloe. "You too, Ms. Smith."

She knows my name?

Chloe blinked. How was she supposed to feel about that? Happy? Bitter? Her grandmother had been instrumental in separating her parents. Granted, she got three siblings out of it, but she'd been raised without a mother or father. Now she was just supposed to show up because her grandmother 'summoned' them?

Char met her gaze head on, lifting an eyebrow in question. Chloe shook her head. She had no wish to meet Mrs. Davenport. Char tossed her hair and looked at Ms. Blakely. "Please inform her we're unavailable."

Hannah stepped back. "Wait, what? You *must* reconsider." She clutched her purse and her face reddened, eyes widening with a hint of concern. "You have to show up. She won't accept no for an answer."

"Then give me her phone number," Char responded.

"What?" Hannah stared in confusion.

"Ms. Blakely, may I have my grandmother's phone number," she said. "Good grief, take a breath, you look ill."

She straightened her shoulders, keeping a tight grip on her clutch. "I can give you her address."

"Please give my sister her number. I'm sure Char will take care of it." Jamie stared at her.

Reluctantly, she rambled off the phone number. Immediately Char punched in the numbers and waited for an answer.

"Yes, this is Charlotte Davenport. I'll wait."

Chloe watched, hoping, wishing…praying for something, but for what she didn't know. *Lord, help in any way you can. Please.* Desperation clawed at her. She wasn't ready to meet her grandparents. They had lost that privilege all too long ago. A part of her knew she should give them a chance, to turn the other cheek, but she didn't have the fortitude to do so at this point in her life.

"Hello, this is Charlotte. Yes, Ms. Blakely just interrupted a family dinner with a summons to your house tomorrow. Thank you for the invitation but we're not coming."

"No, I'm not mistaken and yes, you heard me correctly. We will *not* join you for dinner until you learn how to treat us with the common decency that humans deserve. No, I understood Ms. Blakely. She delivered your message crystal clear. Regardless, we're refusing."

Char set her cell down. "It's been handled."

Hannah's face flamed brighter. She ducked her head and walked quietly away. Chloe almost felt sorry for her. Who knew the reasons why she kept a job that made her so miserable?

"Nice going, Char…" JJ grimaced.

"Now to have a conversation with dear ol' dad when we get home."

"No," Chloe said. "It's unnecessary."

"No," Jamie replied. "It's very much necessary. I'm just glad to see Char agree with me for once."

"Me too," JJ replied somberly.

Tears welled in her eyes as her lower lip trembled. "Thanks, guys."

Thank You for blessing me with family, Father.

Darryl opened his door and smiled at Evan. "Thank goodness you're the first one here."

Evan crutched his way in.

"Is Jo with you?"

"No, she's coming with Michelle. She had a last-minute change in schedule."

"You...drove?" Shock coursed through him. Evan had always refused to drive without a prosthetic. What had changed?

"Yeah, man. It was time for me to take back my independence and rethink what I can and can't do. I don't want to push it, but I don't want the lack of a full leg to hinder me either."

Darryl beamed. "I'm proud of you man."

Evan sat down on the couch, so he followed suit.

"Okay, spit it out. You've been jumpy since I walked in. What's up?"

"I went to lunch with Chloe."

"Like a date?" Evan's eyebrows raised.

"Exactly like a date."

"And *you* asked *her* out?"

Darryl bit back a chuckle and nodded.

"'Bout time. Wait a minute," Evan said holding a hand up. "Does she actually know you're interested in her?"

He was tempted to roll his eyes but didn't want to be accused of acting like a girl. "Yeah, I was going to be straight up with her, but she beat me to the punch." He couldn't stop the grin that stole across his face at the memory.

Evan's low whistle brought him back to his senses. "Wow. I never thought it would happen. Y'all have been tiptoeing around each other since I moved back. Well, in your case since high school."

He smiled at Evan. No way was he going to tell him Chloe felt the same way. It was enough that he knew.

"So what else is up with you?"

This time, he did roll his eyes. "My mother and grandmother ambushed me."

"Hold up. I thought you said your mother."

"You heard me right."

"When did this happen?" Evan sat forward, resting his elbows on his upper thighs.

"The other day."

"What did you do?"

"I walked out." He looked at his friend. Had the man lost his mind? What else did he think he was going to do?

"Wait a minute. You walked out on your mom?"

"No, she took care of that sixteen years ago. I just left the building."

"D, man, you get my point."

"Look," he huffed. "I don't understand why you're bent out of shape. She messed up, not me."

"That she did," Evan said with a nod. "But doesn't she deserve to be treated the way you desire to be treated?"

"Really, Ev? The golden rule?"

"You're a new man, D. So yeah, the golden rule applies here."

Darryl looked away. A comeback remained out of his reach. The logical explanation hit him in the gut, but for once he didn't want to go that route. He wanted to act based on his emotions. His mother had left him without a second thought.

He cleared his throat. "You mean I have to act nicely because I'm a follower of Christ now? Is that what you're telling me? Regardless of her behavior?" His eyes itched.

"Regardless man. I know it's a tough pill to swallow, but look at it this way. If you had done what she did, found Jesus, and then decided to right your wrongs, would you want another chance?"

He squeezed his eyes shut. Too bad he couldn't plug his ears without looking childish. Evan had a point, but he didn't have to like it. It seemed unfair. Why was he, the victim, being punished?

Why, Lord?

Evan cleared his throat. "I know it's a lot to think about."

"It is, but as much as I want to, I can't argue with your logic."

"I'll give you a reprieve and change the subject." Evan chuckled and the tension eased up.

"Change away," he said with a thrust of his arm.

"Would you be my best man?"

His eyebrows rose. "I'd be honored." Darryl leaned over and bumped fists with Evan. "When's the day?"

"September twenty-first."

"Nice. I know Guy said they're tying the knot in July."

"Yeah. I didn't see those two coming."

Darryl snorted. "I don't know why not. The air crackled whenever they were in the same room."

"True. The whole love-hate thing, huh?"

"Yeah, they loved to pretend to hate one another." They chuckled.

Darryl was glad he had taken the plunge and let Chloe know he liked her. Yet he wasn't crazy enough to let her know it was probably already halfway to love. Who said that when they had yet to go on an official date? Lunch at LeeAnn's didn't count in his opinion. No, he wanted to show her the way she deserved to be treated.

Tomorrow's date would be epic.

Chapter Eleven

*C*hloe glanced at the clock for the umpteenth time. Darryl said he would be coming to pick her up at four. In true fashion, she had been ready thirty minutes early. So instead of reading her Bible, texting on her phone, or some other normal routine, her gaze remained fixed on the clock.

Another minute passed. *This is insane.* How was she supposed to pass the other twenty-nine minutes until his arrival? She blinked as her doorbell rang. With another glance at the clock, she made her way to her front door. Her one-bedroom apartment allowed her to make the trip in seconds.

Wrenching the door open, her mouth dropped open in shock. "Darryl." He was early. Twenty-nine minutes early. A grin broke out across her face.

"Hey." He ducked his head, sliding his hands into his pockets. "I couldn't wait any longer."

She chuckled softly. "Glad to know I'm not the only one."

"I see you're ready to go."

"Yes."

"Shall we?" He motioned to his car with his head.

She nodded and grabbed her satchel and house keys off the hook.

Ever the gentleman, he held the car door open and his fresh scent beckoned to her. What would he do if she just leaned into him? If she wrapped her arms around him and kissed him?

Since when do you focus on the physical?

"You okay?" Darryl murmured.

"Yes." She smiled, hoping to erase the images of her wrapped around him. Before he could respond, she got in the car. Since she was wearing her white capris and yellow tunic top, she didn't have to worry about flashing him in a dress. Sometimes pants were really the best option.

When he got in the driver's side, she glanced at him out of the corner of her eyes. For a moment, she missed the way his curls used to flop over. Then again, the new haircut allowed her to see all of his face.

Lord, he's so handsome.

She cleared her throat. "Where are we going?"

His grin split wide and his teeth gleamed in the sunlight. "My boat."

"You have a boat?" What else didn't she know about him?

"I do. I bought it a few years ago. Summer is the perfect time to bring it out."

She looked at him. "So, this is going to sound crazy."

"Go for it." He shifted gears.

"I've never been out on the lake."

His mouth dropped open and his head swiveled toward her. "How can you live in this town without going out on the lake?"

"My grandmother couldn't swim, so we never went. The closest I got was at the park. Of course, as an adult I've walked the trails around the lake. I just didn't go into the water." Would he think her ridiculous? Sheltered? She wouldn't argue those points, but it was still rather embarrassing.

"Well, that's not too surprising. My grandmother doesn't know how to swim either. I learned in elementary. My dad insisted." Gone went the smile as creases appeared on his forehead.

What was he thinking about?

Darryl gripped the gear shift like his life depended on it.

"Do you want to talk about it?"

"What have you heard? Freedom Lake is small enough, I'm sure you've heard some rumors."

"Just that he was arrested and sentenced to prison. Even though our grandmothers were friends, they never said anything that I might have overheard. That rumor was just from the local gossip mill."

He snorted. "Well, they got one right. He was arrested when I was fifteen."

How awful. Was that one of the reasons he thought he wasn't good enough? She'd be the first person to sympathize, not condemn. No one wanted to be lumped in with their parents, especially when they had a bad reputation.

"How did you come to live with your grandmother?"

His jaw flexed and his hand shifted, tightening again. "My mom left town once the hearing was finalized."

"What do you mean?" Surely he couldn't mean what she thought? Then again, why was she surprised? Her mother hadn't raised her either, but at least she abandoned her from the get go and not midway through her life.

"She got in her car and drove away. Apparently she had already talked to my grandmother and had the paperwork in place for me to stay with her."

Chloe blinked, trying to hold back tears. Something told her he wouldn't think too kindly of them. "Why are parents so awful?"

"That's the million-dollar question."

"Have you seen her since?"

A bitter chuckle fell from his lips. "Yes. Unfortunately, she's in town and wants to talk. Evidently she wants to be a mother now."

She opened her mouth, then promptly shut it. This was the point where she should encourage him to get close to his mother. Maybe even relay a Bible scripture. Except she couldn't. Her mouth shut as she realized how much she agreed with him. Why was he supposed to pick up the pieces after a parent...an adult, ground their hopes and dreams into powder?

"What are you going to do?"

He put the car in park. "I want to ignore her, but her face keeps popping up in my brain at the most inopportune times." Darryl looked at her. "Why should I be the one to make things right? She left me, Chloe. Poof." His hands made a vanishing move.

"I get it." She placed her hand on his arm, licking her lips. Now would be the perfect time to tell him about her father. "You know how I said I just met my half-brother and sisters?"

He nodded, his eyes looking straight at her. What would it be like to look into his face every day? She stared at her hands trying to refocus. "Turns out my biological father is white."

"Wow, how did you feel when you found out?"

She stared up at him in amazement. "I'm still trying to figure that out."

He pulled gently on a curl, and it was all she could do to prevent herself from leaning into him.

"Have you met him?"

"He doesn't want to see me."

Darryl's eyes darkened, resembling the sky when thunder was running rampant. "How could he not want to meet you?"

She shrugged, but the hurt widened. Like a chasm that couldn't be closed, couldn't be healed. "I don't know. I'm just happy my siblings do. Jamie, she's the youngest, she's been great."

Darryl shifted in his seat and rested his forehead against hers. She swallowed as his minty breath fanned against her face. He continued playing with her hair. Thoughts fled her until the only thing left was her and Darryl.

"We're a pair, aren't we?" he asked softly.

"Pathetic."

"Ridiculous."

"Pitiful."

"Wretched."

Silence fell.

"My mind's blank," Darry said sheepishly.

She laughed, moving away. Chloe met his gaze and wondered if he'd kiss her. His eyes wavered back and forth, as if searching for something.

"Come on," he said. "You'll love the boat."

He hopped out the door, and she watched in amusement as he slid across the hood, bowed and opened her door.

Laughing, she took his hand and stood. "You do that often?"

He grinned. "Nah, I just practiced a lot." His hand closed around hers as he led her to the boats.

A few boats were docked along the pier. Which one was his? He led her to the one in the middle. The words "First Love" were painted on the side.

She pointed to the name. "You're in love with your boat?"

A bark of laughter erupted from him, his teeth gleaming. "No, I bought it from one of my patient's parents. I just couldn't figure out what to rename it, so I didn't."

Darryl helped her in, his hands warm against her sides. She swallowed, trying to focus on not sliding and falling on her face. She wasn't the most graceful person on land. No telling how it would be on a boat.

A few minutes later they were out on the lake, the breeze whipping her curls back. She felt a little ridiculous in the life jacket, but it was a Freedom Lake rule that anyone in a boat wear one. Chloe closed her eyes and tilted her head upward, letting the sun's rays caress her face. The scents of water and summer drifted over her, chasing her cares away.

It was the perfect date.

Slowly, the boat came to a stop. She turned and watched as Darryl made his way toward her. He sat down next to her and propped his feet up.

"This is my favorite spot on the lake. The breeze is always perfect. Not too many boaters come out this way, so we don't have to worry about rocking motions."

Taking a risk, she slowly leaned into him and rested her head against his shoulder. His arm came around her and she sighed in contentment.

This was the life.

～～

Life couldn't get much better than this. Darryl had prayed that she would like being out on the boat as much as he did. He hadn't dared to dream that it would be like this. The feel of her in his arms was hypnotic. And he couldn't get enough of touching her curly hair. His fingers played with the curls as she rested her head against his shoulder.

In the car, he'd been worried his father's criminal status would ruin his chances with her. Instead, Chloe met his gaze with understanding. How the two of them ended up with the worst parents boggled the mind.

He thought back to a Bible study where Jo had said their experiences helped them comfort others who went through the same thing. Right now, he believed her. If it had been any other woman he doubted they would have been okay with his past.

She still doesn't know what you did.

He swallowed. Okay, so maybe he wasn't 100 percent sure Chloe could handle everything. For now, he would treasure the acceptance she gave him about his parents. All that mattered was the feel of her in his arms. They'd have an hour of uninterrupted bliss before he took her to the next surprise.

The boat had already been stocked with their dinner, but he had plans beyond that. He wanted this date to be memorable, and he'd found the perfect gift to commemorate it a few days ago. Darryl let out a breath of air. *Lord, please let her like the gift.*

As if sensing his nerves, she sat up and met his gaze. "Are you all right?"

"Yeah, just thinking about a surprise I have for you." Her eyes lit up and he grinned. She was so adorable.

"What is it?"

"You'll have to wait until later." He put his feet down and stood. "Are you hungry?"

"Famished," she said, her dark eyes twinkling in the sunlight.

"Good. I have an array of food ready for our dinning pleasure."

Darryl headed aft toward the stern where he'd stashed the picnic basket he borrowed from Ms. Luella. It was filled with goodies from LeeAnn's.

When he returned, Chloe was in mid-stretch, her arms trying to reach the sky. His mouth dried out. Silly to become captivated by her stretching. A few times, he had thought she wanted him to kiss her. He had to stay strong and not give in. He had already mapped out a plan so that he wouldn't ruin his chances. Everything had to be perfect, including their first kiss.

He brought up his mental calendar. The first kiss wasn't scheduled until date four. *Lord, help me make it that far.* He hadn't counted on the insane chemistry that enveloped him whenever he stood within touching distance. The honey scent that was hers alone lured him closer and closer every time. Back in his car, he'd had no choice but to lean his forehead against hers. It was that or kiss her senseless.

Slow down, D. You have all the time in the world to romance her. Show her how much you care.

"I hope you're hungry." He set the basket in the center of the deck. Opening it, he motioned her over. "LeeAnn gave us some nice options. There's chicken salad, a fruit-and-yogurt platter, veggie and humus, and to splurge, oatmeal raisin cookies."

"Oh, I love oatmeal raisin."

"Me too." LeeAnn had given him an earful on their similar eating habits.

They sat in companionable silence as they ate their food. He startled from his thoughts as Chloe nudged him with her shoulder.

"Thanks for taking me out on the lake. This has been wonderful."

"Anytime." And he meant it. He would love to have more moments of just relaxing. His schedule was so hectic, moments of relaxing were treasured.

She eyed him. "Can I have my surprise now?"

"What if I don't have it here?"

"Then where is it?" Her brow wrinkled, and he smoothed it away before he could think.

Quickly, he removed his hands and grabbed another cookie. Anything to keep his hands to himself. *Stop moving fast, D.*

"Darryl?"

"Oh, right." How could he forget her question? He snapped his fingers. "Right, your surprise. It's not here. It's waiting for us at another location."

"When are we getting it?" She bounced in her seat as she turned to face him.

"Calm down." He smothered a laugh. "It won't go anywhere."

"If I can guess what it is, can we leave now?"

"Not yet." He squeezed her hand.

"Spoilsport." The grin, accompanied by the rolling of her eyes, showcased her humorous side.

"Silly Chloe is pretty cute."

She froze and met his gaze. "Cute?"

The way she squinted her eyes told him cute wasn't the appropriate adjective to describe her.

"Adorable?"

"What am I? A puppy?"

He slid a finger down her smooth cheek. "In all honesty, you are breathtaking. The moment I hear your voice, my heart picks up speed. When you smile at me, it drops down to my toes." He leaned forward, resting his head against hers, trying to keep his hands in proper places. "You make me believe in love at first sight. In soul mates. In the possibility of two hearts melting into one."

"Darryl."

Her voice caught and it was his undoing. He cupped the back of her head, taking care. His lips touched one cheek and then the other. Slowly, he pulled away waiting for her eyes to open so that she could see, truly see, how he felt about her before he kissed her.

Her eyelids blinked and her dark eyes melted into his.

A chime peeled the air and his back pocket buzzed from the vibration of his phone. Biting back choice words, he pulled away and answered his cell.

"Dr. Jones."

"Dr. Jones, this is Alayna from Just Right Answering service. You have a message from one of your patients. A Brianna Stephens."

His heart dropped. Not Brianna. She was still recovering from her surgery. "Thanks, Alayna, I'll give them a call. What's the number?"

Quietly, he repeated the number as he dialed Brianna's mother. He turned to Chloe. "Work."

She nodded.

"This is Dr. Jones returning a page."

"Dr. D, Brianna has been acting funny. It's like she's asleep but not really."

Crap. "Get her to the hospital right away, Mrs. Stephens. I'll meet you there."

He turned to Chloe. Of all the ways his date would turn out, a medical emergency hadn't been in his plans. "I'm so sorry. It's one of my patients. I have to meet them at the hospital."

"Go. I'll call Jo or Michelle. You do what you have to do."

As soon as he docked the boat, he was out and running toward his car. He couldn't believe he had to abandon Chloe. He sent up a prayer to God for his budding relationship and for the life of his patient.

Chapter Twelve

*C*hloe padded quietly down the hall. Who could be knocking on her door so late? She clutched the snow globe tighter, just in case the person on the other side of the door had ill intent. With a silent prayer, she opened the door slowly…and blinked.

"Hey, Chlo, sorry it's so late." Darryl's hang dog expression started her heart a flutter, but the little black puppy in his arms turned it into a puddle.

"Aw." She placed the snow globe on the entry table and reached for the black puppy. "Where did you get…," peeking at the puppy, "him from?"

"One of my patient's miniature schnauzer became a mother. She needed a way to pay me, so…"

Her eyebrows rose of their own accord. "You let someone pay you with a puppy?"

The object in question gave her a lick. She giggled. He was so adorable and smelled like…like Darryl. "Why does he—" She stopped not wanting him to know how she recognized the scent. It's not like fresh linen smell was a cologne.

"How does he what?"

"He smells like he just came out of the laundry."

Darryl's deep chuckle sent shivers of awareness up her spine. He leaned against the doorjamb and for a moment she wanted to invite him in. *That's not a smart idea, Chloe.*

"He got into my satchel of potpourri."

"I didn't know you were a potpourri kind of guy."

"A gift from another patient's parent. She makes those little satchels to put in your dresser drawer and make it smell nice." He shrugged a shoulder. "And I didn't want it to go to waste so..."

"Another payment for your services?"

He grinned. "More like a tip."

Chloe loved the way his eyes crinkled at the corners. She buried her face in the dog's fur to hid the blush making its way into her cheeks. Instead, they warmed further as Darryl's scent enveloped her. The mystery of his scent was solved. "Well, hey if you haven't named your new friend, you've got a name already made."

"What?" The quizzical look on his face tugged at her.

She wanted to run her hands over the lines in his forehead. She swallowed, bringing her focus back. "Your puppy. Call him Satchel."

He chuckled. "That's a good name, but he's not my puppy."

She looked down at the now sleeping ball of fur then back at Darryl. "Now I'm confused."

"I don't have time to take care of a puppy. When I saw him, I thought he'd be a perfect companion for you."

"Me?"

Satchel shuddered in her arms as a soft snore shook his body.

"Surprise," Darryl said softly.

She gasped. "He's my surprise?"

"Is it a good one?" Darryl looked at her cautiously.

"Definitely." She leaned on her toes and kissed his cheek, inhaling the fresh linen smell. "Thank you," she whispered.

"You're welcome." He ran a finger down her face. "You make me wish I was a better man."

She stared in confusion as her face tingled from his caress.

"Sweet dreams."

Her heart thumped with trepidation as he walked away.

✥

Darryl watched the scene play out, as if it were yesterday. The dream more vivid than technicolor, only it was like he watched an out of body experience.

"I'm more of a man than you'll ever be. I'd never place my hands on a woman." The words echoed, etched in the darkest recesses of his being. Seared into his soul.

He watched as his father flung his mother aside, focusing solely on him. The old man took a few menacing steps toward him, but he refused to back down. He was done being silent. Done being an enabler in their dysfunctional family drama.

"Hank, no!"

He watched as his mother rose, grabbing his father's arm to stop his movement. A look of disgust darkened his father's eyes to soulless coals. With little effort, his father snatched his arm from his mother's grasp and swung it backward.

The slap rang loudly in his ears as he watched his mother crumple to the floor. Darryl stood transfixed as he watched the scene play out.

"Don't touch her!" Rage turned into something darker. Thought fled. There were only raw emotions coursing through his body. A roar tore from his throat as he charged his father, legs pumping in action. Never again would his mother be used as a human sparring partner. Adrenaline pumping through his veins, he leaped and rammed into his father with his shoulder. His father's eyes widened, arms splaying out as he landed with a thud.

Disdain turned to fear as Darryl began punching him. Finally, his father would know what it felt like to be beat on. Only it wasn't enough. His father needed to suffer as his mother had. Darryl *needed* to make sure his father paid for every slap, closed-fist punch, and derogatory statement tossed at her in fury.

With herculean effort, he dropped his weight onto his thighs, exerting the pressure on his father's torso. He wrapped his hands around the man's neck, willing his hands to squeeze tighter, to cut off the precious air that the man lived on to spew his venom and demean his mother.

His father's arms grew slack and triumphant coursed through Darryl's body.

"Let go, let go, let go!"

Darryl shot up in bed, the memory of the Freedom Lake Sheriff department storming through his house waking him from the recurrent dream. He sighed, wiping the beads of sweat on his forehead. It had been a couple of weeks since the dream continued in its entirety.

Well not completely in its entirety. He never dreamed about the endless hours in the sheriff's department speaking to the deputies and the on-call psychologist. Darryl hadn't been charged with any crimes. And the domestic violence charge hadn't kept his father in jail for very long. No, something else held him in there now.

He blinked, remembering the judge's order for therapy with a promise to seal his juvenile record upon completion. At Darryl's last anger management session, he'd promised to use his hands for good. Since then, he'd been trying to atone for his sin. That was until he repeated the prayer of salvation. He was thankful for his friends who had shown Him the way to God and the need for the gift of salvation from IIis Savior. Accepting God's grace went against all logic, but his soul thirsted for it.

He squeezed his eyes shut. Was he really worthy of Chloe? He had done a Bible search and read that his slate was clean...as white as snow. The image brought comfort, yet the voice inside his head told him he would never deserve Chloe. He'd die if his hands ever touched her in anger.

Wasn't there something in the Bible about the sins of the father? If he had even a remote possibility of turning into his old man, he didn't know if being in a relationship with her was worth it.

Hence the dog. Satchel—he shook his head, what a name—was a peace offering. No, more like a farewell gift. As much as he cared for her, maybe even enough to think the l-word, he couldn't risk hurting her.

The reoccurring dreams reminded him of the truth. Evil lurked inside of him and he wasn't sure God's grace could eradicate it. He would use the gift of grace for good. It was probably what had saved Brianna and allowed her to come out a diabetic coma. His professional life was covered. Now he needed to distance himself from Chloe. She deserved so much more than he could ever offer in a personal way.

∽∾

Chloe walked slowly around the trail hugging Freedom Lake's curves. Satchel took off, chasing after a butterfly. From the excited barks, she couldn't decide if he wanted to talk to it or eat it. The frantic edge to his tone would be laughable if she didn't feel so miserable.

She exhaled and glanced at her watch. Jo had promised to meet her. The anxiety that had dwelled in her insides the past week had slowly but surely morphed into rage. Darryl had dropped off the face of the earth.

Oh, she knew he was in Freedom Lake, but he acted like he didn't know her. He hadn't called her. Hadn't answered her texts about his patient. He didn't even ask about Satchel. Somewhere between their romantic date on the boat and the gift of Satchel, something had changed.

A bite of her lip redirected the ache in her chest. She scanned the lake's surface. What did she do? Had she misspoken? They'd never kissed...could that be the problem? With a groan, she kicked a rock and watched as it launched in the air. It startled the butterfly and it flew away. Satchel sat down in puzzlement as he stared off into the sky.

"You have a dog?!"

She whirled around, thankful Jo had finally showed up. "Yes. Jo meet Satchel. Satchel meet Jo."

He cocked his head.

"Satchel, say hi."

He barked.

Jo laughed. "You're teaching him tricks?"

Well, she was trying. "That's the only one he'll do on command. Sometimes he sits, but only if I have a treat."

Jo bent down, and Satchel rolled onto his back. She rubbed his belly as his legs twitched in the air. "Where did you get him?"

"Darryl gave him to me."

Jo's eyebrow raised and she stood. "So things are working out?"

"No," she replied sharply. She bit down on her tongue, willing the tears away.

"What happened?" Jo's eyes darkened in concern.

Chloe spilled every pent-up emotion as they strolled along the path. She told her about their date. About Darryl dropping off Satchel, and then the awful silence. Finally, when she exhausted her own ears with complaints, she stopped and met Jo's gaze. "What do you think happened?"

"I have no idea." Jo's hands settled comfortably into the pockets of her overalls.

Thank goodness she had a friend who would pause in her busy work schedule and listen to her vent. "I thought things were going so well, Jo. He said he's liked me since high school. So why do I suddenly feel like the teenage outcast?"

Jo rubbed her back. "I'm sorry, Chlo. Maybe he's still uncertain about the relationship. You did say he thought he wasn't good enough. Maybe it bothers him more than he let on."

"He's a doctor for heaven's sake. If anyone should feel unworthy, it's me." She gasped.

"What?" Jo's brows furrowed.

"I told him I was half-white. Do you think that's what it is?"

Jo's mouth dropped open. She quickly snapped it shut. "No way, he's not racist."

"Really? Then why haven't I heard from him? He acted like it was no big deal, now all of a sudden it is."

"Chlo, I'm sure there has to be another explanation."

"Really? Because I don't think there is."

"There has to be. Do you want me to get Evan to talk to him?"

She shook her head. "We're adults. I should...or we should be able to do this without running for help."

A light in Jo's eyes dimmed. *Oh no.* She hadn't meant to insult Jo. She placed her hand on Jo's arm. "You listening to me vent is enough. I'll handle the rest. And if I can't...then you can call Evan."

"Fair enough."

❧

"Dr. Jones." Darryl slid the phone to his ear, holding it there with his head and shoulder. He continued typing up his notes as Luella informed him he had a visitor.

He sighed, glancing at the clock on the wall. It was supposed to be his lunch hour. The mound of paperwork sitting on his desk had dwindled the time but not enough to warrant a break. If he wasn't careful, he'd skip lunch and would run on empty before the day was over.

"Who's the visitor, Ms. Luella?"

"Chloe Smith, Dr. Jones."

A groan escaped before he could muffle it. "If she needs assistance with the décor, she can see Dr. Kelly."

"Dr. D, she specifically asked for you." Luella's voice dropped to a whisper. "I think she's upset."

Great. Most likely she'd figured out he was avoiding her. Something told him she wouldn't accept the excuse that it was for her own good. "Send her back."

He quickly hit the save button as he ran a hand down his polo shirt. With a quick prayer, he stood just as his office door swung open.

Chloe met his gaze, her face flushed with what he assumed was anger. Her curls hung down, begging to be touched so he stuffed his hands in his jeans. He had no right to touch her.

"Hey, Chloe." He swallowed, hoping he sounded nonchalant. His intestines felt like a contortionist on display for all to see.

She closed the door and set her purse on the edge of his desk, and then folded her arms across her chest. The light blue sweater made her skin glow, reminding him of a summer's night. Or how she looked on his boat.

Her floral skirt swirled around her, accentuating her femininity.

Darryl focused on his breathing, trying to ignore the daggers she threw his way. "How's Satchel?"

Her eyebrow rose. "Do you care?"

"Of course I do."

"Really, because I haven't heard from you since you gave him to me. Eight days, Darryl, eight."

And sixteen hours and seven minutes but who was counting? "I've been swamped." With guilt. He had thought about telling her his reasons but didn't dare give himself the opportunity to change his mind.

"Oh yeah? Seems to me you hired a third doctor to avoid that issue."

Right. He had given her the wrong response. Maybe it was time for the truth. "Look, Chloe—"

"No, you look." Her finger flew up, pointing at him. "I was willing to give you the benefit of the doubt. To assume you were indeed swamped. But then Jordan mentioned how quiet the office was the other day. Then I saw you at LeeAnn's yesterday. It wasn't until I talked with Jo today that I figured out the reason you've been avoiding me."

How was that possible? He hadn't said anything to Evan or Guy. Was Jo some kind of mind reader? Did she know deep down that he wasn't good enough for one of her best friends? Plus, he *was* swamped today. He had lots of paperwork from the hospital to get through.

Darryl crossed his arms ready to still himself from the potential onslaught she presented. "I doubt Jo knows everything."

"Oh, you're right. I'm the one who figured it out. I didn't want to believe it, but it's the only thing that made sense. You're a racist."

Darryl froze. *What on earth was she talking about?* "Come again?" The words came out raspy as if he choked on his own disbelief.

Chloe nodded with certainty. "I told you I'm half-white and then the next thing I know...poof. You're gone like the white rabbit."

Without even realizing it, he'd moved from behind his desk. "That's insane! I couldn't care less that you're biracial. I've liked you since high school so why in the world would you think that I care about the color of your skin? It hasn't changed colors since I've met you."

A look of confusion crossed her face. "But you haven't talked to me since I told you. It's the only thing that made sense."

"No it's not. Come on. I know we don't know every little detail about each other, but you mean to tell me, you would even entertain the idea that I'm a racist for more than a second?" He rubbed his chest as if she actually stabbed him. He couldn't believe it. She thought he was racist. It would be laughable if it wasn't so absurd. If it didn't call into question his character.

"Then what?" Her stark whisper roared in the silence. "Why are you avoiding me?"

"Because I'm not good enough for you." The words tore free. He inhaled. "Every time I'm around you, I'm more aware of that fact. You...you..." He paced back and forth trying to find the words to get her to see the truth.

"Darryl," she stepped forward, laying a hand on his arm, stopping him in his track. "You're a new creation. Whatever is in your past no longer matters. God gave you a new slate."

The words were like a lifeline. He wanted to believe them, but he knew the truth. Knew the statistics of how many times the cycle of abuse continued despite the victims desiring to be different.

"If you thought God created a new me, you would have never entertained the thought that I was racist." The words tasted bitter, still harsh in their accusation.

She stepped back, regret darkening her eyes. "I'm sorry."

What was he doing? "Don't worry about it." He rubbed his eyes with the palms of his hands. He was so sick of his conflicting emotions. "I'm sorry for trying to make you feel guilty. Just know that I'm truly not good enough for you."

"You know what? I think you're just scared. Scared of the responsibility of being in a committed relationship. Scared to answer to another person."

He stared down at his hands. She was so far from the truth. "You're wrong."

"Then prove it."

"What?"

"Commit to our relationship. Date me and only me. Show me God created a new you. Let go of the hold your past has on you."

"But—

Once again, she cut him off. "No buts, Darryl."

He stared at her, his heart pounding...from fear. "If I ever hurt you," he whispered, "I'd never forgive myself."

"Then be with me. Because not being with you *is* hurting me."

"Aw, Chlo." He cupped the side of her face. "It hurts me too."

Her eyes searched his. "Don't quit on us, Darryl."

Could he commit? Would God prevent him from hurting the one person he cared about? "Okay. I won't."

She smiled, and for the first time in eight days he breathed easily.

Chapter Thirteen

"CeeCee, I can't believe this is the same room."
Chloe grinned at Jamie. They had finished decorating her living room. It was amazing how much the room had brightened with the pastel sheer drapes and bright floral canvas prints. "You have a good eye, Ames."

"I learned it from my sister."

They grinned at each other, twin smiles of goofiness on their face. Chloe loved having a sister. It was nice to have someone take an interest in her passion.

"Wait 'til Char sees it. She's coming again in two weeks, right?"

Jamie nodded, and wiped at her forehead.

She looked a little peakish, but Chloe didn't know if it was her place to say anything. She still had trouble navigating the dynamics of their relationship. Hopefully Jamie was simply tired from pushing the furniture pieces around.

"Will JJ come too?"

"I hope so." Jamie held up a finger, pulling out her cell phone, and grimaced. "Hold on, our father is calling."

Chloe bit her lip as Jamie answered her cell. Would she ever meet the man?

"Hi, Dad. I'm fine. Yes, I'm sure. I'm not lying."

Chloe frowned. Did Jamie have a chronic illness she hadn't told her about?

"No," Jamie whispered, turning around. "I like it here. Freedom Lake is beautiful, Dad. Why don't you come for a visit?"

Chloe twitched in her seat, trying hard not to eavesdrop. Okay, she wasn't really trying, she was hanging on every word.

"Dad, please stop worrying. I'm fine. Didn't JJ and Char tell you?" Jamie glanced at her then looked away. "Look, I'm hanging with Chloe. I'll talk to you later."

Jamie took a few more seconds to end the call. She let out a sigh. "Sorry about that."

Chloe looked over her little sister, noting the pallor, the sweat beads on her upper lip. Did their father have a valid concern? "Is everything okay?"

"Sure, he's like a mother hen sometimes, always hovering." Jamie looked down at the coffee table, avoiding eye contact.

"Does he have a reason to worry?" Chloe asked softly.

Jamie picked up her sketchpad. "What do you think of this idea?"

"Jamie, what's going on?"

Her little sister bit her lip, tucking her hair behind her ear. "I may have a health issue that makes him worry."

Chloe frowned. "What kind of health issue? Are you diabetic?" And why hadn't she told her?

Jamie shook her head, her hair falling like a curtain, shielding her face.

Chloe swallowed, suddenly feeling a tightness in her chest. "What's wrong?" Her voice cracked as she repeated the question.

"I may happen to need a kidney." Jamie glanced at her before looking away. "I found out recently."

"What?" The weight of Jamie's words rooted Chloe to the spot. She stared at her sister. Her vibrant, goofy, take charge, loveable sister. "What does that mean? Are you okay?" She shook her head. "What am I saying? Of course you're not okay, you need a kidney. Should I take you to the hospital? I'll call Darryl, he'll know what to do."

Jamie laid a hand on her arm. "Relax. I'm alive, and I plan on staying that way for years to come. I've had a kidney problem since birth." Jamie looked at Chloe as if to say what can you do. "Now my kidney has decided to bail on me."

Tears welled in Chloe's eyes.

"It's okay." Jamie squeezed her arm. "I promise."

"But you need a kidney." Her vision blurred. Chloe had just found Jamie. She couldn't lose her. Not another person. *Lord, please don't make me lose another person. I can't handle it.* "How can you be so nonchalant when you need a kidney?"

"I'm hopeful. Plus, modern medicine makes some things doable."

"What do you mean?"

"Dialysis. It'll suffice until a donor can be found."

She blanched. "Ames." Was that why she looked so awful today? Had she recently had a treatment? How come she hadn't noticed before?

"CeeCee," Jamie mimicked. "I'm okay. Seriously."

The words rang false. A person wasn't on dialysis for no reason. She swallowed, panic nearing the surface, threatening to take over.

She stared at her little sister. Although they hadn't grown up together, Jamie had quickly inserted herself into Chloe's life. She couldn't imagine life without her. Didn't want to imagine life without her. Somehow, someway, she had to figure out a way to get her little sister a kidney.

***

The chime announced Chloe's entry as she marched toward Tanya's desk. She needed to talk to someone now. *Asap.* Before she busted at the seams with worry. She had tried for the past fifteen minutes to talk to God and calm down, but it wasn't working.

Lately, talking to Him didn't give her the usual peace it did in the past. *What's wrong with me?* Because she knew the problem rested with her. God was perfect. Was it because she subconsciously blamed Him for being abandoned by both parents?

"Hey, Chloe. Can I help you?"

Tanya's greeting snapped her out of her thoughts. "Is Michelle here?"

"No, sorry. I think she's having lunch with Guy."

The bell tinkled, announcing another visitor. She turned and sighed in relief. Michelle took one look at her and the smile left her face. She quickly rushed over, hands gripping her own. "What's wrong?"

"It's about Jamie," she whispered, too overwhelmed from stuffing her emotions back inside. Now was not the time to lose control.

"Come on back."

She followed her friend to her office, wondering what she would say. Would Michelle be able to calm her down? Should she have called Darryl? He was a doctor after all. She quickly shook the notion away.

No, she needed to talk to her friend first. She wasn't used to being able to call a man about her problems. It seemed strange.

Michelle put her Prada bag on her desk. "What's going on with Jamie?"

"I just found out she needs a kidney."

"What do you mean?"

"She's apparently has some kidney problem and needs a new one."

"Oh, Chlo, I'm so sorry."

Tears spilled over as the words of sympathy washed over her. They fell quickly, picking up speed as the weight of the situation cast a gloom over her soul.

"I want to help her."

"Of course you do, sweetie. That's the kind of person you are." Michelle gave a sympathetic smile.

"No, not like a prayer or holding her hands for dialysis treatments." She wiped her face, willing calm to enter so she could get through this conversation. "I want to give her one of my kidneys." There she said it. It had been circling around the back of her brain since Jamie mentioned her need. She just found her family, she wasn't ready to lose anyone. Not for another fifty plus years.

Michelle stared at her in shock. "That's serious, Chloe. It's not something you should jump into without thought and prayer."

"What if you just found out you had more family; that you weren't alone? Then the rug was pulled out from under you because it was possible someone was ill. To the point of needing an organ transplant...would you stop to pray or act?"

Silence blanketed them. Chloe watched the battle in Michelle's hazel eyes. Saw the need for her to affirm Chloe's feelings but prevent her from harm as well. She stepped closer, the need to beseech her friend for support overwhelming in its need. Her throat ached from crying and the emotion of the day. "I have to try, Chelle. She's my sister. Part of me. And it's that part that makes me hope that I can help her."

"I understand," Michelle said on a sigh.

Chloe knew she did. If anyone would, it was Michelle. Her friend had been orphaned and alone for far too long. If family was out there waiting for her to find them, Michelle would jump at the chance, and then do anything to help them. That's why Chloe had come to Michelle first. Jo was the wild card. The girl hated hospitals more than anyone. It brought too much trauma to mind. If for some reason Chloe had complications from the transplant—provided she was a match—Jo would lose it.

"What are you going to do?" Michelle watched her.

"Find out how to go about donating one."

"Are you going to tell Jamie?"

She shook her head. "I don't want to give her false hope. I want to find out everything I can before I mention it."

"Then I'll help."

"Thanks, Chelle." She hugged her friend, thankful that their businesses were right next door to each other. She would need her support in the upcoming weeks.

Darryl sauntered toward the front door with a smile on his face. He had a dinner date with Chloe. He'd thought about inviting her to his house for dinner, but something stopped him. Evan would probably say it was God's voice, but he wasn't sure if that was true. Did God still talk to people?

He grabbed his keys from the foyer table and opened the door.

There stood his mother, her fisted hand hovering in the air. Guess he beat her to the knock.

Her face flushed as her hand dropped to the side. "Hello, son."

For some reason, he couldn't pry his jaw apart to return the greeting.

"I see you're on your way out." Her hands dropped to his keys. She swallowed before continuing. "I was hoping I could talk to you. Do you have a few minutes?"

He glanced at his watch. Anything to avoid her gaze. He had twenty minutes before he had to meet Chloe, but his mother didn't have to know that. It would be so easy to fake tardiness.

Do you really want to lie to her face?

Darryl bit back a groan. "I have a few minutes." He crossed his arms lest she get the idea she was welcomed inside his home.

She shifted on her feet. "Okay. If it has to be done out here, I can do this."

Was she talking to him or giving herself a pep talk?

"I'm sorry for abandoning you." Her brown eyes seemed contrite, but he didn't know if he was ready to trust her. "I was so broken and so messed up that the only thought I had was to get out of Freedom Lake."

"Without your son?" His jaw muscles clenched, and he had to remember to relax them.

"Darryl, you looked so much like Hank I couldn't handle it. I thought it would just take a few months to get right, and then I could return and be the mother you needed."

"So what happened. By my calculations it's been more than a few months."

Her watery gaze met his. "I know, and I'm sorry."

"You said you're married."

"Yes. His name is Robert."

Robert. "How long have you been married?"

She gulped. "Ten years."

What? "So let me get this straight. You abandoned me. Left me without two parents so that you could get right." He used air quotes, hoping to keep his fist from balling up in anger. "Instead of a few months, you go beyond a decade before gracing me with your presence. And now I find out you've been married for ten years? Am I hearing you right?"

She nodded, tears streaming down her face.

"Do you have any other kids I need to know about?"

Again, she answered with a wordless shake of her head.

"Wow. You're a trip. You weren't ready to be a mother, but you could be a wife again? After having so much trauma from your first marriage?"

"Darryl," she whispered. She laid a hand on his arm.

He stared at the offending member, then met her gaze. "Do not touch me. You have no right."

She withdrew her hand quickly but not before he noticed the trembling. Did she think he would hit her?

"News flash." He snorted in disgust. "I may look like my father. Imagine that, considering how DNA works. However, I am *not* my father. I'm a doctor, and I use my hands for healing not for hurting."

Anger surged in him as it searched for good, devouring it on sight. *Lord, help me. I'm losing it.*

How he managed to form the words he'd never know. But it pushed some of the anger back. The red faded to a haze.

"I know you're not your father."

"Apparently not. I have to go."

He stepped outside, closing and locking his front door without sparing her a glance. He turned to walk toward his car, but stopped. He swiveled around to look at the woman who gave birth to him.

"I'd prefer it if you forgot you had a son again and go back to your new life."

Ignoring her and her response, he got in his car and drove off. Rage rushed over him in waves. He wanted to punch something, yell into the sky, but he couldn't. He wanted to be calm and cool when he showed up at Chloe's. Now was not the time to lose his cool.

Still, it simmered. As soon as his *mother* informed him of her ten-year-old marriage. Did her husband even know she had a kid? And if so, what kind of man would let a woman neglect her child why they lived happily ever after?

He snorted in derision, running his hand over his hair. Pressing the steering wheel call button, he told his Bluetooth to call his grandmother. She couldn't possibly want him to speak to his mother after he shared this bit of news.

"Hello, Darryl."

"Grandmother, did you know she's been married for ten years?"

Silence greeted him. He winced. He had skipped over the niceties...the manners his grandmother had drilled into him.

"I'm sorry. Hello, Grandmother."

"I...no that's not why I was quiet."

The shock was evident in her voice. "Then you didn't know?"

"No, I did not. Ten years, really?"

"Yes," he rasped out. He hadn't really expected his grandmother to validate his feelings. Now that she had, his emotions vacillated between sadness and anger.

"I'm so sorry, Darryl. She told me she wanted to make things right. Have you been praying about the situation?"

He closed his briefly. "Not like I should."

"You've got to. The devil will come at you now that you're a believer. Arm yourself with prayer."

Funny how he never gave the devil a thought in all the times he went to church or studied the Bible with his friends. Did the devil really attack people? Persuade them to follow him? He supposed it was as possible as the very real presence of the Lord. He had a lot to learn, and he couldn't depend on their group study to give him all the information.

"Thank you, Grandmother."

"You're welcome…and Darryl."

"Yes, ma'am?"

"Give her a chance to right her wrongs. Tomorrow isn't promised to anyone."

He sat in the parking lot of Emilio's for a few minutes trying to ground himself.

Lord, I'm a mess. I don't want to go in there and show Chloe how messed up I am. Can you help me fake it 'til I make it?

Tell her.

He blinked, the rest of his body frozen in confusion. Had the words been whispered or was his mind speaking loudly?

Lord?

Tell her.

This time, he realized it wasn't actual words, but the thought was very real. He had the overwhelming urge to unburden himself. Would Chloe be able to handle it? Would it make her look at him differently? Would she think him weak?

Yet with every question spinning in his mind, the thought to tell her never left, but became more urgent and insistent.

Okay, I'll talk to her.

He could only pray that it was the Lord's urging and not the devil's.

Chapter Fourteen

*C*hloe glanced at the front entrance of Emilio's again. Darryl was rarely late and she had a sinking feeling that something was wrong. He'd already changed their plans from picking her up to meeting him at the restaurant. She twisted the cloth napkin.

Lord, I pray nothing's wrong, but if there is, please give me the wisdom to know how to handle it. I also pray for peace and calm for our date, and of course, happiness and fun. Thanks for listening Heavenly Father. Amen.

She looked at the door again and sighed in relief. *He's here.* Her heart picked up speed as she took in his appearance. His white collared shirt had been rolled up his forearms, a black leather vest over it, laying open. She raised an arm, hoping to get his attention.

He scanned the restaurant then stopped, meeting her gaze across the room. Her breath caught. Something was wrong. Gone were the laugh lines that creased his eyes. Instead, lines drew his mouth down in misery.

It was like someone had hit a switch, changing him into a different person.

"Sorry I'm late." He sat down across from her.

"Everything okay?" She searched his face. What could it be?

He sighed. "Not really." He grabbed the glass of water at the table. "My mother's back."

"Again?"

"Again," he stared morosely at the tabletop. "She dropped a bombshell on me." He rubbed his face. "I still can't believe it."

"What did she say?" And how could she tell him about Jamie now?

"She's been married for the past ten years." His lips twisted. "Can you believe that?"

Chloe shook her head. The bitterness in his voice tore her apart.

"That's why I was late. Called my grandmother and she was just as shocked."

"Do you want to mend your relationship?"

"My grandmother thinks I should. She said we aren't promised tomorrow."

His grandmother had a point, but what about the years of neglect. Did that mean nothing? A thought popped into her head. "Hey, what if you email your mother?"

"What?" The look of confusion on his face was adorable.

"Obviously, you're not ready for a face-to-face conversation. Why don't you try email? Sometimes it's easier to say what you want when you write it versus actually saying it."

"Huh, that's definitely something to consider."

He reached for her hand. She intertwined her fingers, loving the way goosebumps raced up her arms, as if to see how fast the touch could reach her heart. She loved the way his thumb stroked the back of her hand. His touched soothed and excited her.

"Are you ready to order?"

Chloe barely held back a laugh as the same server from the last time she was here seemed to materialize out of thin air.

"Do you know what you want?" Darryl asked.

She shook her head. She'd completely forgot to look at the menu.

"A few more minutes?" the server asked.

"Yes, please." Darryl nodded his thanks.

"Very well." The server bowed.

Darryl glanced from the menu back to the spot the server had occupied. "What in the world? How did he leave so fast?"

Chloe snickered. "He did that the whole time I was here with my sisters and brother." It felt wonderful to say that.

"How are they?"

"Great. Jamie's been dying to meet you." Chloe winced.

She hadn't meant to say it *that* way. She stared blankly at the menu. Did that mean she should tell Darryl about the transplant idea? Would he object to her idea? *Only one way to find out.* Taking a breath of courage, she informed him of Jamie's health and her desire to donate a kidney.

He sat back in his seat, his mouth parted in surprise. It took a few moments but he finally spoke. "You're amazing."

"What do you mean?" Her face heated up. Not the reaction she was expecting.

"You've known her for what, two months now?"

Chloe nodded.

"And you're ready to donate a kidney to her?"

"She's my sister."

"Most people wouldn't feel like that considering you only share one parent."

How could they not? They still shared blood. Family was family, right? "I think you'd be surprised. I can't be the only one who thinks that way."

"No, but I only know you and I think you're amazing." His lips curved with pleasure. "If that's what you want to do, I'll support you. First thing is to be tested to see if you're a match."

They spent the rest of their dinner talking about the transplant process. She was surprised at how much information he knew. Turned out, he had wanted to specialize in surgery for transplants but ended up specializing in pediatrics after doing a tour on the pediatric floor. The more she learned about him, the more her heart dipped into that precarious valley of love. Would her heart make it through unscathed?

She could only pray he wouldn't abandon her like everyone else had.

～

Dropping the anchor, Darryl headed for the bench seat on his boat. The night sky was lit up with stars, the perfect time to unwind. The perfect time to think and talk to God. Besides getting a haircut to signify his new self, he hadn't changed much. He was still full of anger. Still irate by the injustices his parents had committed. He wanted retribution so badly it invaded his sleep on a nightly basis.

However, the desire to be rid of the bitter feelings outweighed the need for vengeance. He was so tired of being angry. Tired of everything triggering the emotion in him. His grandmother had urged him to pray. Chloe wanted him to pray. Even his boys had asked him to pray. It was time to learn how and to get used to speaking to God so that it would be his first response instead of anger.

He bowed his head, closed his eyes, and clasped his hands loosely together. "Lord, this is new to me, but I want it to be like second nature. I don't want to let anger rule me. I've accepted Jesus as my Savior, but I've been holding on the reins of my life. Please, help me surrender all to You. Please help me to seek You first. I can't take this anymore."

Silence fell over him, but for once he didn't feel like the Lord was ignoring him. The sound of the current soothed his soul. Why hadn't he thought to come out here sooner? His mood always improved on the water. Just unburdening himself to the Lord took away some of the weight he'd been harboring. He leaned back, sighing as quiet wrapped around him.

"Lord, I have to do something about my mother." He gulped. Hearing the word aloud unnerved him. "I don't know how to even talk to her without feeling resentment. This can't be what You want for me."

He purposely pictured his mother. She'd put on some weight, but there seemed to be a peace that followed her. Except for the times she tried turning on the water works to illicit his sympathy. How was he supposed to forgive a woman who had walked away? With his father in prison, she'd left him without a parent. Without love.

Not that his grandmother hadn't done a good job. She had helped him with homework, attended every basketball game he played in. She had always been there, but lacked affection and nurturing traits. She wasn't his mother, and he had felt the loss daily. That is until he stuffed it down into the dark recesses of his mind, with a promise to never dwell on it again.

His phone vibrated. He pulled it out, noticing it was the paging service. Another patient needed advice. Hopefully it wasn't Brianna.

Chloe smiled as she stared at her sketch. It had been awhile since she'd drawn for the sheer pleasure of it. The house stared up at her as if saying job well done.

"What's that?"

She peered up at Jamie. "Just something I drew."

"You drew this?"

She chuckled, not at all offended by the question. "I like to do it in my spare time or just when my brain needs a recharge."

"That's amazing, CeeCee." Jamie picked up the sketch, examining it. "I wish I had that kind of talent."

"Are you kidding me? The way you designed the Millers' master bedroom is nothing short of amazing." She bumped her sister's shoulder. "I love having you work with me."

Jamie grinned. "Really?" she asked softly.

"Really. I'm so glad you sought me out."

Jamie squeezed her hand. "I have a huge favor to ask you."

Uh oh. Although Jamie smiled like it would be no big deal, Chloe's mouth dried with trepidation. Somehow she had a feeling the request wouldn't be an easy one. "What is it?"

"Come with me to Ohio."

Her stomach dropped to her toes as if she rode a roller coaster.

"Don't look at me like that," Jamie said. "I want Dad to see you. Maybe if he does, he won't deny you any longer."

And maybe he'll push the knife in a little deeper. Ironically, her heart broke for her sister. Jamie had a huge heart and wanted everything to work out for good. Unfortunately, life didn't always work out that way. "It's a wonderful thought, Jamie, but it's quite obvious he wants nothing to do with me."

"But if he saw you, I know he would change his mind."

"How could you think that?"

"Because you two are so alike."

"What?" Panic seemed to reach out, clawing at her, trying to draw her under the cover of darkness. How could she be anything like him? She'd never met him. Never seen his face. All she had for a measuring stick was her half siblings. Sure, they all had similar features, but they were all individuals. They didn't seem to have any similar quirks or habits.

"You both stare at your hands when you're gathering your thoughts. You bite your lip the same way."

Chloe met Jamie's gaze, forcing herself not to look at her hands. Did she really do that so often? And worse, did her father really do it too? Before she could form a question, the store bell chimed, announcing a visitor.

She turned toward the door, barely concealing a groan. Her grandmother's secretary was back. Hannah Blakely gave a forced smile.

"Ms. Blakely, how's it going?" Jamie gave her a sunny smile.

Why couldn't Chloe fake a smile? Unfortunately, the presence of Ms. Blakely just added fuel to the already tense atmosphere. She was ready to crawl back into bed and declare this day a loss.

"It depends on what you have to tell me."

"She can't really be asking to see us again." The words slipped out, chock full of bitterness. Chloe barely recognized herself these days. It was like her life had spiraled out of control from the moment she found out her father didn't want her. Didn't even want to acknowledge her. All because of Mrs. Davenport.

Hannah smiled sadly. "Mrs. Davenport does not ask. She will not take no for an answer this time, even though Charlotte and John Junior have left Freedom Lake."

149

"Yes, they'll be back in a few weeks." Jamie said cautiously.

"I'll be sure to pass that along. As it is, Mrs. Davenport requests your attendance for dinner tonight."

Chloe darted a glance at Jamie. Jamie met her gaze as if to ask "should we?" She wanted to object, but wouldn't it be better to find out why her grandmother objected to her mother in the first place? Would she be able to find out why her father didn't want to acknowledge her? It seemed odd that her grandmother wanted to meet her but her father didn't.

"Fine," she said. "We'll be there."

Hannah closed her eyes in gratitude. "Great. Dinner will start at six sharp. Please don't be late."

"We won't, Ms. Blakely." Jamie said.

Something told her that Ms. Blakely's job would be on the line if she and Jamie didn't show up tonight.

With a wave, Ms. Blakely left as quietly as she arrived.

Chapter Fifteen

*D*arryl dropped into his chair, propping his feet up on the corner of his desk. The elementary school had a stomach flu passing through the kids. It seemed like every student had traipsed through the clinic doors all day long. The need to shower and ensure himself that no germs lingered repeated in the back of his mind, but fatigue won out. The way he felt, it would be awhile before he removed himself from his chair.

His stomach rumbled, alerting Darryl to his neglect. Lunch had merely been a thought. Now dinner called to him, begging for a portion worthy to sate his appetite. He was tempted to call for takeout but that meant moving.

The phone rang.

He groaned, cracking an eye open. Was it another parent with a kid losing their lunch? *Briiing.* Maybe it was his grandmother. *Briiing.* Could be his mother. *Briiing.*

Springing forward, he grabbed the phone. "Dr. Darryl Jones."

"Hey, what are you doing still at work?"

"Chloe," he breathed out. He leaned back, thankful no one could see his ear splitting grin. "How did you know I was at work?"

"I called your cell first."

He pulled it out of his pocket. Why had he placed it on vibrate? "It's been a rough day. Stomach bug going around."

"Uh oh."

"How was your day?" His grin stretched wider. He was finally in a position where he could ask. Could life get much better?

"Interesting. I had two requests from family members and neither of them appealing."

"Do tell." He held the receiver between his ear and shoulder, relaxing back into his chair.

"Jamie wants me to go to Ohio with her to meet my father. And Ms. Blakely came to summon us to my grandmother's house for dinner."

"Who's Ms. Blakely?"

Chloe told him about the woman's previous visit. He'd forgotten Mrs. Davenport was her grandmother. Probably because his brain was mush. He stifled a yawn as she continued on. When she paused for breath, he rushed ahead. "Are you going?"

"Which one?"

"Either of them."

"Yes to my grandmother's and no to my father's."

He could understand that. "I get the no, but do you think you should consider it?"

"Are you going to talk to your mother?"

The question held a bit of a bite.

"I've been thinking about it. Praying about it." *And praying for you.*

Her sigh caressed his ears. "I needed that reminder."

"Are you...are you having trouble praying?"

The words felt foreign to his tongue. He would never have thought that Chloe would have trouble praying.

"A little. I've wanted a family for so long and now that it's within my grasp, it's even more difficult. I don't understand what God's doing in my life."

It was good to know he wasn't the only one that felt that way. However, he hated that Chloe sounded so lost. So sad. "Do you want me to come with you?"

"Oh, Darryl, thank you so much for the offer. I'm going to go to dinner with Jamie. However, if I make that big step to see my father, I think I would like a hand to hold."

"Then I'll be there."

"Thanks. Go home and rest."

"I will. I'll be praying about your dinner."

"Thanks."

He hung up the phone and bowed his head.

Lord, I hate to hear her so sad. If you could somehow make something good come from this dinner, I know she'll appreciate it. And if for some reason You don't...please help me be there for her. Be who she needs. In Jesus' name, Amen.

Chloe stared at her reflection, wondering if she was dressed appropriately. She had draped a cream colored cardigan over her purple floral dress. The dress had a 50s style silhouette and came with pockets. Was it dressy enough? Better yet, did it show that she was confident despite the fact that none of her parents wanted to be tied to her?

She shook her head at the thought. *Wow.* She'd really allowed her thoughts to spiral. Where were her prayers? Once upon a time, a prayer would have flown from her lips without conscious thought. Now it was a struggle.

It seemed she only spent her time thinking of praying instead of praying.

Oh, she still read her Bible daily, but the reverence, the peace, the desire wasn't there. Once she had lived to wake up each morning with a cup of tea and her Bible. Now she'd been simply going through the motions. Every time she passed the Good Book on the bookshelf, it seemed to call out.

Did it know she was going through the motions? God certainly did and the thought shamed her. *But not enough for you to change.* What would draw her closer to God? What would make things in her life right? She closed her eyes, thankful she could no longer see her image, but overwhelmed by the tide of her emotions. Her life had been swinging back and forth like a pendulum. She wanted it to stop. She wanted her old self back.

The one who knew who she was and trusted the God she served.

This Chloe wasn't her. This version had let the uncertainty of an ethnic box make her question her very identity. This version second guessed every decision. This Chloe could no longer see comfort in staring at her hands to gather her thoughts. Instead, it spiraled downward, mocking her, letting her know she was a fraud.

Because she was. If she wasn't fully African-American, then what was she?

She had been raised Black. Had been teased for being Black. Had been immersed in the culture from birth, never questioning its truth and familiarity. She had been raised as the grandchild of April Marie Smith, daughter of Charlotte Smith. Freedom Lake was her home, where her roots ran deep.

Except tonight, she was none of those things. She would be showing up as grandchild of Geraldine

Davenport, daughter of John Davenport, sister of Charlotte, John Jr, and Jamie. As awkward as those titles were, it was a role which she had no choice but to be in. Taking another quick glance, she decided that her outfit would have to do. She needed a reminder of who she had been raised as.

The drive to her grandmother's house was over in a blink of the eye. Staring at the turret jutting from the roof above the bay window, nerves froze her to the driver's seat. Why hadn't she driven with Jamie? Unity would be much better than walking up the sidewalk by herself.

Chloe drew in a ragged breath. *Come on, girl, get out of the car. You can do this.* She *had* to do this. Before she could change her mind, Chloe opened the door and smoothed the sides of her dress as she stepped out of the SUV. With whispered encouragement, she took one step forward, then another, and still another. Before she had a chance to ring the doorbell, the door opened. An older gentleman graced the foyer.

"Good evening, Ms. Smith. Mrs. Davenport is expecting you. Is Miss Davenport with you?" He peered over her shoulder.

"Uh, she'll be here shortly." Her words stammered over one another as her mind came to grips that the Davenports had a butler. What decade were they in?

"Very well. Please come in."

She gulped and stepped over the threshold.

"This way, Ms. Smith." The butler led her down the hall.

Antique furniture lined the hallway. She slowed as she passed a curio cabinet with Victorian figurines. Her grandmother's house would be a gold mine for the antique market. She faced forward just as the butler turned left into a room. She followed quietly and looked around the living room. Velvet couches appeared as if it were the nineteenth century, not the twenty-first. An eerie sensation crept along her neck, raising the hair on her arms. It was like an episode of the Twilight Zone. How far back in time had she gone? Still, it was nothing compared to the vision sitting on the blue loveseat before her.

A woman—who Chloe could only assume was her grandmother—stared at her, her white hair twisted into a chignon, emphasizing the point in her chin. Her eyebrows had been drawn in, accenting the natural arch in her eyes. Her makeup appeared to be flawless, adding and not hindering from her looks.

But it didn't detract from the haughty attitude that permeated her being. Chloe was aware of every judgment that rested in her grandmother's eyes. With a tilt of her chin, cool disdain shone forth in her ice blue eyes. Her elegant ring finger was graced with a huge bauble. Chloe prayed it was fake and not real. It would only expand the differences between them.

"Ms. Smith has arrived, Mrs. Davenport."

"Where is Miss Davenport?"

"She has not yet arrived, Mrs. Davenport."

"You're dismissed, Gilbert," she said with a flick of her wrist.

Her legs were crossed at the ankle, her hands resting on top of her lap. "Have a seat."

Chloe nodded, trying to show confidence instead of the rabid fear keeping her heartbeat at a frantic pace. *Where is Jamie?*

Her grandmother took in every movement.

It took every ounce of willpower not to fidget. It was like she had been summoned by the big, bad principal—known for her lack of mercy. Somehow, she couldn't imagine leaving unscathed.

Say something!

"You look like your mother." Annoyance filled her grandmother's face.

Okay, not what she was expecting. "Thank you?"

"Don't thank me. It was merely an observation." Her grandmother pulled out a cigarette case, removing a slender stick. She lit it, inhaling before blowing a puff of smoke. "I do believe your face is too round. Otherwise, it would appear you've inherited the Davenport chin."

The sound of the doorbell echoed through the older home.

Please, let it be Jamie. She desperately needed reinforcements.

"I despise tardiness."

She discreetly checked her watch. "It just turned six o'clock, Mrs. Davenport."

"As I said," she said with an arched eyebrow, "I despise tardiness."

Lord, how am I supposed to make it through an entire dinner of this nonsense? Never had she met such an uptight, miserable woman in her life. If she had met her in the streets, a chill would be left in her wake. As it was, she was trying hard not to shiver in her cardigan. Being around the infamous, reclusive Geraldine Davenport was a lot to take in.

"Miss Davenport has arrived, Mrs. Davenport."

"Thank you, Gilbert." She flicked her wrist as ash fell into her cut glass ashtray.

"Sit down, Jamie Lynn."

Jamie sat down next to her. "Everyone calls me Jamie, Grandmother. Jamie Lynn sounds kind of old."

"I thought it sounded a little country but your father did not seek my approval when naming you. The women in our family have always had more...feminine names."

Her grandmother turned and met Chloe's gaze. Chloe stared back, praying she wouldn't blink.

"I'm surprised to hear your name isn't after some vehicle or alcoholic beverage."

"Excuse me?" Her mouth dropped open.

Jamie laid a hand on Chloe's arm. "Grandmother, I'm sure you didn't mean anything negative by that comment."

"Of course not, Jamie Lynn. Just merely making an observation."

Jamie squeezed her hand and Chloe squeezed back. Dinner was going to be a long, tortuous state of affairs.

Chapter Sixteen

I f Chloe was brave enough to face her grandmother, then Darryl could face his mother. He jogged up the steps of the B&B. He slowed as the front door drew near. With a huff, he turned away, staring out onto the lake's surface. Maybe he wasn't ready. He'd never written that letter Chloe suggested. Perhaps he should just leave. *Think of Chloe. Just knock.*

But the old hurt and anger rose within him like an inferno ready to burn to the ground everything he had work so hard to build. Was his new self in that precarious of a situation?

Lord, I need Your help. I can't do this on my own. Please help me. With a whispered, "Amen," he whirled around and rang the doorbell before he could change his mind.

The door opened and Mrs. Carter stood in the entry way. A beam replaced confusion. "Darryl, what brings you by here?" She shook her head, her small locs swinging freely. "I almost forgot. She's in her room. Give me a moment and I'll let her know you're here."

She started down the foyer and then stopped, turning back. "Would you like some privacy? If so, the library is free of any guests."

"Thank you, Mrs. Carter. I know the way, if you don't mind."

"Of course, make yourself at home."

Mrs. Carter continued walking, advancing toward the stairs. He went down the hallway to the back of the B&B where the library was located. He dropped to the loveseat, sliding his palms down his jeans. They always became clammy when he was nervous. It wasn't a very masculine trait…at least he didn't think so.

Footsteps echoed in the hall. Was that Mrs. Carter? Or his mother? He closed his eyes, quickly sending a benediction toward heaven. Now was definitely the time for some divine intervention. He wanted to come out here to accomplish what he set out to do, but his emotions felt like a teeter totter. He wasn't sure which way they'd lean.

"Darryl?"

The wonder in his mother's voice had him rising. His hands rested at his sides, unsure of what to do. He stared at her, trying to gauge her mood. Her straight black hair was parted in the middle and tucked behind each ear, showcasing some dangly earrings.

The timid nature that used to guide her every action had disappeared, although the wariness from his surprise visit was quite evident.

"What are you doing here?" She folded her arms across her chest.

"I came to talk."

Her brown eyes searched his face as if seeking the truth. "Very well. Should we sit?" She gestured toward the loveseat and wingback chairs centered around the coffee table.

"Fine."

She sat across from the loveseat in a wingback chair. "What do you want to talk about?"

"Nothing actually. I'm more here to listen than talk. I know I haven't given you a chance to say whatever it is you came to say." He lifted his hands in the air. "I'm ready to listen now."

She nodded slowly. "Very well." She sighed. "I wanted to apologize for abandoning you."

"You said that the last time."

She winced.

Was she scared of him? He hadn't yelled, but his words did have an edge to him. *I'm not my father.* Why did she have to act afraid of him? "What I meant," he stated calmly, "is that you've said that already. If that's all you came for then I don't really need to stick around for an encore."

"No wait." She held her hand out as if pleading. "I…there's more I want to say."

He met her gaze, trying to look nonthreatening because obviously all she saw was his father, which was ironic considering he looked like her. No one had ever thought he looked like his old man. Maybe she was just lumping him into the category because they were men.

No, that didn't make sense. She remarried.

"I was so messed up from years of abuse. The physical side was easy to heal from, but the emotional scars…well, it took years for me to heal. At first, I just drove as far away as possible. I ended up in California. I got a job as a waitress. I mean, I wasn't qualified for anything else. It was there I met a woman who recognized my symptoms. She recommended me to a counselor."

He knew that path all too well. The judge had shoved counseling down his throat as if it would erase the emotional scars he suffered from.

"The counselor helped me deal with past problems by introducing me to God."

He searched for truth in her body language. "You're a believer?"

"I am." Her eyes widened in surprise. Are you?"

"I became one recently."

Her eyes filled with tears. "I'm so happy for you."

Why couldn't he say the words back? It was like he was emotionally stunted where she was concerned.

"Have you been baptized?"

"No." He hadn't even thought about it. It seemed like there was a long list of things he was supposed to do once he became a believer. He wished there was a manual.

Your Bible.

"It's a wonderful feeling. I encourage you to do so soon."

"Thanks for the advice." This time disdain was absent from his words.

She nodded. "I'm going to be here for another week. Maybe we could get together for dinner sometime?"

"Maybe." He wanted to tell her not to push her luck, but that was just him being unnecessarily caustic.

"Thanks for listening, Darryl."

He stood, glad the visit was over. "I'll see you around." He headed for the door but stopped, suddenly remembering a burning question he had. He looked back at her, freezing as he stared in the face of her longing.

"Does your husband know you have a son?"

She blinked, confusion wrinkling her brow. "What does that have to do with anything?"

"Please just answer the question."

She bit her lip, glancing out the window. He watched as she inhaled, as if trying to gather the strength needed for an answer. "No, he doesn't."

"You might want to fix that." He turned away, thoughts going a mile a minute. He thought the response would bring him understanding, but instead it just fueled his anger. How could he believe she changed when she wasn't willing to tell her husband about him?

～

Chloe walked down the corridor of the clinic. She needed to talk to Darryl. Last night's dinner had been a disaster of epic proportions. If she never stepped foot in Geraldine Davenport's home again, then she would die a happy death. Poor Jamie had tried to stick up for her, but their grandmother had been intent on throwing barbs all night long. Unlike the darts thrown in carnival games, hers had found their target each and every time.

She slowed as she neared Darryl's office, and knocked, all the while praying he wasn't busy. He had told her how hectic things could get at the clinic, but it seemed eerily quiet today.

"Come in."

With a twist of the knob, she entered his office. She stopped, surprised by amount of paperwork on his desk.

"Hey."

The grin that lit up his face warmed her heart. She didn't think she'd ever tire of his smile.

"What are you doing here?" He got up, rounding his desk.

"I needed to talk. Last night was horrid."

He pulled her to him and she went willingly, laying her head against his chest. She closed her eyes, letting out a small sigh. This moment was one she had longed for without ever realizing it. She wrapped her arms around his back, thankful for the strength exuding from him. His signature scent wrapped around her.

Darryl ran his hand up and down her back, leaving goosebumps in his wake.

"Want to tell me what happened?"

The rumble of his voice caressed her, sent shivers down her spine. All of a sudden she realized how close she was. She stepped back, giving herself room, her skin heating up with embarrassment.

"It'd be easier to tell you what didn't."

"Ouch," his mouth turned downward. "That bad?"

"Epic failure."

He chuckled. "I thought you saw things half full?"

"Oh, I do. That's why I said epic failure. If I said it was a colossal waste of time, then I'd be looking at it from a glass half empty perspective."

He laughed, the sound pulling an answering grin from her. She never thought of herself as funny, but she was willing to keep trying if it kept his eyes lighting up like that. She stared, mesmerized by the sparkle in them. "No wonder you're a great doctor. All you have to do is smile and the kids are putty in your hands, aren't they?"

"Does my smile charm you?"

She shivered at the lower timbre in his voice. "Maybe."

"Maybe what?" he asked softly, tracing a finger lightly down the side of her face.

"Is it warm in here, or is it just me?" She stepped back, stepping out of his arms. Whose bright idea had it been to visit his office where they could be alone? Obviously her grandmother's tirade yesterday had completely addled her senses.

His warm chuckle skated over her senses. She gripped the windowsill, trying to anchor herself. What she really wanted to do was throw herself back into his arms.

"Since you obviously want to talk, I'll sit at my desk and listen."

She peeked over her shoulder as he settled into his chair. Part of her was thankful for the space, the other part wanted to get closer. Instead, she turned, leaning against the ledge. "My grandmother hates me."

His eyebrow rose. "I'm sure she doesn't."

"Oh, no, she really does." She moved forward, her hands beginning to punctuate her statements. "She was surprised I didn't have a ghetto name."

"No way."

"She didn't say those words, but the implication was loud and clear. Even Jamie was uncomfortable."

"As she should be."

"Then she proceeded to point out the horror I must feel to be in the middle. Not acceptable to both races, because what "European descent" wants my honey-toned skin in their clan and what African American wants a white woman in their mix."

She flopped into the chair in front of his desk. "I'm pretty sure her use of clan was meant with a capital K."

He held his hand out across his desk. With a sigh, she placed her hand in his.

"I'm sorry your grandmother is a racist."

She snorted. It escaped before she could assess the wisdom of snorting in front of a man she hoped found her attractive. "It's really not a surprise, but a part of me hoped her invitation was because she wanted to get to know me."

"Well, if it makes you feel better, I found out that my mother's husband has no idea she has a son."

When her brain was able to formulate a sentence, she blinked before forging ahead. "Okay, you win."

He rubbed a thumb lazily over her fingers. "We're a pair aren't we, babe?"

He called me babe. "Definitely." She cleared her throat, trying to keep her emotions in check. She didn't want a blubber fest from the endearment until she was at

165

home alone with Satchel. But the thought of her sweet puppy and the man who had gifted him made the tears spring up anyway.

Darryl tilted his head. "Are you going to cry?"

"Not from sadness." She cleared her throat.

"From happiness?"

She nodded.

"Because…"

"You called me babe," she blubbered.

Darryl came around the desk once more and gently helped her up. He wrapped his arms around her and held her as she cried softly into his shirt.

So maybe there were some sad tears in the mix.

Chapter Seventeen

*D*arryl hustled down the court, readying himself for a layup. With a jump and swish, he turned around, aiming a grin at Evan. "Wait 'til I tell your team I beat you in a game of twenty-one."

Evan snorted. "Please, I let you beat me." He patted the side of his wheelchair used specifically for basketball. "These wheels are much faster than your legs. I took pity on you. Can't have your girl thinking you can't beat a man in a wheelchair."

A burst of laughter broke free. Darryl had to give it to Evan. The man had overcome the negative stigma surrounding the loss of his left leg. Now he was the high-school basketball coach leading a team that had a shot at nationals.

"It's a good thing I have no intention on telling Chloe we played ball."

"Scared much?"

He stooped over, catching his breath. It was good trash talking with Ev, but the dude had no idea how much he had fought to win their game.

His chair gave him some serious speed and the man already had mad skills. He wasn't the coach for nothing.

"I saw my mom." He sat down on the open court, sparing a glance Evan's way to gauge his reaction.

"Big step. Was it as bad as you thought?"

He ran a hand down across the top of his head. "Worse."

"How so?" Evan wheeled closer, his voice dropping in seriousness.

"Her husband has no idea she has a son."

Evan's low whistle rent the air. "Her husband is not going to be happy when he finds out."

"That's the understatement of the year. Then again, it's not like I'm his son. Maybe the sting won't be so bad."

Evan let out a derisive laugh. "You know how men react in those situations."

He nodded, thinking of the impending explosion. He said a prayer for his mother then paused, realizing where his thoughts were going. Did that mean he was on the road to forgiveness?

"Other than that, how's everything with you?"

"Great. Things between Chloe and I couldn't be better." He nodded his head toward Evan. "You? Ready to walk down the aisle?"

A silly grin came over his face. "I can't wait. We've decided to have it at the B&B, that way we can have the lake as our backdrop."

"Nice."

"Jo's going to build an arbor for it. It'll be a casual affair. No suits and ties."

"Even better."

"I know, right?"

Their laughter faded. Darryl wondered if he would be ready to make that kind of commitment. He gave a mental shake of his head. Of course he would. He'd wanted to be with Chloe forever. Had spent countless hours fantasizing what life would look like if she ever returned his feelings. However, now that they were dating, he'd slowed to a snail's pace. The thought of scaring her off with the depth of his emotions terrified him.

Which was one reason he had yet to kiss her. He wanted to with every fiber in his being, but he didn't want her to freak out. Didn't want her to think he was going too fast or being too forward. If God could guarantee him she would be his wife one day, he'd find her now and kiss her senseless.

But his mind was constantly reminding him how he didn't measure up. Sure, God had given him a clean slate, but that didn't negate his past or the consequences of those actions. He had therapy records to prove it. Deep down he knew he had to tell her about the incident with his dad, but to see the look of horror and fear that was sure to come across her face rendered him mute.

How could he expect her to accept him for all he was? Just because he had a one-way ticket to heaven didn't mean the other passengers would agree with his admission.

"You're doing some mighty heavy thinking over there, D."

"Yeah." He looked at his friend. "Did you ever feel like you weren't good enough for Jo?"

"Countless times. Don't you remember how much I ragged on her in high school?"

"Yes, but we were teens. Isn't that what kids do?"

"She sure didn't think that was a viable excuse. I hurt her in ways I will never truly comprehend. It's enough to remember the loathing I saw in her eyes when I first moved back. And it's a miracle that we're now getting ready to head down the aisle as husband and wife. I *know* I don't deserve her, but God blessed me anyway."

An ache took residence in his chest. The emotion in Evan's voice was unmistakable. It helped knowing his friend had doubts. But as powerful as words could be, they were no match against physical harm.

"I tried to kill my father."

"What are you talking about?" He heard the caution in Evan's tone.

"He slapped my mom one too many times. I snapped. Dove on him. Tried to squeeze the air out of his body. All I could think of was it was time to shut him up. Time to end the madness that pervaded our home. We couldn't eat in peace. Walked around on eggshells all the time. All in hopes that he wouldn't snap. That we wouldn't set him off."

He inhaled, trying to draw in air against the pain of the memories. "He flipped when he came home and my mom served him dinner. Said his vegetables were cold. And for that infraction, she earned a slap."

"Ah, D man, why didn't you tell me it was that bad?"

He met Evan's eyes. "How do you tell your friend your father uses your mom as a human punching bag? I was ashamed. I didn't tell anyone."

Evan nodded, his Adam's apple bobbing up and down. "I'm sorry I never helped."

"What could you have done? You were a kid just like me."

"I knew. I never asked. I never confirmed, but I knew just the same. I'm sorry for not telling someone. I failed you as a friend."

He looked down, hoping Evan would mistake the moisture falling from his eyes as sweat. When he was in elementary school he had desperately wished someone knew what was going on, could somehow make it better. But he never had the guts to say anything. There was no way he was blaming Evan either. He told him as much.

Evan wheeled closer and lightly slapped his back. "Don't carry that guilt with you. Any person in that situation could have reacted the same way. God's forgiven you, now you need to forgive yourself."

But how was he supposed to do that when it haunted his dreams?

∽∾

Chloe stroked Satchel's fur as she read her novel. When she came home after work, her apartment had seemed quieter than usual. Half of her yearned to drop by Darryl's place and spend time with him, but she was so worried about what would happen if they were alone. Growing up with the knowledge that her mother had her as a teen, Chloe had promised never to put herself in the same situation.

Her cheeks warmed as she remembered the hug Darryl had given her at his office. Had he wanted more than a hug? She had no clue what she would do if he ever kissed her. Even though she'd been on dates in the past, she never dated a guy long enough to warrant kissing. She could only pray it was as natural as breathing.

She frowned. Was it okay to pray something like that?

With a sigh, she returned to her book, remembering why she started reading it in the first place: to escape. It was wonderful to forget one's own problems and dive into another's, especially knowing there would be a resolution by the end of the book.

A knock at the door echoed in the silence. She moved Satchel to the side, placing her bookmark to prevent bending any of the precious pages. Wondering who had stopped by, Chloe unlocked the door.

"JoJo!"

Her friend leaned down for a hug. "Hey, Chloe. How've you been?"

She shrugged. It was like God knew she needed to talk to someone, but where did she begin. "What brings you by?"

"I haven't seen you in a while so I wanted to check up on you."

Chloe sat on the couch, folding her leg beneath her. She laughed as Satchel barked at Jo.

Jo watched in amusement. "Poor guy hasn't found his big voice yet."

Chloe nodded. "I know, but I appreciate his efforts. I'm just glad he doesn't bark unless someone comes in. I'd hate it if he spent all his time barking at the door."

"The thought makes me cringe." Jo put her feet up on the couch. Fortunately, she remembered to take off her work boots.

"How's wedding planning coming along?"

A small smile lit Jo's face. "Fantastic. We're on agreement on almost everything. The only thing we argued over were bridesmaids and groomsmen."

She frowned. "What's to argue about? I'd assumed Michelle and I would be the bridesmaids, and Guy and Darryl the groomsmen."

"You'd think. However, by dear fiancé wants to include Vanessa and Darius."

"Why?" Jo's sister and brother might as well be a step sibling versus the real deal. They stuck to themselves while nominating Jo as the family caretaker.

"He says that I will regret not extending the olive branch."

Chloe grimaced. "Well, they are your family, but I just can't see them actually joining in the ceremony. Are they even coming to the wedding?"

Jo fell out laughing, falling sideways onto the couch. Chloe couldn't help but join in. She met her friend's gaze and the sound of their laughter went up an octave and ran longer. Satchel begin barking, running back and forth between them.

Finally, Jo wiped the tears away. "Girl, I needed a good laugh."

"I'm just glad you can laugh about it. Have you ever wondered if you were adopted?"

"Countless times." Jo leaned back against the couch. "Okay, enough about me. How are your family woes going?"

She told Jo about dinner at her grandmother's. Although considering the woman's thoughts toward her, maybe she should just call her Mrs. Davenport.

"I'm sorry, Chlo. I know how much you wanted family."

"I'm not too upset. I mean look at you. You struck out in the family department. I'm lucky to have a sister who likes me."

"So true." Jo sat up, looking as if she had an idea. "Hey, you haven't told me anything about the kidney situation."

She swallowed. "I have an appointment to get tested in a week. Kind of nervous. What if I'm not a match?"

"How bad is her situation?"

She sighed, looking down at her hands. "I'm not sure. She doesn't want to talk about it, but she's been looking more tired lately. I can't tell if she's always looked like that and I didn't notice, or if she's getting worse."

"Illnesses are the pits."

"Amen," she replied softly. *Lord, please let me help my sister. I don't want to lose her.*

Chapter Eighteen

arryl opened the new gate between his backyard and Evan's. He was so happy it was Bible study night. It seemed like forever had passed since the last one. With everyone going through life changes, meeting up the last few weeks had been impossible. Thankfully, they were all able to get together this weekend. Plus, Chloe's kid sister would be coming for the first time. He knew she wanted JJ and Charlotte to come as well, but they weren't arriving in town until tomorrow.

"D, man! Glad you're here." Evan said with a nod, holding a pair of tongs in one hand and his crutch in the other. "Could you grab the vegetable skewers from inside? I don't want to burn the steaks."

"Yeah, no problem." He headed inside, nodding to Jo as she squeezed some lemons into a pitcher. "Hey Jo."

"Hey, Darryl." She looked behind him. "Where's Chloe?"

"She's not here yet?" That wasn't like her. She was usually the first to arrive at a Bible study. Five minutes early was considered late for Chloe.

"Not yet. Hopefully something's not wrong with Jamie."

He sighed, rubbing the stubble on his chin. "Jamie's been looking a little peakish."

"Peakish? Really? Is that an official doctor term?"

"No, but it fits." He grabbed the skewers. "Give me a holler when she gets here."

"Will do."

He sent up a prayer for Jamie's healing. The results of Chloe's kidney test should be coming in any day now. If she was a match, Chloe was planning on taking Jamie out to dinner as a celebration. He was pretty sure the waiting was torturing her.

Guy and Michelle arrived as the steaks finished up. Still, there was no sign of Chloe. He glanced at his watch, stepping away from the group. He hit the speed dial for Chloe. After two rings, it went to voicemail. He took a deep breath, trying to relax his brow. *What could be keeping her?*

He walked inside. "Jo have you heard anything?"

"No." She shook her head, her ponytail swinging. "I've tried to call her a couple of times."

"Same here."

"You have Jamie's number by any chance?"

"Huh, why didn't I think of that?" He dialed her number, thankful she'd made him put it in his contacts list. She had wanted to be able to get in touch with anyone in case she had a medical emergency.

"Hello?" The groggy reply spread relief through him. If Jamie was okay, surely Chloe was.

"Hey, it's Darryl. Have you heard from Chloe?"

"What? No."

A muffled noise greeted his ear. Either she had dropped the phone or she was looking for something.

"It's 7:15?" she exclaimed. "She was supposed to pick me up for Bible study."

A ball of dread spread through his insides. *Chloe hadn't made it to Jamie's house?* His mind whirled, a thousand different scenarios begging for his attention.

"I'm going over to her place right now."

"Meet you there."

He jammed the phone in his back pocket. "Chloe didn't make it to Jamie's. I'm going to her place now."

"I'm coming with you. Give me two seconds to tell everyone else." Jo jogged outside.

He started to head for the front door then remembered he walked. His car was in his own garage. Before he could switch directions, Jo came running in.

"We can take my truck."

"Thanks."

They dashed out of the house. His hands shook as he reached for the door handle. He didn't know what he would do if something had happened to Chloe. He lived and breathed for her, of that he was certain.

Lord, You know I'm new at this prayer thing, but I beg You not to let it make a difference today. Please let her be okay. Please let us find her. I'd much rather laugh about being ridiculously freaked out for nothing than for something bad to have happened. Please, I'm begging You, let her be okay.

∾

Chloe closed her eyes in horror, feeling the heat come closer. Her bedroom had been engulfed by flames. How it even started she had no idea. All she knew was that Satchel had awakened her from her nap with frantic barks. At the time, the fire had been regulated outside her room. She'd learned that the hard way when she'd checked the doorknob. Her hand still burned, but it was the least of her worries.

She was trapped.

Her lips trembled as her back hit the tiled bathroom wall. She blinked rapidly as the flames licked the edge of the doorway. Her hands shook as she held Satchel tightly to her chest. The poor thing hadn't stopped whimpering since she'd awaken.

Lord, please get me out of here. I don't know what to do. If she burned, or worse died, Jaime would never be able to get a new kidney. She needed to get out of the apartment intact. *Now!*

Satchel licked her cheek as he whimpered.

"It's okay, boy. Help will come." She hoped. *But how?* her insides screamed. She couldn't call anyone. She'd left her cell on the nightstand when dashing to the bathroom. It was probably a melted mess by now.

The flames crept closer and Chloe set Satchel down into the tub floor. "Time to help ourselves, boy."

She reached up on her toes and aimed the shower nozzle toward the door. She grabbed the shower curtain and pushed it against the opposite wall so that the nozzle had a good aim. With a quick prayer for favor, she turned the shower on.

The flames hissed and drew back slightly. Satchel barked as he tried to get away from the water that dripped into the tub. His feet slid. She stared at him, and then the water. They needed to get wet in case the fire came all the way into the bathroom. She had no idea if her friends were out looking for her or if a neighbor had called the fire department.

All she knew was she wasn't going down without a fight.

༺✦༻

"Oh God, no," Jo uttered in horror.

Darryl stared at the smoke billowing in the sky above the apartments. His lips moved in a silent prayer. His heart beat erratically as they drew closer. Firefighters were going back and forth from the firetruck to the apartment. It seemed like chaos, but he could tell from their faces that they had the dance with the fire down to an art.

He hopped out of Jo's truck before she could park and headed straight for the fire chief. Chief Barnes' children were his patients.

"Chief, did someone get Chloe Smith out?"

The chief whirled around, looking perturbed by the interruption. "We have men going through the apartments now looking for any occupants. What apartment number is Chloe?"

He gave him the number then watched as the Chief relayed the information over the radio attached at his shoulder.

The walkie-talkie squawked back in an unidentifiable reply.

"My guys are about to go in that apartment now."

"Is that where the fire originated?"

"No, looks like it happened a few doors down. It hasn't gone past her apartment so hopefully that's a good thing." The chief moved away, barking orders as he went on.

A tap on Darryl's shoulder made him turn around. Jo met his gaze, her eyes filling with tears. "Where's Chloe?"

"They're doing a check in her apartment right now."

"Oh, no," she whispered, clasping her hands in a silent prayer.

Lord, please let her be okay. I don't know what I'd do...

He kicked at the ground, needing something, anything to distract him from his thoughts. He watched her apartment, hoping for a sign, any sign that she was okay.

That she was safe. A flutter of movement caught his eyes.

Chloe emerged looking like she was glowing. *Wait, was that steam?* He didn't think, he took off running before he even realized he was moving. Chloe looked up and saw him and ran toward him.

The force of her weight knocked into him as he wrapped his arms around her, resting his chin on the top of her head. He vaguely wondered why she was wet, but he didn't care. She was alive.

Thank You, God.

Satchel barked and they broke apart. She placed the dog on the ground. "Stay."

Chloe rested her head against his chest, her face buried into his shirt. He stroked her back, more to calm his nerves than hers. He didn't dare think how close he came to losing her.

"Are you okay?" he asked softly in her ear.

"I am now." Her arms tightened around him. "Please don't let me go."

The fear in her voice rent his heart in two.

"Never." He kissed the top of her head. "It's okay," he whispered, to help her realize she was safe and sound. "I'm so glad you're safe."

"Me too."

He pulled back, still holding on tight. "Are you sure you're okay? Do we need to go to the ER?"

"No," she said with a quick shake of her head.

He stared into her liquid brown eyes, thankful that the evening hadn't turned into tragedy. He brushed her bottom lip with his thumb. She shivered in his arms, her lips parting in anticipation. He stared into her eyes, asking permission.

She stepped closer, and he took it as a yes.

Before he could think, before he could temper his reaction, his hands delved into her curls and his lips met hers.

She gasped, but quickly kissed him back.

She's kissing me back.

The thought triggered his emotions and he deepened the kiss. He slid his right arm around her waist and tilted her slightly. Her hands cupped the back of his head and he groaned with pleasure.

He jolted backward, realizing where his thoughts were leading him. He watched as she struggled to regain focus, her breath coming out in short puffs, her lips full and rosy from his kiss.

"About time you two broke it up," Jo said, holding Satchel in her arms. "He was about to make a run for it."

He had no clue how long she had been standing there. He stepped back and Jo moved forward, hugging Chloe in a rocking motion.

"Girl, you had us worried."

"I'm so glad you came looking. My cellphone melted on my nightstand."

His guts twisted. How close to the fire had she been?

"What happened?" Jo asked.

"Satchel woke me. Thankfully my bedroom door was closed, but I couldn't get out so I hid in the bathroom."

"Is that why you're all wet?" he asked.

She blushed, folding her arms in front of her. "I didn't want the fire to burn us while we waited for help. I showered us with water and then aimed the nozzle toward the door."

He opened his mouth to ask a question then shut it as the chief strolled toward their little group.

"Ms. Smith, we need to get your statement. Plus it's mandatory for us to look you over and make sure you don't need medical attention."

"I just hurt my hand is all." She held out her hand, blisters already formed.

"Babe," Darryl hissed out. He gently took her hand as he looked it over. "I can take care of this."

"Not a problem, Dr. Jones, but my guys still have to follow procedure."

"Lead the way, Chief." There was no way he was letting her out of his sight.

Chapter Nineteen

*G*iving up the fight, Chloe opened her eyes. There was no way she was going to fall asleep any time soon. Every time she closed her eyes, she smelled smoke. Saw flames as they danced their way across her bathroom floor. The majority of her apartment had been charred beyond recognition, which was why she was now in Jamie's guest bedroom.

Who knew when she helped her pick out furniture that she'd be the guest enjoying the comfortable trundle bed. Jamie had been half hysterical when she arrived at her apartment. She'd held her so tight, Chloe had to beg for air. She still felt sore from the death defying hug her little sister had bestowed upon her. But it was so nice having someone care. Never in a million years would she have imagined that someone being a sister. It had been a comfort to hug someone without being the one to hold the other person up.

Her face heated as she remembered Darryl's embrace. The safety and affection she'd felt pouring off from him had righted her world. And then she remembered she was all but wrapping herself around a man in broad daylight. So not her M.O. but maybe adrenaline was to blame. If she hadn't come so close to death, she'd be mortified by the public display of affection. Only she couldn't help but be grateful for his kiss.

The power of it had nearly knocked her socks off. She'd felt like Sandra Dee in *I'd Rather Be Rich*. Only her shoes had already been off...probably melted and charred under her bed.

"Oh no," she muttered. She was going to have to replace an entire wardrobe. One she was quite fond off. Her collection of dresses and cardigans had taken years to accumulate, but one small fire wiped away her apparel.

Tears brimmed at the surface. The injustice smarted, but there was no use in shedding any more tears over everything she had lost. It wouldn't bring her clothes back. Her interior design tools she kept at home. Nothing could be recovered.

How was she so unlucky to have experienced two fires?

Despite her efforts, the first tear fell freely. Then the next one, until she couldn't distinguish between them. Her body shook from the force of her sobs. Covering her mouth, she curled into her pillow, letting the tears have control.

A knock on the door interrupted her.

"CeeCee, are you okay?"

She sighed, wiping her nose and tears away. "I'm okay," she croaked. She grimaced. No way would Jamie believe that.

A creaking sound confirmed her suspicions. The bed dipped, then an arm circled her waist.

"Shh, don't cry." Jamie smoothed Chloe's hair back from her face. "Everything you lost can be replaced. I'm just glad you made it out alive."

"My last photos of my grandmother are gone," she whispered. Why hadn't she scanned them and saved them in some cloud?

"Oh, man, I didn't even think of that. Go ahead and just let it all out."

So she did. Jamie stayed, hugging her until the last tear fell. She fell asleep with her little sister rubbing her back and whispering words of encouragement.

∼

Darryl rubbed his eyes as he reread his colleague's email. Jordan had put in her request for vacation. She and her fiancé had finally set a date and she wanted to take a week off for the honeymoon. They were going to Barbados.

People still visit Barbados? Where would Chloe want to go on their honeymoon? He froze, shocked by his line of thinking. Was he really ready to tie the knot? To make that type of commitment?

He leaned back in his chair. There was no denying the depth of his feelings. It had become quite obvious as he held on to her after the fire. Chloe was the only one he wanted to spend the rest of his life with. But did she feel the same way? She was committed to him now, but he couldn't help wondering how she would feel if someone better came along. Because there were definitely men out in the world who were better.

But only I can love her the way she needs to be loved.

With a quick click of the mouse, he pulled up a jeweler's website in Kodiak City. If he took the plunge and proposed to her, he wanted a ring in hand. He clicked yellow to narrow his choices. She deserved a ring that spoke to her personality, and a yellow gem would definitely fit that criteria.

He scrolled down the page, then paused. A sparkling yellow diamond stared at him, flanked by two white diamonds. He clicked on the link hoping for more information. *Emerald cut.* He had no clue if that was a good cut or not. Who could he ask for advice without giving anything away?

"Knock, knock."

He looked up as Jordan walked into his office. "Hey, Jordan. I saw your request."

"Do you think it would be feasible?" Her eyebrow quirked in question.

"Definitely. That time of the year isn't too jammed pack with appointments. Now if it was close to the new school year, I'd object." He chuckled to make sure she wouldn't take any offense.

Her shoulders dropped and a look of relief lit up her face. "Thank goodness. Mark was really worried about my vacation time." She sat down in a chair. "How's Chloe?"

"She's good. She had some second-degree burns on her hand, but that's it. All things considered, she's good."

"I'll bet you're relieved."

He nodded, then glanced at his computer before glancing back at Jordan. "Hey, could I ask you something? It can't leave this room."

"Sure," she sat forward. "What's up?"

He spun his computer monitor around. "Is this a good ring?"

She gasped. "It's gorgeous! Colored gems are becoming all the rage lately. Does she like yellow?"

"Loves it."

"Then I'd say you've got a winner."

He huffed out a sigh of relief. "It's emerald cut. I wasn't sure if that was a good thing or not."

"It really depends on the girl. No cut is bad unless it's not her preference. Does she wear rings so that you can get an idea?"

He thought about her hands, slender and dainty. They were always devoid of any jewelry, well except for her watch. "No, she doesn't wear rings."

Jordan shrugged. "Well pray about it. I'm sure God will clue you in."

"Thanks Jordan," he said with a chuckle.

"No problem." She headed for the door. "Hey, the next time there's a Bible study, could I bring Mark?"

"Definitely. We're all dying to meet him."

"Likewise." With a wave, she left his office, closing the door softly behind her.

With a sigh, he leaned back against his chair. *Lord, some guidance on marriage and a ring would be much appreciated.* He stared at the ring in question, then at the price. He could afford it. Saving was as easy for him as a drive around the lake.

But would she like it? Better yet, would she say yes?

He shuddered at the thought of a "no." If only there was a way to find out her feelings on love and marriage before baring his soul. Women had it easy. The guy did all the work in the relationship; all they had to do was be present. It was rare for a woman to plan the romance and, of course, pop the big question.

Then again, if Chloe asked him, he'd be bummed he didn't get the chance. He laughed to himself. Who was he kidding? He would die from happiness if she asked him. Whether she asked him or not made no real difference as long as she wanted to marry him. He needed a plan to find the answers before he took the plunge.

∿

The doorbell peeled.

"Could you answer that" Jamie called out from her bedroom.

"Sure." Chloe ambled toward the front. Most likely it was Char and JJ. They were due to arrive any moment.

She twisted the knob, swinging the door open and froze, staring in confusion. The man standing before her was definitely not JJ or Char. His brown hair was streaked with gray matching his mustache and beard. His chocolate brown eyes reminded her of her own, except the guy was white.

"May I help you?" Maybe he had the wrong place.

"Chloe?"

She straightened up, gripping the doorknob. Her mouth dried as her heart picked up speed. She had to ask, even though she knew the answer in her heart. "Do I know you?"

He grimaced, making his eyes appear smaller. The look on his face reminded her of the way she looked whenever she was agitated. The muscles in her stomach clenched.

"No, we've never met."

Not the answer she was looking for. "Are you here for Jamie?" Her head swam as her heart continued its rapid pace.

"I'm her father."

She inhaled, trying to suck in oxygen, but it wasn't enough. Her breath came in short puffs, increasing the surreal feeling.

She was looking at her father.

The father who refused to acknowledge her.

What was she supposed to do? To say?

"May I come in?" His voice was quiet, hesitant. The low timbre of his voice made her wonder what it would have been like to listen to him growing up. Had it soothed her siblings in nightmares?

Turned stern in discipline? She knew nothing about it other than it sounded nice.

"Dad!"

Chloe whirled around as Jamie came bouncing down the hall. Her little sister threw her arms around him. "I'm so glad you're here. What are you doing here?" Jamie gasped, turning to stare at Chloe. "Are you okay?" she whispered.

She nodded, incapable of speech. "I think I'll go to my room...I mean yours...uh, the guestroom."

Jamie grabbed her hand. "No. This needs to be settled now. Let's go into the living room."

Jamie continued to hold her hand as if afraid Chloe would dart off at the first opportunity. And her little sister wouldn't be wrong. She sat down next to Jamie, thankful they were all on the same sofa. Since they were seated in a row, she didn't have to look into her father's eyes. Searching for similarities, searching for answers to questions he was unwilling to answer.

Yet her soul cried out, begging to know why he didn't want her.

"I'll start, since no one seems to be jumping into the conversation." Jamie's sardonic comment sliced the air.

What conversation? The tension in the room was hot enough to finish the job that global warming had started in the Arctic circle.

"Dad, this is Chloe Anne Smith. It has been confirmed that you are her father thanks to the DNA test that we did. No thanks to you."

Chloe wanted to laugh at the mock growl in Jamie's voice, but she couldn't move. This was like some twisted out-of-body experience. It was like she had been transported to a set of the Maury Povich show.

"She has a huge heart, a crazy talent with design, including the artwork that any one rarely sees. Her faith is the cornerstone of her personality.

"And she loves family. Loves us to the deep, even if we don't deserve it."

Tears sprang to her eyes as Jamie waxed poetic. She didn't know when her little sister had become such an expert on her, but it felt good to have someone recognize who she was inside. To see past the curly hair, light skin, and smile.

Chloe squeezed Jamie's hand in gratitude.

"She's also in need of a father. One who would embrace his role in her life and treasure it. The same one who taught me to be the best person I could be. I don't think it's fair that she missed out because her skin is a different hue."

"Are you done, Jamie?"

Chloe shivered at the sound of her father's voice. He sounded mildly perturbed, but unfortunately she had no experience to back that on.

"I am if you're done acting immature." Jamie rushed on. "And I mean that respectfully and not at all snarky like it could be perceived."

He chuckled. "I know you do."

Chloe sneaked a peek to the right and froze. He was staring straight at her.

She sat up, pulling her hand from Jamie. If he had something to say, she would meet it with courage and confidence. Even if she had to fake it.

"Nice to meet you, Chloe Ann."

She nodded, but inside she was shaking with rage. A rage she had never experienced before. *How dare he act like this is just an ordinary meeting.* All the shows she had ever watched where people got to meet their biological parents came rushing to her. Where were the hugs? Where were the tears? And why was this white-hot rage washing through her?

Her father looked at Jamie then back at Chloe. "Ames, I think you better give us some alone time."

Jamie met her gaze, her eyes asking if it was okay.

"I'll be fine." *I hope.*

"I'll be in the backyard if you need me."

Jamie stood up, her bare feet leaving no trace of sound. Chloe wanted to turn around and beg her to come back, but he was right. She needed to talk to him alone. A chance to express every emotion she had ever felt surrounding the word 'dad'.

"Jamie means well, but she doesn't understand that sometimes we need to do things in our own time, in our own way."

She stared at her hands. For the first time since she read the DNA test, they felt like her normal hands. It was the strength she needed. Her courage bolstered and words flew from her mouth. "How could you ever deny me?"

With a turn of her head she met his gaze. He averted his, staring down at his own hands. The move was so reminiscent of her own behavior. She inhaled sharply, tears stinging her eyes. Wasn't that all the proof she needed?

"I have no excuse."

"No," she said with a shake of a head. "I don't deserve that cop out. You owe me an explanation. Do you realize how differently my life would have turned out if you hadn't denied me?"

"Most likely Jamie wouldn't be here."

A tear spilled over. "That's not fair."

"No it's not, but it's the truth."

She stood up, moving away from him. This wasn't going anything like she had imagined. She had hoped he'd beg her for forgiveness. Offer words of regret and a request for a second chance. Instead, he sat there like a bump on the log while she was forced to relive her disappointments.

"Chloe."

She squeezed her eyes tight, her back to him.

An audible sigh reached her ears. "I was young and impressionable. My mother knew what buttons to push. Unfortunately, she shared some information about your mother which I now know to be false. It was enough for me to break up with your mother and ignore her pleas about the pregnancy."

Chloe swiped away the tears, and then turned around. "Let's say I believe you. What does that have to do with present day? Why would it keep you from ignoring *my* pleas when I contacted you?" *Let him come up with some trite excuse for that.* She tapped her foot.

"My wife."

"What?"

"I didn't know how she would react when I told her it was possible I had a grown daughter from a previous relationship. It's not a conversation any man wants to have with his wife."

She bit her lip, hating that she could sympathize with him. He didn't deserve her sympathy. Yet, the part in her that had been rooted in her faith, knew much more than sympathy was required of her.

"Have you told her yet?"

"Yes, that's why I'm here." He gave her a sheepish look. "She kind of chewed me out."

It sounded like she would like his wife, but her dislike for him grew. He needed permission to do what was right? "So now all of a sudden you're ready to own up to your paternal rights because your wife made you?" Part of her hated the cantankerous tone of her voice, but she didn't want to moderate it either. She wanted him to know how badly she hurt.

"Jamie told me about the fire. It hit me like a punch to the gut that my daughter could have died and I've never seen her face." He stood and walked to her, his hands in his pockets. "But looking at you now, I know that every time I stared at myself in the mirror I saw you." He paused. "You have my eyes."

His gaze searched hers as if asking for forgiveness. She wanted to yield. Wanted to capitulate to the emotions rising in her.

"I grew up without my mother as well. She turned to drugs when you left."

He let out a groan, his eyes darkening with regret. The frown lines that appeared at his mouth showed the heartache he was experiencing.

Was it on her behalf or at himself?

"I'm so sorry. I had no idea."

"Why would you? You left Freedom Lake and never glanced back."

He swallowed. "I did look back."

"What do you mean?"

"I came back to visit one time. It was before I had met my wife. I wanted to know how Charlotte was doing. I didn't know where to look so I went to her mother's house. I saw you...you must have been around three. You looked so much like Charlotte it was mind blowing."

He had seen her?

"I don't remember ever seeing you."

"I didn't go in. I convinced myself there were no features of me in you, that you couldn't have been my child. Still, there was always that 'what-if' in the back of my mind. So every month I sent some money to your grandmother. Never signed it, just put cash or a money order in the envelope."

Was she supposed to feel gratitude? "I...I need some time to process this."

He nodded. "I'm staying at the Carter's B&B."

"I'm surprised you didn't pick a fancy hotel or your mother's place." The words flew out uncensored, but she didn't care. She was too busy wondering why he wouldn't welcome the chance to live the life of luxury. Having a personal assistant, cook, and butler all at his disposal.

"No. I haven't spoken to her in years."

"Did Jamie tell you about dinner at her place?"

His eyebrow raised. "You had dinner with my mother?"

She laughed. She couldn't help it. The look of utter shock on his face was enough to push her emotions over the side to slightly hysterical. "We did. Suffice it to say, I won't be going back anytime soon."

Her father chuckled. "I can only imagine. Not too many people can stand five minutes alone in Geraldine Davenport's presence, let alone eat dinner with her."

"Is the laughter a good sign?"

Chloe turned at Jamie's question. "We're not killing one another if that's what's got you worried."

Jamie grinned, looping her arm through hers. "I'm not worried, big sis. I am curious as to the laughter."

"Chloe said you ate dinner with your grandmother."

Jamie blew air, her hair fanning away from her face. "That was pure torture. Thank you for keeping us away from her growing up." Jamie's eyes widened and she clapped a hand over her mouth.

Chloe laughed. Then her father. And then Jamie joined in until tears ran down their faces. Maybe they really would be all right.

Chapter Twenty

arryl knocked on Jamie's door. He hadn't warned Chloe that he was coming over. Hopefully, she wouldn't mind. He needed to see her. He hadn't come up with a concrete plan to find out if she was thinking happily ever after with him, but he wanted to at least find out something.

The door opened and he stared in shock at the man who answered. Even though he was older, his height was impressive. The man had to be at least six one or two. It put his five feet nine inches to shame. Was the guy Chloe's father?

"Um, is Chloe here?"

"She is." His low rasped was laced with surprise. "And may I ask who you are?"

"I'm Darryl Jones."

"Dad, move out the way. Let Darryl in." Jamie's voice carried from the back.

Mr. Davenport stepped back, making a motion to enter. Darryl nodded his thanks, but he only had eyes for Chloe. How was she dealing with this? Both of them had a lot to figure out when it came to their parents.

Hopefully she fared better than he had.

Chloe walked down the hall, offering a small smile. He searched her face for signs of stress, but there was none. Either she was a great actress or she really was fine with her father's presence.

"Hey, Darryl."

Her soft voice was like coming home. "How's everything?" He raised an eyebrow hoping it was pointed in the direction of her father.

Unfortunately, he couldn't tell by her laughter if he was successful or not.

He took hold of her hand. "Want to go out on the boat and talk?"

"Yes." The swiftness of her grin stole his breath. "Is it hot or will I need a sweater?"

"Very hot." He drew in a steady breath, trying to get his heart to slow from a gallop. He was such a goner. If she married him, he would do all he could to see her smile daily. Or hourly. Or every time he saw her precious face.

Once they were in the car he let his curiosity fly like a fisher's reel. "So was that your father? How did *that* conversation go?" He glanced at her from the corner of his eye.

"It was difficult. I'm not sure I liked all his answers, but I got the impression he was being honest."

"What did he say?"

As she relayed the conversation, his stomach tied up like a pretzel. Her voice waivered during some of the retelling, the pain of the experience leaking through. He held out his hand in an offer of comfort. She quickly laced her fingers with his.

Was it his imagination or did her voice sound stronger?

"Did he really send money?" He shook his head feeling a touch moronic. "Sorry, it's not like you can ask your grandmother."

"Don't be sorry. I don't actually have to ask her. We used to get what my grandmother called 'rainy day' money. I had always assumed it was from my mother. Proof that she cared an ounce for me."

He swallowed down the lump that appeared upon hearing the rejection in her voice. What would it be like to realize the parent you hoped had cared, didn't? And the one you expected nothing from was the one who showed some thoughts toward her?

Even in his rejection, Chloe's father still provided for her.

"Babe, why haven't you tried to find your mom?"

Her hand tensed in his. As the silence widened, suddenly uncertainty crept into the mix. Maybe he shouldn't have asked the question.

"I'm worried I'll find out she died."

Wow. He had never thought about that aspect. If her mother still did drugs, death was a very real possibility. Why didn't he think of that sooner? "Have you prayed about it?"

A chagrin smile touched her lips. "No. I haven't."

"Hmm. I'm still new at this whole prayer thing, but would you like me to pray with you?" He parked at the dock, unbuckled his seatbelt, and turned toward her.

Her mouth parted in surprise. "Would you?"

"Of course. I'm here to help in any way I can." Holding both of her hands, he bowed his head. "Lord, I'm here to pray on behalf of Chloe. I know you know what's going on with her on the parental front. Please give her wisdom to know what she should do regarding her mother. Also, please help Chloe and her father navigate the waters of their relationship. In Jesus' Name. Amen."

He opened his eyes and stared into Chloe's sparkling brown ones.

"Thank you, Darryl."

"Anytime, babe."

Her cheeks took on a rosy hue and a small smile touched her lips. His eyes stared at them. He met her gaze again, garnering permission, then touched his lips tentatively to hers. This time, he took his time kissing her. Exploring the shape of her mouth with his. The kiss was different from the first one, but no less special.

He pulled away before his senses took him down the difficult road. How he ached to tell her he loved her. Wasn't it too soon? He rubbed a thumb over her cheek. "Ready for the boat ride?"

She nodded, her cheeks rubbing against the palm of his hand. "As long as I'm with you, I'm ready for anything."

He wanted to pump his fist at the comment. He'd take that as the first sign she'd be willing to marry him.

⌇∾

Spending time with Darryl was the epitome of a Calgon commercial. The cool breeze drifted through her hair, fluttering her curls about as waves gently rocked the boat. Chloe sat on the bench, curled up next to Darryl. His hand made lazy circles along her arm. She told herself the goosebumps were from the breeze, but knew she was deluding herself.

Summer had officially arrived in Freedom Lake and temps were running high. It only made sense that the man cradling her in his arms was the source of her puckered flesh, and not the breeze.

Closing her eyes, she thought about the prayer he had said in the car. Never had she dated anyone who actually prayed with her. Then again, it wasn't like she had loads of dating experience. She was picky when it came to the opposite sex. Her grandmother had pressed upon her the importance of choosing a life mate well.

Could Darryl be the one?

They'd only been out on a few dates, but they talked every night. Had been for two straight months. Were the feelings she experienced when he was around love? How did one know with absolute certainty that they wanted to tie themselves to another for life?

The thought of marriage was foreign and a little scary. A healthy marriage wasn't something she saw every day, and neither had Darryl. She swallowed, shifting to a sitting position.

Immediately, she felt the loss of his embrace.

"You okay?"

She blinked at him, unwilling to say yes and unwilling to say no.

"Penny for your thoughts?"

Just talk already! "Do you think our relationship is going too fast?"

Darryl looked around and then back at her. "Sitting on a boat, on a lake, next to each other doesn't seem that fast, so I'm unsure of what you mean."

"You know what I mean." She groaned in exasperation.

He chuckled. "Sorry, you're going to have to be a little clearer." His thumb and forefinger pinched together, a sliver of space between them.

"What's the end goal?"

Darryl sighed and took hold of her hand. "Real talk? No holding back?"

"Yes, please." The words came out a whisper, but that's because they couldn't surpass the ball in her throat.

"I'm praying for a lifetime with you. For a ring on our fingers. Two and a half kids and a white picket fence. What about you?"

She gripped the sides of her head, pushing the curls out of her eyes. *He wanted marriage?* How did he know that already?

"It's been my dream since the first time I laid eyes on you."

Oy.

She had spoken her thoughts aloud. She searched his gaze, trying to remember the moment she first laid eyes on him. An image of Freedom High popped into her mind, the blue lockers lining the way and a boy with a curly mop of hair surrounded by the cheerleading squad. She remembered her junior year accurately.

"You were surrounded by cheerleaders."

"That was the first time *you* noticed *me*. I noticed you the first day in art."

"What?" He had been in her art class? Would she look like a fool if she uttered the thought aloud?

"You walked in wearing a denim skirt, white shirt, and a yellow sweater. You had on Keds and your hair was a lot shorter. You had it in a short curly fro."

Her face heated as she recalled the day. She remembered that outfit fondly. She'd worn it the first day of her sophomore year. "How can I not remember you being in my class?"

"Remember the dorky dude with glasses and short curly hair? Used to button his shirt all the way up to the top button?"

"Oh my goodness." She slapped a hand over her mouth, but not before a snort of laughter escaped.

"Go ahead, laugh it up."

So she did. She let loose, tears streaming down her face as she recalled the nerd who had pestered her daily by asking questions on techniques.

Funny how the memory was so vivid but she couldn't remember his name.

After the laughter subsided, she cleared her throat. "I cannot believe that was you."

He shrugged, his strong shoulders lifting up. "What can I say, summer vacation was good to me. My eye doctor decided my eyesight had corrected itself. Grew out my hair and went out for sports. It was quite obvious I didn't have a talent for art."

She snorted in agreement. "What was that blob you tried to make? Looked like a snowman?"

He fell back against the rail, his laughter ringing loudly. "It was supposed to be a plaster art of my fist."

"Oh."

They continued talking and the subject morphed to their current professions. Suddenly, Darryl became quiet.

"I've actually been wanting to tell you the reason why I became a doctor." His eyes had darkened, worry furrowing his brow.

"Okay." Why did she have the feeling she wouldn't like the direction their talk would go?

He gulped, his Adam's apple bulging in his throat. "I wanted to devote my life to helping people. To using my hands to bring healing and not pain."

"That's admirable."

He was shaking his head before her sentence was complete. "It's not."

She opened her mouth to object, but he held up a hand. Her stomach dropped as she realized it was shaking. Darryl's—the man who she'd always viewed as having admirable strength—hand was shaking. Automatically her hand came to hold his, but he slipped free. Coming to a stand, he faced her.

"I did something horrible when I was young. It marred me, changed me for life. I promised myself that I wouldn't give in to the evil that had tried to claim me, but instead I would do good. Right the wrong I committed by giving my life to heal others."

Chloe nodded, wishing she could voice her thoughts and offer words of comfort. But her inner voice prompted her to remain silent. So she clamped her teeth over her tongue.

"I...I..." he cleared his throat. "I tried to kill my father."

She inhaled sharply. Her heartbeat picked up speed. Not knowing what to do or say, she met his gaze, hoping he would find patience in her gaze.

His eyes darted away, his voice dipping lower, softer even. "He hit my mom for serving him cold vegetables."

A metallic taste assaulted her taste buds. She must have clamped down too hard on her tongue. Her insides quivered at the thought of his mother being beaten.

"I snapped. I couldn't take it anymore. I was done with him terrorizing her. Terrorizing me. I was fifteen, old enough to finally stand up to him. Words were said, but for the life of me, I can't remember them. Before I knew it, he was pinned down with my hands around his neck, squeezing the life out of him."

Tears filled her eyes at the thought of Darryl as a young boy defending his mother. How awful to think she had to be defended from her husband. His *father*. What kind of impact had this had on him?

"I didn't realize how close he was to dying until the cops pulled me off of him. His skin bore the marks of my fingers and I found out I fractured his voice box." His voice began to falter. Began to crack under the strain of his emotions. "The judge ordered me to attend anger management classes and seek counseling with a child therapist. If I met those requirements, then he would seal my juvenile record as if I had no mark against me."

IIis eyes rose, meeting hers, and her heart cracked at the look of defeat on his face. His eyes were dark with pain and regret.

"Although my records are sealed and no one knows about them unless I tell them…do you know the turmoil this has caused? I see it when I see my hands. I know what they're capable of. I know the damage they can cause."

"No." She stood, gathering her sea legs under her, to end his self-deprecating entreaty. "I know these hands as well." She touched them, guiding them closer to her. "They are used to love. To heal. To offer hope to those who are ill and in need of a physician's touch. Sure, you used them in a brutal matter before, but to protect someone who needed it. You shielded her from death. You have to know that."

Darryl stared at her in wonderment. "With all I've told you, you still see good in me?" His voice held a rasp.

She dropped his hands and held his face in her palms. "I see good because that is who you are. Not only that, but you belong to the Lord now. He will mold you to His likeness until all the bad has been smoothed out."

His forehead touched hers and slowly the tension left his shoulders. She kissed his cheek, hoping to soothe him. To erase the hurt and pain he had carried for far too long. His lips met hers, softly, then pressing firmly as if to affirm the truth she had already spoken.

She wrapped her arms around him, praying that he could feel the love and acceptance she had for him.

Chapter Twenty-One

*D*arryl headed down the hallway of Freedom Lake Tabernacle. He had a meeting with Bishop Brown. After unburdening himself to Chloe he needed to speak to someone. Someone who didn't know the situation or him personally. He needed wise counsel and hoped the Bishop would be able to offer advice.

He slid his hands along his jeans before knocking on Bishop's door. With any luck, the clamminess that had taken ahold of his hands the moment he stepped foot in the church would be gone.

"Come in."

Trying to give himself a pep talk, Darryl slowly opened the door.

"Ah, Dr. Jones, right on time." The Bishop glanced at the wall clock for confirmation.

"Thanks for meeting me, Bishop. And you can call me Darryl." He held out a hand, shaking the Bishop's in return.

"Have a seat Brother Darryl. Tell me what brings you by?"

He settled into the soft leather chair, trying to rest his hands along the armrest instead of gripping them for support. "I need some advice."

"Whatever your issue, have you already prayed about it?"

He nodded. For once, he remembered to lay his request at the feet of God. He had waited for a response, but all he could think of was Bishop Brown. He wasn't sure if that was a God nudge or his own flesh speaking. He said as much to the bishop.

"Understand. It's hard to know what is what when we first become believers." He leaned forward. "Tell me what's going on."

Darryl told him about the incident with his father. Funny how retelling it now felt so much easier than when he had spoken to Chloe. It was like she had freed him to talk of the subject without regrets.

"Have you seen your father since?"

"No, sir." Darryl paused, rubbing his chin. "Funny you ask because that's what I prayed about last night. I think I should see him, but I'm not sure why."

"What do you mean?" Bishop leaned forward, his chin resting on his forefingers.

"My grandmother asked me to go see him. To lay to rest the bitterness I carry around. I spoke to my girlfriend…" he paused, marveling at the feelings that ran through him as he spoke those words aloud. He swallowed. "I spoke to my girlfriend yesterday. I felt she had the right to know what happened before committing to me any further. Later on that evening, the urge to see him began to run through me."

"And you want advice on what to do next?"

He nodded, thankful the Bishop understood his problem.

"Let's pray before we go any further."

Darryl closed his eyes and bowed his head as Bishop Brown's clear and strong voice filled the room. Immediately, his heart rate slowed and his hands began to feel like their normal dry selves. Darryl recognized the peace that took over whenever he communed with God in prayer. Thank goodness God gifted them with prayer; a way to seek Him out in this manner. At first he wasn't sure that prayer worked, but the more Darryl used it, the more peace he felt.

"Amen," Bishop said.

"Amen," he echoed.

"Brother Darryl, I think this urge you're feeling is a nudge from the Holy Spirit. Your spirit knows you need to reconcile this relationship. Not that it will necessarily happen, but you need to do your part and leave the rest up to God."

"Sir, I just don't know if I can handle it. It's one thing to believe I need to see him, but to actually go to prison and see him." He huffed out a breath of air. "I have to admit it's a daunting task."

"And it will be. Make no mistake about it, the devil never wants us to do our part. He never wants us to forgive and walk the path of healing. I'm sure the visit will be a difficult one. If you commit your way to God, He'll see you through."

"Okay," he said with a nod. "Would you mind praying for me? Pray that I can follow through and handle the visit however it may go."

"Without a doubt, Brother Darryl. If you don't mind, I can also add you to the prayer list. There are brothers and sisters of this church committed to lifting in prayer those in need."

He blanched, suddenly feeling insecure. The idea that the other congregation members would know his struggles was a little nerve wracking.

Yet the thought of having multiple people praying for him was a comfort he didn't want to pass up.

"Yes, you can add me to the prayer list."

He thanked the Bishop and left his office. He knew what he had to do, the only question was, could he do it?

∽

Chloe sat on the bed, her Bible unopened on her lap. She was a match for Jamie. What were the odds it would be her and not Char or JJ? Her thoughts whirled around in her brain. They were so jumbled up she couldn't make sense of her feelings. This was an answer to prayer, but now she had no clue how to respond.

Her life had literally turned upside down since she had been tested. She'd lost her apartment, every single possession except for Satchel who was curled up next to her, taking a midday nap. All she had was her business and car. Sure, renter's insurance would give her the money to buy material things, but it didn't take away the sting of loss. And why all of a sudden was she apprehensive of giving Jamie a kidney?

When she first found out about her sister's health issues, she'd jumped at a chance to help. Jamie was the sister of her heart before DNA even confirmed the blood connection. The love she felt for Jamie shocked her with its depth. Still, a tiny voice in the back of her mind voiced her fears.

So much could go wrong with a kidney transplant. What if Jamie rejected her kidney? The thought sent shivers of fear down her spine. If either one of them had complications during the surgery she wasn't sure how she would handle it. She would be bereft if Jamie suffered.

Lord, what do I do?

The cry came from the depth of her soul, straight from her heart. She was so confused and knew that right now wasn't the time to be making decisions. However, when would she ever feel stable enough to make that kind of commitment?

She sighed. Maybe Jo would have some good advice. Before she could change her mind, she texted her friend to ask if they could meet up.

Sure. Is This Something You Want Michelle In On?

She texted back: *No. I Know She's Busy Getting Ready For The Wedding.*

Ok. Meet At Leeann's?

Perfect.

Chloe picked up Satchel, thankful he stayed asleep as she settled him into the crate. He hadn't mastered potty training yet. He was so close, but the fire seemed to make him regress. That and they now lived with Jamie. Since he refused to go in his crate, she could leave him there until she returned.

Grabbing her car keys, she headed out of the house. Jamie, Char, and JJ had taken their father out for a family lunch. They had extended the invitation to her, but she still felt awkward around him. She rolled her eyes. *Ninny.* The only way the awkwardness would go away was if she spent time with him.

Only she wasn't ready for that step.

Before the song on the radio finished, Chloe pulled up to LeeAnn's. A cup of iced green tea sounded wonderful about now. The sun seemed to pour out all its energy to heat up her skin. It sapped her energy, yet it could be the whole transplant issue draining her.

Jo waved from the back, settled at a table by the window. Chloe held up a hand and pointed to the order line. She needed a drink before she got up the nerve to tell Jo her feelings.

She exchanged greetings with LeeAnn, placing her order and grabbing the tea. With a thanks, Chloe made her way to Jo. "Hey, JoJo."

"Hey, girl. How are you?"

"Let's skip that for now. How are *you*?" She knew Jo had to be feeling the pressure now that she and Evan had set a date.

"Stressed. My mother is trying to sink her claws into our wedding. No matter how many times I tell her we want a simple one, she still tries to take over." Jo fiddled with the chain on her neck.

Chloe figured as much. Jo's mother was...*difficult*. "Why don't you compromise?"

"How so?" Jo asked warily. Her eyes squinted as if daring her to come up with a horrible solution.

"Let her plan the reception?"

Jo's mouth dropped open.

Chloe chuckled. "Bad idea?"

"No, no, that's actually not a bad idea. If the reception goes over the top, I don't think I'll mind because we'll have already said the vows. The ceremony is the most important part to me."

Jo leaned back in her chair. "I'll have to see what Evan thinks. Thanks, Chlo."

"Happy to help." She raised her drink in a toast and clanked it against Jo's iced coffee. After taking a sip, she dabbed at her lips with a napkin. "Have you finished decorations for Michelle's wedding?"

"Yep. Everything is already. You remember we have to pick out the bridesmaids dresses this weekend."

She grimaced. It had completely slipped her mind. "I remember now."

Jo cocked her head to the side. "What's got you all riled up that you'd forget? You never forget anything."

"I got the test results back. I'm a match for Jamie."

Jo watched her, gauging her mood. "And that scares you, I take it?"

"About the same way going to Geraldine Davenport's house again scares me." She rested her forehead in her hand. "What was I thinking? I don't even like needles."

Jo's hand gently pulled at hers.

Chloe raised her head to meet her friend's gaze.

"You were thinking that you love your sister and want to do something to help her. That's who you are, Chloe. Whenever anyone of us is need…you're there."

"Can I do this? What if she rejects it? What if there are complications and one of us leaves surgery worse than when we went in?" She couldn't bring herself to say the "d" word, but it reverberated in her head like clanging symbols.

"Chloe, you have to let go and trust God. Didn't you say you spent time in prayer before you even tried to get a match."

"I did."

"So why doubt Him now?"

She closed her eyes. "Because I'm terrified."

"Aren't we all? You'd be the first person to remind me of the scriptures that tell you to not let fear take hold."

She smiled. The student had become the teacher. She reached over and squeezed her friend's hand. "Thanks, JoJo."

"Anytime, my friend, anytime."

Chapter *Twenty-Two*

*D*arryl drew in a ragged breath, barely audible over the drumming in his ears. Feeling his hands slide along the steering wheel, he tightened his grip. The closer he drew to the prison, the clammier his hands became. What was he supposed to say? Do? He never imagined himself here.

Or taking the steps to forgive his father.

He parked his car and closed his eyes. *Lord, help me please. I don't know how to walk in there. How to look in his face and try to forgive.* His heart thumped in his chest. Gathering courage, he began the process for visitation.

A slam echoed in the quiet hall. He jumped, glancing behind him to see the steel prison door sealed shut. *One way in, one way out.* If he needed to escape with a quickness, he was doomed. The makers of the prison ensured no one was going anywhere without property authority.

He followed the guard down the corridor, remembering the fact that cameras showed his every move. Property not allowed had been confiscated, and now he was sealed inside a steel prison. He almost felt like a criminal. The urge to run pressed upon him.

Breathe, man. This visit needed to happen, no matter how much his mind objected. Chloe had offered to accompany him, but he wouldn't let her. Forgiveness needed to start with him. Alone.

I will never leave you.

Chills raced down his arms. He wanted to fall to his knees in gratitude. *Lord, be my strength.*

The guard motioned to a booth. "Number eight."

Darryl nodded and sat down in the last booth. A few minutes passed before the door on the other side of the partition opened. Slowly, prisoners shuffled in one by one taking a seat at their assigned spot. The pounding in his head grew more intense.

Calm down. It'll be over soon.

Fifteen minutes wasn't long in the grand scheme of things. Life was over in the blink of an eye for some and seemed to drag on for others. It would be interesting to see how his time with his father would go. He watched as a man came through the doors, hands and feet shackled.

It was amazing how sixteen years didn't erase the knowledge of which man was his father. The drab gray uniform washed out the old man's face, but there was no mistaking his identity. His hair marked the passage of time, gray and white strands mixing in with the black. His beard a mixture of gray and black gave him a hardened edge. It fit his personality to a T.

But he couldn't help thinking how old his father looked. When had it happened?

"Fifteen minutes," the guard shouted.

Darryl swallowed, wishing he had been able to bring a bottle of water inside. The dry feeling in his throat intensified. He blinked, unsure of how he felt. Half of his lifetime had passed since he'd last seen his father.

Going to the trial hadn't been an option. His mother insisted he not miss a single day of school. At least that was the excuse his mother gave him. The last time he had seen his father was when the police had dragged him off of him and escorted his father out of the house. After he'd been released for abusing his mother, his father left town. He knew from his grandmother that he'd been in and out of prison since then.

The old man froze, his eyes locking onto Darryl's face through the clear partition. He looked around, as if wondering if he was there to visit anyone else.

"Have a seat at number eight, Prisoner 10902."

An indescribable looked appeared on his father's face. Slowly, he lowered himself onto the wheeled rounded stool. They reached for the phone at the same time.

Darryl exhaled, wondering what to say.

"Never imagined you'd come for a visit." The low rasp wasn't the same voice of his childhood.

Guilt slammed against Darryl. He was the reason his father would never talk above a whisper again. A fractured voice box had led to his low tone turning into a rasp. Bad memories warred with the good ones, each one vying for dominance in his brain. He exhaled again.

"How've you been?"

Shocked by the question, Darryl answered with a squeak. "I'm a doctor now."

He coughed trying to erase the evidence of strained vocal chords. The sound that had greeted his ears was reminiscent of his pubescent years. He didn't want to seem like a child but a grown man. One who had arrived to adulthood and turned out just fine…despite the lack of a father. And without following in his abusive footsteps.

"A doctor, huh? I knew my mother would shape you up."

He bit his tongue to keep bitterness from spewing.

"Did you know she came to see me?"

He nodded. *Why had he bothered to come?* "Why did you do it?"

"Do what? Are you talking about your mother?"

"No." He swallowed. *The reason you're here this time.*

His father had only been sentenced to three years for domestic abuse because Darryl had been a witness. Apparently the state didn't take too kindly to a man beating his wife in front of the kids. When he had been a teenager, the guilt and shame ate at him constantly. In his head, he was the reason he had no parents. If he hadn't been present, his father could have received a fine or a year in jail. Instead, he was sentenced to three years in prison.

"Look boy, if you're not going to talk, there's other things I can be doing with my time."

Just like that, his father had reduced him to a child. He straightened up in his seat. "Right," he snorted. "I'm sure you have things to do and people to see. Prison is a happening place."

The slam of a fist against the counter, echoed starkly in the prison.

"First warning, Prisoner 10902."

His heart slowed as his father nodded in acknowledgement. Darryl spoke before he could change his mind. "Why did you kill that man?"

"Look. I needed money so I acquired it." His father shrugged. "I had no intention of killing anyone." His brow furrowed. "Why do you care anyway?"

Because he had been left alone. In the back of his teenaged mind, he thought his father would get out of prison a better man. Return home in search for forgiveness for his sins. He would beg his forgiveness, and then search for his mother to seek hers as well. Only it never happened.

A month after being free, his father had been arrested for theft. Then armed robbery. Eventually, for killing a store owner in a robbery gone wrong.

Each time it had been like he'd been abandoned all over again.

But he couldn't say that. Couldn't let the old man know how much it hurt. How much he wanted to have a family again. "I never thought you'd kill anyone."

His father smirked. "Nah, that's more up your ally."

"I've never killed anyone."

"Just like to rough them up a bit?" A sardonic look took over Hank Jones' face.

Darryl stared at his old man. For once, a barb had bounced off leaving no anger, no bitterness, no regret. His father just wasn't capable of behaving rationally. "I save lives for a living."

"Sure. But deep down you're the same as me." His finger motioned back and forth between them.

"No." He shook his head. "I'm redeemed by grace. I'm a new creation." Darryl wasn't sure if he was saying that for himself or his father.

A derisive bark of laugher echoed in the visitation room. "You've found Jesus, huh?" His old man shook his head in shame. "Them freaks are crawling all over this place. You'd think you'd be able to catch a break but too many of them use it as a crutch in here. But I'm not fooled. They just want extra privileges."

"They want freedom."

"They're in prison!"

He froze, startled by the ferociousness coming from his father. When would he show he wasn't afraid anymore? He leaned forward. "Yes they are, but they no longer have to be imprisoned by their behavior. Dad—"

"I'm not your dad. And don't you forget it." His father pointed a finger at him. "If you think you came to say you forgive me and to seek Jesus' forgiveness, then you're wasting your breath and wasting my time." His father dropped the phone. "Guard."

His yell was loud enough to wake the dead, but the guard got the point. He opened the door, and his father shuffled away without a backwards glance.

∽

Chloe stared at the greeting cards. None of them were appropriate. You would think with all the illnesses people suffered from, someone would have written a "I'm-giving-you-an-organ-surprise" card.

Of course the blank ones filled her with anxiety. She had no idea what to write, that's why she was in the greeting card section in the first place. Closing her eyes, she laid her hand on her forehead.

Get it together.

Who said she needed a card in the first place? Maybe she'd just buy some flowers and tell Jamie 'surprise' that way. It was actually a genius idea. She walked away from the greeting cards and headed straight for the floral department.

Luckily the store owners were smart and put the two sections near one another. She stared at the flowers, looking them over. Roses weren't appropriate. They screamed romance to her. Tulips? *No, too sunny.* More of a flowers-just-because occasion. She slowed as she came to the lilies.

They were such beautiful flowers. Almost exotic in their brilliance. She smiled and reached for the yellow lilies. They would suit Jamie perfectly. She picked out a tall skinny white vase. *Perfect.*

Chloe pulled up along the curb since Char and her father's vehicles were parked in the driveway. It was a real family affair. Should she tell Jamie quietly or in front of the whole family? She bit her lip.

Lord, help me please. I don't know how to say it. What words to use. I need you desperately.

Part of her wanted to turn away and wait until it was just her and Jamie. Her father still made her nervous even though he had finally begun to make the effort. So far their conversations sounded like a questionnaire you'd see floating around on social media.

Her hand hovered over the door and she blinked, realizing Jamie had given her a spare key. She pulled out her keychain, staring at the small fish. Was God with her in this? Had she truly heard His voice lead her down this path?

She wished there was a way to be a hundred percent sure. Jo had helped her lay down her fears, but now knowing what lay on the other side of the door had them clutching at her again.

Breathe, Chlo, breathe.

Before she could change her mind, she inserted the key in the lock and stepped into the house. A cool breeze drafted over her thanks to the air conditioner.

"CeeCee's here," Jamie's exuberant shout could be heard over the raucous laughter. She stepped further into the house to see them settled around the coffee table playing Monopoly.

"Oh, flowers," Char said with a smile.

"For Jamie." She handed the flowers over to Jamie, who greeted her with a hug.

"These are beautiful. What's the occasion?"

She swallowed, looking into her sister's face. She glanced away only to find her father, Char, and JJ staring at her.

"What's wrong?" her father asked.

"Nothing. I just…"

He stood up and made a motion with his head. "Let's give them some time alone."

Charlotte looked like she wanted to object, but one look from him silenced her.

"What's wrong, CeeCee?" Jamie took ahold of her hand.

"I want to give you one of my kidneys."

Jamie giggled. "This isn't a game of Operation. You can't just hand over a kidney. There's a process to it."

"I know. I'm a match."

Jamie's eyes widened as they flickered back and forth, searching Chloe's. "What do you mean?" Her voice had gone quiet as if hope wanted to reign but fear held it back.

"I had to do something. I couldn't just let you be sick and not do something. You've welcomed me with open arms. Been there as I sludged through doubt and rejection. You've been my little champion and all I know is I can't lose you. You're the best of me, Ames."

Jamie put the vase down on the counter. "You really got tested?"

"Really," she replied with a nod. "I got the results back yesterday. I'm good. We're good. I can give you a kidney."

A tear slipped down Jamie's face and her arms flew around Chloe's neck, squeezing her tightly.

She returned the embrace, thankful words weren't necessary. The tough part was over. She'd half been afraid Jamie would object.

Thank You Lord.

Chapter Twenty-Three

 arryl knocked on his grandmother's door. When he left the prison, he'd been intent on seeing Chloe. He wanted to share how the meeting went. Instead, he ended up parked in the senior community center parking lot.

It was time to have a heart-to-heart with his grandmother.

His grandmother cracked the door and peered at him. Her eyes darted back and forth as if she wanted to see into his soul.

He gulped. "Hello, Grandmother."

"You did it." Her voice rang clear with assurance.

"Yes, ma'am."

She nodded and opened the door wider. "I imagine you need a stiff drink."

He chuckled. "The thought crossed my mind."

She sat down in her favorite recliner as he took up space on the couch.

"Wasn't a pretty sight, was it?"

Darryl shook his head. He had no words to describe his 'visit.' That was about as close as he got to admitting aloud that he had sat in a jail for almost fifteen minutes to talk to a man who had no desire to speak to him.

As much as he had prepared himself before going there, it hadn't been enough. The ache of being yelled at and kicked out as much as his father could kick anyone out of a prison...had weighed on him the entire ride back. Even though he had made something of his life, he still wasn't good enough for his father. Still couldn't be accepted by the man who was responsible for half of his DNA.

The thought was baffling. "Why doesn't he like me?

"Something's broken in him."

He looked at his grandmother. "I've always thought something was wrong with me."

"Oh, Darryl. You're a fine young man. A terrific doctor and a great grandson. I couldn't be prouder than if you were actually my son." His grandmother glanced away.

He waited, wondering if she would continue speaking or if she was done. Just when he was ready to interject, she met his gaze.

"I can't tell you how sorry I am for failing you."

"What?" He sat forward, arms resting on his thighs. "You took me in when no one gave two thoughts about my wellbeing. I'll always be grateful for that."

"Yes, but did I encourage you? Did I give you the love and affection you deserved?" His grandmother shook her head. "No, I'm not proud of the way I raised you. I can only tell you this. I was petrified that if I raised you the way I raised your father, then you would turn out just like him. I failed as a mother before, so I thought I would try a different tactic." She pointed her finger at him. "You turned out well because of the fire and smarts inside yourself. It had nothing to do with me and everything to do with you. So be proud of yourself. Don't measure yourself next to people who aren't worthy."

He stared at his grandmother hearing the words she said. Mulling them over in his brain. He'd never thought she would say something so eloquent and heartwarming. Without another thought, he rose and bent down to give her a hug.

"I love you. I'm sorry I never said it before." He pulled back.

She placed her aged hands against his face. "And I love you, Darryl Jones. Look to God for your identity and you'll be just fine. You're learning a lot sooner than I did, so I have high hopes."

He chuckled and moved back. Maybe something good had come of his visit after all. It had forged a bond between him and his grandmother that had been lacking before. The hurt he had toward his father would be dealt with another time.

"Grandmother, I think I'll come back soon. I'd like you to meet a friend."

She grinned, her eyes twinkling. "Female friend?"

"Yes."

"Friend or something more."

Darryl bit back a groan at the twenty questions. "Something more."

"Are you going to tell me her name or make me ask you more questions?"

He chuckled. "Chloe. Chloe Smith."

"Oh, April's granddaughter." She paused, cocking her head to the side. "Funny, you two being together."

"Why do you say that?"

"When you were about two, I used to hang around April all the time. Took you with me because I knew she had Chloe and figured she needed someone to play with.

"In fact, I have a picture somewhere of you two holding hands and you offering her a flower. You were smooth with the ladies even back then."

He laughed. He couldn't believe his grandmother. "I'd like to see it if you can find it."

"Give me a second." She held up a hand. "You know I don't remember much, but I do know where I place everything."

She went to the bookshelf, pulling out a blue photo album. His grandmother had to be the only person he knew who still owned albums. He couldn't remember the last time he looked through one. Then again, he really didn't take a lot of pictures. The last one he had willingly taken was of Chloe so that he could set it as his background on his phone.

"Yep. Still there."

She opened the clear sheet and removed a picture, then smoothed the clear overlay back in place. After putting the album back, she walked over to him, holding out the picture.

He grinned, looking at a young Chloe. Her hair was full of curls, and she wore a white romper. His grin turned to laughter as he gazed at his younger self. His head was full of curls and his white shirt and yellow shorts emphasized his chubbiness. He held out a yellow wildflower to Chloe as he held her hand.

"Thank you, Grandmother."

"You're welcome. You make sure to give me warning before you bring her over. I need to look my best."

"You always do."

⧵⧸

Chloe tapped her nails softly against the tabletop. She resisted the urge to glance at her watch. There was something about the waiting process that always sucked her into a downward spiral of doubt and insecurity. Darryl thought he wasn't good enough for her and she thought she wasn't cute enough.

No that wasn't it. She knew she was cute, but so were puppies, and who wanted to be described that way. No, she wanted him to find her irresistible. Breathtaking even. Alluring. She smiled to herself as the adjectives got better and better.

Deep down, she just didn't see herself that way and couldn't imagine he would either. But he was with her. Wanted to be with her even though he thought she was better than he. The thought was laughable.

The care he took with his patients and his friends. The way he was determined to do well, and that surrender of giving his life over to the Lord. Not to mention the sweet puppy he'd gifted her. The care in which he took with her made him a dream catch.

She sighed thinking of the conversation about his father. The wounds were deep, very deep. *Lord, please bring healing to Darryl. I can't imagine being put in that situation where I wanted to kill another person. Then again, I can imagine protecting someone I love.*

She bit her lip, fighting tears. Hurting his father, having his mother leave. All of it had to tie into his feelings about not being good enough. And boy could she identify with that.

Her life had become so complex. Growing up, she'd had moments of longing to have two parents, but she had gotten used to being raised by her grandmother. She'd meant everything to Chloe. Had been her mother for all intents and purposes.

Now she had a father, a brother, and two sisters. It was mind boggling at times. Sometimes she wanted to hide from everyone, overwhelmed by the number of people around her. She had grown up in a house with two people. *Two.* That was it. Sure, she would occasionally have sleepovers with Jo and Michelle, but that was fun and didn't last more than an overnight stay.

She shouldn't gripe about the excessive amounts of people around her. Would God shake His head, thinking her ungrateful? Because she wasn't, but a little quiet here and there would be nice. Like now, where her thoughts could run free and in whatever direction they wanted to.

Her musings came to a halt when she caught a glimpse of Darryl entering LeeAnn's. This had become their favorite place to get together, besides relaxing on his boat. Her heart picked up speed as his mouth spread wide in a smile, just for her.

Darryl sat down in the chair across from her. "I feel like I haven't seen you in a while."

"I know exactly what you mean."

She wanted to kiss him. To show him how much he meant to her. Maybe meeting at LeeAnn's wasn't such a great idea. No way could she give in to a public display of affection. She'd be mortified. Yet, meeting in the midst of people kept her honest and helped avoid temptation.

"How have you been?"

"Good. I told Jamie about the kidney."

His eyes lit up. "I'll bet she was overjoyed."

"That's putting it mildly."

"What did the rest of your family say?"

Family. She gave a happy sigh. "JJ said it was decent of me. Char cried..." her voice trailed off as she remembered the look on John Davenport's face.

In that moment, they had connected. His gratitude had added a sheen to his eyes that couldn't be mistaken. He'd gripped her hand and whispered his thanks, because his voice had been too choked up to talk.

For a moment, she'd taken his gratitude the way a daughter would accept thanks from her father. He had held her hand in one and Jamie's in the other. *Accepted* had been the word ringing in her head.

Would it fade away the moment Jamie received her kidney? Would she be placed on the back of the shelf, not noticed? Instead of voicing her thoughts, she told Darryl how they were all thankful.

"I can imagine. Not everyday someone willingly gives up a kidney."

She inhaled trying to calm the nerves that assaulted her. It was like every time she brought it up her body wanted to hyperventilate and wig out. *Please be cool, Chloe. It's for Jamie.*

She'd lost count how many times the pep talk had echoed in her head. "I'm a little nervous." *Understatement!*

Darryl nodded, his eyes searching hers. "I understand. How can I help you through it?"

This man! He'd stolen her heart with the strength of his character. She knew her feelings and heart were safe with him. He hadn't given her any reason to doubt. "Just pray. And be willing to listen when I need to vent before I completely spaz out."

He chuckled and reached across the table to hold her hand. "Do you need to vent now?"

"No, I'm good." Because the moment his hand had touched hers, calm centered her.

"Want to go for a walk around the lake?"

"Yes, let's get out of here." They stood, pushing in their chairs.

"If I didn't know any better," Darryl cocked an eyebrow. "I'd take this as a sign you want to be alone with me."

"Uh…" her face heated. Not alone in *that* way, but alone nevertheless.

"Don't worry. I feel the same way, babe." He whispered as he pulled her into a hug.

Chapter Twenty-Four

The blank piece of paper lay there, waiting for words to form from the pen. Except Darryl had none. He'd gotten the bright idea to write a letter to his father saying he forgave him. It was a step he needed to take. The urge to bridge the gap of bitterness with an olive branch had echoed in his heart since he'd left the prison. Unfortunately, the memory of choking his father had visited him in his dreams.

Well...flashback more than anything.

Lord, I don't want to be chained by this bitterness anymore. I need to forgive him for how he treated me growing up. How he treated my mother. His abandonment. Everything. I just don't know what to say.

Divine intervention was the only thing that could get this letter written. He tapped on his chin with the pen, trying to figure out how to start. Maybe if he could figure out that part, the rest would soon follow.

Did people use 'dear' as an opening anymore? He snorted. People didn't even write letters. How sad was that? He exhaled and ran his hand over his head. *Dear Father.*

No.

Dear Dad.

No, his father had been quick to refuse that title.

Dear Mr. Jones.

Too formal.

To Hank Jones.

His lips twisted. It wasn't perfect but it would have to do.

To Hank Jones,

I hate the way we left things. I'm sorry that you didn't want to hear anything I had to say because there's so much I need to say. I hope that you'll read this and hear me out on paper.

Darryl took a deep breath, searching for the words needed.

I would like to say that I forgive you, but I know that I'm still working through all my feelings over my childhood and the role you played. But I want you to know, that one day, I'll be able to clearly say, I forgive you.

He had to hope that God would make it possible. No way he wanted to live in a state of unforgiveness. Darryl recalled a Bible study he and his friends had done on forgiveness. It had seemed impossible, but now he knew only God could complete it.

I want to be a better man than I have been. God has shown me how much I tried to do life on my own and how impossible that route is. I need Him desperately. I've asked His forgiveness for trying to kill you. At the time, all I could think was I wasn't going to let you hurt us anymore.

He winced at the words on the paper. It was undeniable as he stared at the word 'kill.' "Lord, thank You for Your grace and forgiveness." He bit his lip and continued writing.

I had no right to lay hands on you. When my time on earth ends, I'll have to answer for my actions. What I did, it's haunted me for years. As much as I hated you at the time, I still loved you.
Darryl gulped.

You're my father and that means I should honor you as such.

Please forgive me for what I did. Please forgive me for every hateful word I ever threw at your feet. I'm sorry.

If you decide you would like to develop a relationship, here's my address. Thank you for taking the time to read this.

Always,
Darryl Jones

Chloe opened the door to the wedding shop. She couldn't believe they were here to pick out their bridesmaid dresses for Michelle's wedding. Soon, Jo would follow and then she would be the only one left. Unattached. *Well, not married at least.* Darryl had hinted at marriage, but was she ready to think that far?

Jo had teased her about having a double wedding. Sure, she and Darryl had known each other for a while, but they had only entered this stage of their romance a few months ago. Wasn't that way too soon to be talking about weddings?

Wasn't it?

"Okay, ladies. I don't care about your feelings, whatever I pick, you'll be wearing." Michelle's no-nonsense tone of voice couldn't be mistaken, but in case they had any ideas of disagreeing, the hand on her hip added emphasis.

"Chelle, please just let me wear a pantsuit," Jo mumbled out.

"Not on your life. You aren't even allowed to wear one on your wedding day."

Jo crossed her arms, her lips pursed in irritation. Jo reminded her of a petulant two-year old. Chloe laughed. She loved her friends.

"Oh, I know you're not laughing, Chlo. Cardigans are not allowed either."

Her mouth dropped open as Jo cackled in laughter.

"She's got you there, Chlo. Do you have one for every outfit?"

"I did. They'll have to be replaced since I'm pretty sure they turned to ash." Her tone was even despite the ache that filled her chest. Before the fire, she had made sure to have a cardigan in every color. Sometimes she liked to switch them up a bit. She shook her head. *Pathetic.*

What if Michelle picked a strapless gown? Nerves flying, she asked the question.

"You wouldn't make us wear strapless, would you?" Jo's eyes grew wide in horror.

Michelle laughed. "As tempting as it is to torture you, I promise I won't pick strapless."

Thank You, God! She would feel terribly exposed in a strapless gown.

"What colors are you going for?"

"Champagne," Michelle answered with a smile.

"Figures," Jo grumbled.

"Look, JoJo. I get you like pants and dressing like a female is akin to torture for you. But please, pretend to enjoy this. I'm only getting married once, you know."

Jo's eyes watered. "I know. I'm sorry for being a pain. Life's changing." She sat down on an ottoman.

"I'm looking forward to married life, but I also know our friendship will never be the same again. We'll be married ladies."

Michelle sat next to Jo. "So we'll enjoy married life together. Yes, our lives are all taking different paths, but it won't negate the years of friendship we've had. Friends to the end, Jo Ellen Baker." She looked at Chloe. "And you're next."

They huddled up for a group hug. *Lord, please bless their marriages and our friendship.*

❧

The nerves were going to eat her alive. Chloe had tried on three dresses, five different skirts and had yet to settle on any of them. Why was dressing to meet Darryl's grandmother so difficult? She flopped onto the bed, emotions vying for her attention, threatening to plague her with tears. Meeting Darryl's grandmother was big time. The woman had raised him and still remained in his life. The relationship with his mother was tenuous at best and not something to elicit the thousands of butterflies dancing around in her stomach.

But Ruby Jones was a force to reckon with. She remembered the woman as a pillar of strength and determination. More like judge and jury and less like a welcoming committee. She shuddered. Darryl was excited about the day and had told her as much on the phone last night. He had stressed not to worry, but her mind refused to take the advice. Her fear and nervousness hadn't been hard to miss since her voice had quavered as if she'd skinny dipped in Freedom Lake in the dead of winter.

Lord, please help me out here. I'm terrified she'll find me lacking. Wanting in some area.

Exhaling, she looked at her clothes one more time. She pulled out a navy blue skirt with flowers on it and grabbed a yellow cardigan. Yesterday's shopping trip yielded great results. She'd come home with four new cardigans. Not enough to satisfy her, but enough to feel like her wardrobe was recovering.

If she wanted to make a good impression, she needed the boldness of yellow to bolster her. To give her the courage she lacked. Just one of the reasons why she loved the color. That and it was impossible to be gloomy wearing the sunny shade.

By the time Darryl knocked on Jamie's front door, Chloe was ready. The slow look of perusal darkened his brown eyes and widened the smile on his face. She sighed with pleasure as crinkles appeared around his eyes. *Gorgeous.*

"You look wonderful." His husky voice sent shivers down her spine.

"Not as wonderful as you." And what an understatement.

The compliment staggered from her lips under the force of his magnetic eyes. His white collared shirt fell across his shoulders, emphasizing the broadness. Hinting at muscles underneath. It was enough to tease her senses.

He must have had similar thoughts because his arm snaked out and closed the gap. His lips were on hers before she could form a coherent objection. Was it faux pas to arrive to a person's house looking like she'd been thoroughly kissed? Before she could explore the subject any further, he deepened the kiss until all she could think about was the firmness of his touch, the gentleness of his lips, and the heat emanating from him.

She loved him.

Whole-heartedly without reserve loved him. She tensed then pulled back. Coming to the realization and uttering the feelings out loud were on different ends of the spectrum. *What do I do, Lord?*

He sighed, running a hand through his curls, unaware of her emotions. "Let's go before you sidetrack me again." His wink took any sting out of his words.

They arrived in front of the senior center with a quickness that set her stomach to rolling. It was like going from zero to sixty seconds on a roller coaster ride. When would the nausea end? *Please don't let me be ill in front of Ms. Ruby, Lord. And please let me sound coherent.*

"Ready?" Darryl squeezed her hand.

"Yes." She knew her smile didn't reach her eyes but she was just thankful it managed to curve her lips upward. The ache in her stomach intensified with every step.

Darryl guided her through the community area and toward the hall of apartments. He came to a stop and knocked on the door.

After a moment, it opened slowly and there stood Ruby Jones. She looked just as Chloe remembered. Darryl's grandmother stood ramrod straight as if her spine were made of steel. Her gray hair was twisted into a bun, showcasing the aristocratic nose God had blessed her with.

"Good afternoon, Darryl." She offered her cheek for a kiss. "Please, bring your friend in."

Chloe closed the door behind her and turned.

"Mama?"

She froze at the husky sound of Darryl's voice and studied the unexpected addition to the visit. Not only was she supposed to meet his grandmother, but his mother had joined in the party too? *Great.*

∾

Darryl couldn't believe it. Was nothing sacred to his mother? After over a decade of silence, her constant appearance had worn thin. This wasn't how he pictured the day going. He wanted to bring Chloe to get to know his grandmother. She was a big part of his life and he recognized that. Unfortunately, introducing Chloe to his mother hadn't even crossed his radar yet. Sure, he had made the effort to go and see her, but he wasn't ready to jump back into a relationship with both feet.

Reaching out to her had been more of a pinky finger type of effort. This...this reached daunting proportions he wasn't ready to endure. He could only imagine what Chloe thought. She'd been terrified as it was. He turned and saw her standing by the door, a look of worry on her face.

When his gaze met hers, it hit him square in the gut. She was worried for him. *Him.* Not herself. The darkening of her chocolate brown eyes and the way her teeth worried the edge of her lip pointed at signs of distress, but her gaze had never wavered from his. He held out his hand and pulled her gently to him as she took hold.

"Are you okay?" Her whisper reached his ears, and he squeezed her hands in response.

He felt her relax and shift closer. He wanted to laugh at her efforts to hold him up, but was too grateful. It had been awhile since someone was ready to stand beside him as he faced his battles.

"Your mother came to say good-bye before she left, and I told her of our upcoming meeting."

He met his grandmother's gaze, wondering when she had developed the annoying habit of meddling. Who would have thought he'd miss her hands-off method? It had been irksome and often lonely. Yet he preferred that to the nose-in-every-aspect-of-his life method.

Lord, save me from old ladies trying to get into heaven.

He winced inwardly. *I didn't mean that maliciously, Lord.*

Darryl cleared his throat. "I appreciate that, Grandmother." What he thought was a lie, came out as a half-truth. He did appreciate her efforts and maybe this visit would save him from future ones with his mother.

"I thought you would." His grandmother looked him square in the eye, and he resisted the urge to fidget and look away.

A staring contest had always been her method of intimidation.

He nodded in concession.

"Great, have a seat while I get some refreshments. Mrs. Nelson was in a baking mood yesterday, so I have chocolate chip cookies. And I made some lemonade."

An eyebrow raised before he could tame it. Since when did she make lemonade?

"So how is your business going, Chloe?" His grandmother sat down a platter of cookies as she lobbed her question.

"Great. I'm not sure if Darryl told you, but we finished giving his exam rooms a face lift. The office looks much better."

He smiled at Chloe, remembering the day she touched his hair.

"Plus, I had some other clients who moved into the area. They all seem pleased with the results thus far."

He squeezed her hand. "She did an awesome job in our clinic. The kids seem more relaxed now. It helps a ton having them comfortable, considering some of the pokes and prods illicit complaints."

His grandmother grinned and directed her question to Chloe. "What are you working on now?"

"Actually, I was trying to decide if I wanted to buy a place myself. I'm not sure if you heard but my apartment kind of burnt down."

"Oh, no," his mother said. "Were you hurt?"

"Just some minor burns. Considering what could have been, they seem like nothing."

The blisters had faded from her hand, but Darryl could still feel the residual scar. It shook him to the core when he thought of how close he came to losing her. He shifted a little closer, verifying what his mind knew already…she was safe.

His mother looked back and forth between them. "You two seem awfully close. Have you given any thought to sharing a place?"

His mouth dropped open, and Chloe tensed beside him. Probably from shock. "Mother!"

"What?" She asked with wide eyes. "You have a place, and she needs one. Obviously the two of you are dating or you wouldn't be introducing her to your *grandmother.*"

The emphasis on grandmother did not go unnoticed. He inhaled. Exhaled. Counted to ten. "Mother, we're Christians."

"Okay." It came out more like a question then a statement.

He rubbed his forehead. "We're not going to share a place together. I would never think of asking her that."

"And I certainly wouldn't agree to it."

The edge of steel in Chloe's voice was kind of cute. Rarely had he seen her get angry and judging by the look in her eyes, anger had come and gone, letting something fiercer take its place.

"I meant no harm. I was just saying."

"Mother, I know you've been out of the loop for a few years so there are certain things you don't know." He shifted in his seat. "I recently accepted Christ as my

Savior and I'm taking the steps to live accordingly. I would never put Chloe or myself in that kind of situation. If we ever live together, she'll have a ring on her finger."

Chloe gripped his hands. A part of him hoped it meant she wanted to be married and not a sign of strength to continue this conversation.

"I need some air," she whispered. "Take all the time you need." She met Darryl's gaze before standing and turning to his grandmother. "Ms. Jones. I thank you for the invitation. I would love it if you would join my family and I this weekend. We're having a barbecue at my sister's place. Darryl knows the time and place."

"Thank you, my dear."

With a nod, Chloe left the apartment.

Darryl watched her leave. Somehow he didn't think Chloe was as ready for the next step as he wanted her to be.

Chapter Twenty-Five

*D*arryl leaned forward, his elbows resting on his knees while his hands pressed the buttons on his controller. Selecting a play, he manipulated his player with his game console. After a long day of work, playing the football game on his Xbox helped relieve his stress. His brain operated on autopilot, allowing him to think.

A truce needed to be made with his mother.

The thought had repeated itself over and over in his head until he'd sickened of it. Chloe would probably say it was the Holy Spirit, and Evan would convince him to pray. Guy would smile and remind him God could handle his emotions. Darryl wasn't even sure he could handle his emotions. Forgiving his dad seemed to be more about forgiving himself and what he'd done to his father. But his mother...

Seeing your mother after she decided that parenting was no longer her job was enough to make a grown man cry. Not that he had shed any tears. No, he refused to do that. So instead, he would play his game until all thoughts of a truce ceased or he capitulated.

It would be interesting to see which side won.

⌒⌒

Cloe knocked on Jo and Michelle's bungalow. Instead of a bachelorette party, Michelle had opted for a night of chick flicks and fairy juice. The fairy juice, made from rainbow sherbet and sprite, was a staple of their get togethers.

The door opened and Jo stood there in her overalls, her hair cascading down her shoulders. "Chlo's here!"

She shook her head, ears ringing from Jo's yelling. "Isn't this a one-story bungalow?"

"Yes." Jo's brows wrinkled in confusion.

"Then why do you feel the need to shout as if you're still living in your mother's place?" Jo's family home was a huge two-story home.

Jo chuckled and shrugged. "Old habits and all."

Chloe shook her head. She loved Jo, but the girl was a tad bit loud at times. "I figured we'd watch this first." Chloe sat her tote down and pulled out a movie.

"Ohhh, I love 'My Big Fat Greek Wedding.'"

"Remember the first time we saw it?"

Jo nodded. "This is going to be great." She turned. "Chelle!"

This time her shout had gone down a decimal or two.

"I'm coming, I'm coming."

They both looked at Michelle and time stopped. There she stood in a white wedding gown. The top was all lace, sleeves going down three quarters length. The skirt was made of chiffon and swished with every step. Chloe sighed at the romance of it all.

"Gorgeous, my friend."

She twirled around. "Right? Guy's mother took me dress shopping. She wanted it to be just me and her." Her face puckered up. "You guys aren't mad, are you?"

"Course not," Jo stated. "Making memories with a mother is good for you."

"You too, Jo Ellen." Michelle replied back.

"No. I'm sure my mother is going to drive me mad. I'm half tempted to run away and elope."

Chloe snorted. Her eyes widened as her friends stared at her with equal looks of shock. "What?"

"Did you just snort?"

"What's eating you?"

Michelle and Jo laughed as their questions bounced in the room.

"I did *not* snort. It was a chuckle. And I'm listening to you two and your tales of woe over motherhood and realize I have you beat."

"Do tell." Jo folded her arms across her chest.

"Darryl's grandmother is like his mother, and she's scary in her own right." She suppressed a shudder at the memory of Ruby Jones. "As if that wasn't bad enough, Mrs. Lee acted like she deserved the mother-of-the-year award."

"Who's Mrs. Lee?" Michelle sat down, a look of confusion marring her face.

"Darryl's mother."

Jo's low whistle pierced the air. "That sounds like a fun day."

She stared at her nails, thankful the polka-dotted nail design distracted her from looking at the scars on her palms. "She asked if we would shack up."

Michelle chortled. "Did you just really say that? Girl, that's such an outdated term."

As if the term mattered. Chloe had been insulted. Embarrassed.

Jo met her gaze with sympathetic eyes. "Maybe my mom isn't so bad after all."

Chloe's eyes welled in response. She looked up at the ceiling, hoping to stall the tears. "I don't know why it got to me, but I was furious." She swiped at the trail of tears that had leaked out despite her best efforts.

"You haven't been yourself lately," Michelle said softly. "Do you want to talk about it?"

She stared at her hands. "I don't know who I am anymore. I thought I was Chloe Smith, granddaughter of April Smith and daughter of Charlotte Smith. I thought I was African American but I'm not. I thought knowing who my father was would answer all the questions I ever had. But instead, I feel more lost." Her body shook under the weight of her emotions.

Arms reached out and wrapped her in a hug. Vaguely she recognized that her girlfriends had wrapped their arms around her. The words they whispered didn't register but the love did. And for now…it was enough.

Today the yellow accessories were failing her. Chloe's yellow wedge sandals did nothing to perk her up. It was like walking on the yellow brick road, clueless as to what awaited her. Jo and Michelle had tried their best to cheer her but without much success. Instead, she'd put on a brave face and celebrated Michelle's upcoming nuptials. Now all she wanted to do was get through the work day.

"Excuse me."

When had the door chimed? She blinked. Because of the midday sun's location, the woman was aglow. She rose, coming around her table to greet the customer. "Hi, I'm Chloe, how can I help you?"

She stepped closer then stopped. She had no trouble looking at the customer now. A woman who strangely resembled the woman she had last seen almost eighteen years ago.

"I don't suppose you know who I am?" The woman bit her lip nervously. Her black hair hung straight underneath a straw hat. She had a mixture of bohemian flair and millennia style.

"Charlotte Smith." The words tasted strange on Chloe's tongue. As if she had eaten some exotic fruit and couldn't decide if it tasted good or not. Her stomach however had picked the side of 'not.' It sent waves of nausea rolling through her gut as if she was on the boat headed toward Gilligan's Island.

"You do know me." Something like relief crossed her face.

"I remember you from the first and last time I saw you. It was at Gran's when I was in eighth grade." The girl scout trip had ended early, but that's not why she remembered. It was because she saw her mother for the first time since she had been born. Seeing her strung out on drugs had been the proverbial icing on the cake.

Charlotte's head dipped down in regret. "I'm sorry I don't remember that."

Chloe wrapped her arms around herself. "Why are you here?" *And what are You doing to me? I don't understand, Lord.*

"I...I just wanted to introduce myself." She shrugged as if to say she hadn't planned anything beyond this point.

Why couldn't Chloe think, or at least say something? Her brain felt like mush, her hamster struggling to turn the wheel. "I met my father." The words flew from her mouth faster than a speeding bullet and the regret came as swiftly.

She had no idea if her mother was clean or if the news would somehow destroy her fragile self.

Charlotte blinked. "That's good. How is he?"

"Married." The words were tinged in bitterness.

What is wrong with you? She groaned inwardly, wondering at the sorry state of affairs of her words. Since when had she lost the ability to speak with compassion?

Her mother chuckled softly. "I imagined so."

"Gran died a few years ago."

This time tears welled in her eyes. "I know. I came."

"What? How?" Why hadn't she seen her?

"I had a friend who knew how to get in touch with me and let me know."

Anger and bitterness swirled inside of her. *Her mother kept in touch with friends?!*

"I…I'm staying in the city. It seemed too weird to lodge in town. Here's my number. In case you'd like to reach me." She held out a folded piece of paper.

Chloe took it, too upset to speak.

"Well, I'll get out of your hair." Her mother waved stiffly then vanished as quietly as she had entered.

She stared at the door, wondering when her life had turned into a reality TV show.

ౚ

Darryl glanced at his office phone as it rang. He'd been enjoying his lunch quietly. Now that Jordan had joined the practice, he had more down time and was able to actually use his breaks effectively.

His private line blinked at him, regaining his attention. "Dr. Jones."

"Darryl?"

"Chloe?" His guts twisted at the sound of misery in her voice. "What's wrong?"

"Could you come to my office? I need you."

"I'll be right there."

The ride to Chloe's office seemed to last an eternity. What could be wrong? Nothing could be worse than the fire that burned down her apartment building. Yet she had sounded like the world was coming to an end.

He inhaled sharply. Was it Jamie? He had almost forgotten that her sister needed a transplant. Maybe she had gone into renal failure. He stepped on the gas, praying Guy and his crew weren't out policing the streets. Being detained was the last thing he needed.

Finally, he pulled up in front of The Space. Putting the car in park he hopped out, almost forgetting to lock the door. He rushed through the door but stopped short.

Chloe sat there staring at the wall. No music was playing. It was like walking into a tomb. He approached her workstation cautiously. "Chloe?"

She turned to him.

The despair on her face ripped his heart in two. "What happened, babe?"

"I saw Charlotte today."

His mind rushed to figure out who she was talking about. "Charlotte?" *Her sister?*

She nodded. "She came by as if she happened to be in the neighborhood. Gave me her phone number." She held up a folded piece of paper.

He bent down on one knee and took ahold of her hand. "Baby, which Charlotte?"

"My mother."

She turned in her chair, resting her head in the crevice of his neck. He rubbed a hand down her arm. "Are you okay?" Despite his soft tone, the stillness in the office amplified his voice.

Her head shook, her hair tickling his face.

"How about we go out on the lake?"

She looked up and nodded. Never had he seen her so beaten by life. Like she let it steal her joy.

Lord, I don't know how to help her. I don't know what to do. Please guide me and restore her joy in You.

The whole time he readied the boat, Chloe sat quietly. A word hadn't passed her lips since they left her office. Thankfully, Martin and Jordan readily agreed to cover his patients for the rest of the day. Darryl dropped the anchor, quickly glancing over his shoulder. She faced the lake, her back toward him. He grabbed his cell and turned it to silent. Then he sent a group text to Michelle, Jo, and Jamie. They needed to know what happened. Hopefully they would know how to cheer Chloe up if the boat trip turned out to be a bad idea.

One by one, replies filled his inbox. Jo and Michelle let him know they would be waiting at Jamie's house for her return. Relief flooded his heart. He closed his eyes asking for wisdom and guidance again. With a deep breath, he headed toward her.

As he sat next to her, he took in her appearance. Even her profile was breathtaking. He couldn't remember ever being so entranced by another woman. He trailed a finger down the side of her face. "Do you want to talk about it?"

She shook her head no then leaned over and rested her head on his shoulder. He wrapped an arm around her. She shivered Before he could ask her if she was cold—although how could she be in the middle of summer—he felt a wet spot on his shirt. Looking down, he saw tears slide down her cheeks in a seamless stream.

"Babe, don't cry," he murmured softly.

Her sobs increased.

He rubbed his hand up and down her arm trying to offer comfort, but the cries only increased. They turned to sobs and a keening sound erupted from her lips. He felt his eyes water. He'd never seen her like this.

"Why is He doing this to me?" she cried out.

For a moment, he sat stunned. By her emotions. By the question. He never thought she would be one to question God. All her life, she had walked closely with the Lord. He figured she had a better connection with Him than anyone else. If she felt her prayers were going unanswered then what chance of hope did the rest of them have?

Help! I don't know what to say.

I will never leave you.

"What is it you think He's doing?" The tentative sound of his voice made him wince. Shouldn't he sound more confident? What hope could he offer her if he sounded like a prepubescent adolescent?

She pulled away and her eyes flashed fire. "My life is in upheaval. My apartment was burned to the ground. My sister needs a kidney. My father didn't want to have anything to do with me, but as soon as I mention the kidney he warms up. Then to top it off, my mother comes waltzing back into my life as if she was gone away on a trip for vacation. Life was supposed to get better, not worse."

"Says who?"

Her mouth dropped open. "What do you mean says who?"

"I mean exactly what I said." He held onto her hand praying she didn't snap at his question, but seriously, why did she think life was supposed to be easy? "We weren't promised an easy life. No one is."

"But I'm a Christian. I believe in God. I believe that I've been saved by the blood of Jesus. He came to give me an abundant life. If that's not a promise of a good life I don't know what is."

"Oh it is a promise of a good life." That scripture had been in his reading plan just the other day. Maybe in preparation for this very moment. "It's a wonderful gift and hope. But that's not a promise that life is going to be a cake walk or any other clichés you can think of. It's a promise that we'll always have help, and He will always be there for us.

"But babe, it's not a promise for an easy life."

"Don't you think it's about time that something goes right in our lives? Your relationship with your parents is about as screwed up as mine. There's nothing abundant about that."

"Oh, really? Didn't you just gain three siblings? Find out that you're not alone in this world? That you have family who cares for you? Please tell me what's so messed up about that?" He swallowed, trying to gain control of his emotions. He didn't want to argue. Didn't want to fight, but he had to make her see the silver lining. Who threw a pity party because their mother wanted to establish a relationship?

Realization struck him still. Hadn't he complained about the same thing? His mother wanted to right her wrongs, establish a relationship, and he had shut her down. How many nights had he stared out into the night sky wishing his mother would come back? And now that she had, he walked around with a chip on his shoulder.

He stared at Chloe. "We've been going about this all wrong, Chloe. We've been accusing God of upsetting our lives when instead, He's been trying to restore it." He paused as the truth rang in his head. It felt too right not to have come from the Holy Spirit.

"Then why does it hurt so bad?"

"Because we still haven't forgiven them."

Chapter Twenty-Six

Tomorrow was Michelle's wedding day. Chloe sighed. It should be a day of celebration. Thoughts of excitement and well-wishing should be running through her head. Instead, she sat with her journal, wondering what to say to the Lord. It had been awhile since she attempted to be still. She'd been walking around so angry, so hurt, that she had ignored God's prompting.

What Darryl had said felt like a blow from a gloved fist. Was she really harboring unforgiveness? The thought never crossed her mind until he'd suggested it. At first, she was indignant. She'd been a Christian longer than he. How dare he suggest her behavior wasn't befitting of her faith?

Still, his words echoed over and over in her head. In her heart. And then she knew, he was right. She had let unforgiveness turn into a bitter root in her life. And the only way to destroy the root was to ask for forgiveness.

And to forgive.

But how could she when she'd been living like this for so long? Three decades of thinking she was above the trauma and drama that her mother and father had caused. Thirty plus years of hating the woman who abandoned her. Three months of anger that her father wanted nothing to do with her.

She turned at the knock on her bedroom door. Jamie probably wanted to make sure she hadn't gone off the deep end. "Come in."

The door opened and Jamie peeked her head in. Chloe stared in shock. Her sister looked...sick. Her face was devoid of makeup and for once, she realized how sick she must be. "Hey." She shifted to rise but Jamie waved her back down.

Her sister sat next to her. "You feeling better today?"

"Getting there." She examined Jamie. "What about *you*?"

"I'll be fine soon." A light lit her brown eyes.

They had scheduled the transplant for after Michelle's wedding. Chloe bit back nerves and smiled at her sister.

"The wedding should make you feel normal, right?" Jamie watched expectantly.

Chloe should be thrilled, but happiness seemed far away right now. Forgiveness would be a long road, but one necessary to make so she could go back to her normal self. Chloe redirected her thoughts. "Michelle will make a beautiful bride."

"Right," Jamie said with a grin. "I want to be Michelle when I get older."

A laughter escaped, half rusty from unuse. "Michelle's one of a kind."

"That's what I like about her. What you see is what you get. Guy's lucky, but then again, so is Darryl." Jamie nudged her with her elbow.

"I don't know. Sometimes I feel so messed up. Maybe I should let him go find some woman who has it together."

"You don't mean that." Jamie's wide eyes stared at her.

"No," she replied softly. "I just don't want him to wake up one day and tell me my emotions are too much for him." She wiped at an errant tear. "I can't stop crying. I can't feel happiness. Joy seems like a myth. What's wrong with me?"

Jamie put a thin arm around her. "What would your God say about this?"

"Count it all joy." The verse was there without a thought. She'd read the Bible more times than she could count. Knew it like the back of her hand. For the first time, she knew what that verse meant.

"My brethren, count it all joy when you fall into various trials, knowing that the testing of your faith produces patience."

She need to let patience have its perfect work.

"Then count it all joy, big sister."

Chloe wrapped Jamie in a hug and kissed her cheek.

Darryl pulled his car alongside the curb and parked. He stared at the white house with a picket fence. It was a little cliché, but screamed his mother through and through.

Get out of the car. You can do this.

He swallowed and sent a prayer heavenward. God wouldn't fail him, but he still wasn't sure of his mother. In fact, he wasn't exactly sure why he made the trip to visit if he was going to just sit in the car staring at the front porch. Would she welcome him?

Would her husband?

His mouth dried in apprehension. Drawing in a deep breath, Darryl let it out, mentally praying for guidance. After the incident with Chloe, he realized he needed to do his part. His mother had tried to make amends. He just had to accept them. Running a hand through his curls he wrestled with indecision.

Just get up.

He turned the car off, pulling the key out of the ignition, and opened the door before he could change his mind. One step at a time brought him up the walkway before his brain could halt his body.

Lord, please be with me.

He knocked on the door, thankful there was no doorbell. Maybe they wouldn't hear his knock and he could leave knowing he at least tried. But if he took the coward's way out, was he really trying? He knocked harder, this time hoping the sound would carry and give his mother the chance to invite him in or send him packing.

"Just a moment."

The sound of a man's voice reached his ears through the door. In all his scenarios, the idea of his mother's husband answering the door hadn't been one of them. *Well that was shortsighted.* He didn't know if he should be thankful or grimace at his bad luck. Feeling the need to give himself another pep talk, he prayed instead.

Lord, I'm not sure exactly why I'm here. Yes, I do. I feel that you've been tugging me toward this visit for a while now. I know I need to put my words into action and begin the process of forgiving my mother. Please help me with the words, because I have no clue what to say when I see her.

The door swung open. "Can I help you?" The man's brow wrinkled up into his forehead, emphasizing the lack of hair on his head.

"I'm Darryl." He waited to see the man's reaction. He was surprised at the silent nod in response.

"I see. Come on in." He opened the door wider.

Darryl held out a hand in greeting. "Nice to meet you, sir."

"Nice to meet you as well. I'm Marvin. Marvin Lee."

They shook hands and Darryl let out a little sigh, glad that was over. "Is Alice…my mother…is she here?"

"Yes. She just put my grandson down. I uh…have a daughter from a previous marriage."

Darryl nodded his understanding. "How old is your grandson?"

"Five months."

Wow. He couldn't imagine his mother acting like a grandmother. He still hadn't thought of her as a mother. Would she want to be around if he married and had children? The thought seemed so foreign. His mind had kept her frozen in his brain as the timid woman who cowered at every loud noise that echoed in the apartment. Especially the ones coming from his father.

"I'll go let her know you're here."

He looked around the house as he waited. It had a homey feel to it. The brown couches looked soft and inviting with the green throw pillows on them. Or maybe they were blue. He angled his head trying to get a better look.

As he took in the space he noticed little things that had been forbidden in his home growing up. There was a throw blanket draped across the smaller sofa. His father hated blankets out in the living room. Insisted they cluttered up the place.

Plus, there were candles and pictures everywhere. He drew closer to the one above the fireplace. It looked like it had been taken on vacation. His mother stood smiling in the arms of her husband.

Yeah, a picture like that would have never been hung when he was younger. His father didn't object; it was his mother's doing. She didn't want any object within reach of her husband's angry grasp.

"Darryl?"

He whirled around. His mother stood there, hands clutched together. It was her signature anxiety pose. Funny how the mind remembered what the heart chose to ignore.

"Hello, Mother."

"Hello." Silence filled the room. She stood there frozen, but her eyes had a sheen that gave a hint to her emotions. "I can't believe you're here."

He shrugged. "You said I could come and visit. So here I am." The thumping of his heart betrayed his feigned nonchalance.

"I did." She smiled. "Come, let's go in the kitchen and I'll fix you something to eat. I remember how much you ate as a boy."

"All right." He patted his belly, but truthfully he didn't know if he could eat right now.

It had been so long since he had eaten one of her meals. Too long. He should welcome the idea of breaking bread with his mother. Isn't that what Jesus would have done? Probably so, but awkwardness flooded his being.

Darryl figured his mother's intensions were to fix him a snack, but the table was set when they walked into the kitchen. Unfortunately, he hadn't looked at the clock when he drove to Ohio. He'd arrived just in time for dinner. So now he would sit with his estranged mother and her husband.

Yep, awkward didn't cover it.

Marvin—which is what his mother's husband asked to be called—coughed into the sleeve of his arm. "How do you enjoy running your own practice?"

"It's great. It's what I went to school for."

The lasagna sat unappetizingly on his fork. He ate a forkful. It was like it had no texture. Thankfully, his movements were steady, going off of muscle memory.

"And you have partners or…"

"Partner, well, partners now. Martin and I went to the same school. And we recently hired a third doctor and are considering making her co-owner as well."

He dabbed at the sauce at the corners of his mouth.

"Darryl's a wonderful doctor." His mother beamed at him then at her husband.

"How would you know that?" The words flew before he could check them. Before he could consider the ramifications of the question he asked.

It was too late to take it back. The tears that ran down her face were testament to the fact. Slowly, she set her fork down. Her chin raised as she met his gaze. Her eyes didn't blink. Her gaze didn't waver.

"I may not have been there daily, but I do know what you've accomplished. You graduated magna cum laude from the University of Indiana. You completed your internship at Kodiak Hospital. Became the co-owner of Freedom Lake Pediatrics at twenty-seven. No, I wasn't there daily, but I know that you're a wonderful doctor."

She pushed away from the dining table, calmly picked up her plate, and left the room.

He closed his eyes, vacillating between indignation and remorse. Had he been too harsh? Why was restoring relationships such a pain?

Chapter Twenty-Seven

*I*t seemed surreal that today Michelle would become Mrs. Guy Pierre. One moment Chloe had been giggling over crushes with Jo and Michelle. The next, they were waiting to walk down the aisle to celebrate Michelle's marriage. *To Guy.* Chloe didn't know how she would make it through the day without falling apart. Her friend deserved all the happiness in the world. But she couldn't help but be a little envious.

Chloe could quote scriptures warning about the evils of envy, but it didn't stop her emotions from experiencing the sin. Her life was in shambles and Michelle's was perfect. *Your time will come, Chlo.*

She still lacked peace. The calm she wished for remained elusive. Chloe stared at the champagne colored bridesmaids' dresses hanging on the hook of the dressing room door. The strapless gown had a lace overlay that promoted modesty. It fell right below the knee and embodied the classy ways Michelle was known for. Chloe was just glad it would keep her cool in the summer heat. Thankfully, the wedding was scheduled for sunset.

The heat of the day would pass by as they pampered themselves. Michelle smiled at her from under the portable hair dryer. Her short bob was being transformed into a French twist. She planned on using the silver hair comb that her mother had worn when she married her father.

Remembering the scene earlier, she sniffed, holding in tears. Michelle had broken down, feeling very much the orphan. It was a big day and one where she'd felt her parents' absence acutely. Thankfully, Michelle had forged a strong relationship with Guy's mother. The woman had been instrumental in planning the details surrounding the wedding. Chloe believed she wanted to make up for the lack of people attending on the bride's behalf. Maybe Mrs. Pierre would institute a sit anywhere policy.

Mrs. Pierre had made the cake, catered the food, and hired people needed to take care of everything else. Chloe thanked God that the in-law relationship would be a blessed one. Despite the melancholy that hovered over her spirit, Chloe couldn't wait to see all the preparations come together.

Each person had contributed something for the outside wedding. Jo had built a wooden trellis to act as the arbor. Jamie had been wonderful, assisting in the décor. Guy's twins had made tissue paper bouquets for Michelle and the bridesmaids. Darryl and Evan had paid for a honeymoon to Boston. And Guy's mother was more than happy to watch the girls during their trip.

Chloe thought of her own contribution. She let Michelle borrow her grandmother's pearl teardrop earrings. Chloe had wept when she remembered they'd been safely tucked into her fire safe along with her important papers. The earrings looked great on Michelle, who had broken down in tears at the gift. She smiled.

Closing her eyes as her hair was manipulated into an up do, she said a prayer. *Heavenly Father, please bless Guy and Michelle's union. Please help them become one. Guide them as they raise the twins and any other children they may have. Help me not intrude on their marriage but be an encourager. In Jesus' Name. Amen.*

Today was going to be a good day, no matter what.

ও

Michelle inhaled then exhaled. *Breathe, girl.*

She stood, holding her tissue paper bouquet that Rachel and Rebekah had presented to her after she donned her wedding dress. Now all she needed was the music to cue her entrance. It would be a little strange walking out there by herself, but it had to be done. If she couldn't have her parents, then she'd walk with the strength the Lord blessed her with.

Taking another breath to steady herself, Michelle blinked back tears. She. Would. Not. Cry. *Lord, may Your presence propel me forward and comfort my heart.*

The only tears she wanted to shed today were ones of joy. Being able to marry Guy was a dream come true. *Literally.* Even though her parents weren't here to join in the celebration, God had blessed her with a make-shift family. Her mother-in-law to share in feminine moments and provide motherly wisdom. Two beautiful girls who loved to play with her and hang out. Friends who would be with her through thick and thin.

Bless the Lord, o my soul. She smiled and tilted her chin up as the music began. Slowly, she began her walk down the path to their lakeside wedding. When she turned the corner, her heart stopped as Guy came into view.

Handsome wasn't a strong enough word to describe him. He stole her breath in his black tux with his champagne colored tie. His face split into a grin as he met her gaze. She watched as he took in the dress. She loved the way the lace top fell to her elbows. From the waist down, the chiffon material shifted in the breeze as she took step after step down the aisle.

Michelle paused to hand her bouquet to Jo as she took Guy's hands. He squeezed them and threw a wink her way. She tried to listen as Bishop Brown went through the pleasantries, but her body pulsed with excitement. Today she would be Mrs. Pierre, wife to Guy and mother to his children. God had blessed her more than she'd ever imagined.

"And now, the two will exchange their own vows. Guy, please go first."

"Chelle Belle, I promise my heart to you, knowing it's in safe hands. I promise to love and cherish you as long as there's breath in my body. I promise to lead our family in spirit and in truth and to raise our children in the same manner."

She sniffed, trying to hold the tears in. *How she loved this man!*

"Michelle, your turn."

"Guy Pierre, I promise to love and respect you with God's strength. I promise to be the safe place you can rest your head when you are weary. I promise to be the best mom to Rachel and Rebekah and any other children we may have. And I will treasure the gift of family you've given me."

The friends and family on Guy's side of the aisle cheered.

"With this ring, I thee wed." Guy looked into her eyes as he placed the love knot on her finger.

She blinked, holding the tears back. She didn't want anything clouding her vision.

Jo handed her his ring. "With this ring, I thee wed." She pushed the gold love knot on his finger.

"The couple also wish to present gifts to their girls."

Michelle took the love knot necklace from Jo as Guy took one from Evan. She motioned to Rebekah and put the necklace on her neck as Guy did the same for Rachel. "Love you, sweetie."

"Love you." Rebekah smiled shyly. She hugged Rebekah, and then Rachel.

Once more, she and Guy held hands and waited for the bishop's prompting.

"You may now kiss the bride."

Guy slid his hands around her waist, and then dipped her. Her heart picked up speed as his scent enveloped her. "*Mwen renmen ou,* Chelle belle."

"And I love you."

When his lips met hers, she knew she would love him until the day she died.

Chapter Twenty-Eight

*F*t was funny how a new day began. The sun rose while the moon made its descent as usual. But today was special and creation had missed the proverbial memo. Then again, why would the birds and the trees alter their purpose to recognize the day she gave up a kidney to extend the life of her little sister?

Strangely, Chloe had awakened stress free. All the worrying that had been present leading up to this day was absent. She knew this was what God wanted her to do. This step signified her decision to walk in faith. And how could she not after seeing Michelle's beautiful wedding, knowing all her friend had been through to even get to that point. It was time for Chloe to remember who she was.

The faith that existed deep down in her core. It had been there from childhood and carried her through life, but now it required more from her than attending church and reading the Bible daily. It needed her to be a doer. Staying in her bubble of safety was no longer an option.

Blaming her parents for a life she didn't have needed to stop. Chloe could finally say she was thankful for finding her father.

Her family had embraced her with love and affection. Of course there were times it was downright awkward, but she could tell they cared. If her heart had any doubts, the flowers in her hospital room proved it.

Char had French braided her and Jamie's hair last night in preparation of the kidney transplant. She knew the funny blue cap they'd give her would wreak havoc with her curls or not even hold them all. Since she had been a girl scout, becoming proficient in braiding had been a necessary skill. Still, it had shocked her to the core when Char had offered.

Chloe had figured Char would change her mind once she tackled the curls, but she had done so with ease after wetting Chloe's hair. It was after the braid had been complete that Char shared her secret. Every morning, she straightened her hair into its sleek bob. Curls were smoothed out in the process.

It made sense that if Char dealt with curly hair on a daily basis, she would understand Chloe's. The moment had brought them closer. Their relationship required more work than her and Jaime's, but maybe that made it more special. It was amazing how God used braiding to bring them together.

As if that wasn't enough, JJ's gift had touched her heart. He gave her and Jamie an iPod filled with their favorite music. The fact that he downloaded every contemporary Christian and gospel song she loved moved her to tears. Their relationship had remained a little aloof, but the gift bridged the gap. There was no way he knew all her favorites, which showed her how much trouble he had gone through. Never had she felt so loved in her life.

It was what her heart yearned for. Now if she could only mend her relationships with her parents.

Her relationship with John Davenport was at a stalemate. Maybe because Chloe kept calling him by his name in her head, she couldn't accept him as her father. Since she made the announcement of giving her kidney, he hadn't spoken beyond the initial thanks. A part of her wanted to know what he thought, the other was terrified at the prospect. She didn't want to be rejected again once Jamie had a working kidney.

What did she even *want* from him? What would it take to feel comfortable with him? To feel a kinship? To feel anything but apathy or hurt from the years of rejection? With a sigh, she shifted in the hospital bed. It was time to leave those thoughts behind and focus on her upcoming surgery.

Her clothes had been traded in for an oversized hospital gown. Thankfully, no one would see her behind since she was laying on it. The sheets were more comfortable than she'd imagined. They were pulled up as high as they would go. She wished they would have given her an extra blanket. The room had a draft that skidded goosebumps along her flesh.

"Knock, knock."

She froze at the low sounding timbre. John Davenport—no, her *father*—had come after all. "It's safe." She winced at the croak that emanated from her. Would her emotions always be so obvious?

"Hey there." He stood there in jeans and a white polo, his hands in his pockets. He looked like an older version of JJ, with a touch of uncertainty.

"Is Jamie all set?"

He nodded. "Yep, her eyes look like they do on Christmas morning."

She laughed. "Great visual."

Silence settled between them, filled with awkwardness.

He sighed and ran a hand over his beard. "Are you sure you want to do this, Chloe?"

"Yes. Why wouldn't I?" Her eyes widened in surprise. "Wouldn't you if you could?"

"Without a doubt. I'd do anything for my kids."

She nodded, trying not to let the sting of bitterness steal her joy.

"Any of my kids," he repeated. "My brain can't reconcile one kid giving up something for the other."

She looked up at him. "What do you mean?"

"I was just in there when the doctor went over the list of precautions. It's pretty daunting but Jamie is an adult and I can't make her decisions. I asked the doctor the potential dangers you could encounter. It's worse."

"I...I know them." She thought she'd be nervous when the doctor went over them, but calm had greeted her. She was doing the right thing. "He already went over them with me. He had to in case I changed my mind."

"I know that. I'm not asking as Jamie's father. I'm asking as your father. The list of possible complications..." he cleared his throat. "It's enough to make my skin itch. Are you sure you want to go through this? No one is going to think ill of you, least of all me."

Tears welled in her heart. He cared about her. "Thank you for that. I'm good. I'm sure this is what God wants for me."

He nodded, a sheen darkening his eyes. "Okay then. We'll be waiting for you when you get out." He stepped next to her bedside. "I'll be waiting." He squeezed her hand.

Thankful for the olive branch, she held his hand until the ER tech wheeled her away.

∽∾

Darryl leaned back into the waiting room chair. He glanced around, thankful that Chloe had support. Her father, sister, and brother occupied one half of the room and Jo, Michelle, Guy, and Evan, the other half. Michelle and Guy had come back the day before from their honeymoon. He knew how much Chloe appreciated all the support. She was loved and accepted no matter what she thought. Even his grandmother had asked him to keep her updated. The church had added her to the prayer list as well. Everyone wanted her to do well.

The only problem was the waiting.

He yawned and leaned back against the wall. His doctor mind wanted to go over the list of things that could go wrong. Probably why he wasn't a surgeon. He didn't have the stomach for it.

The sound of footfalls reached his ears. He sat up and noticed everyone else doing the same. Tension filled the room. He glanced at his watch. It had only been a half hour. That wasn't a good sign.

A woman appeared in a floral maxi dress. She froze as the group eyed her warily. She licked her lips in a nervous gesture. "Are all of you waiting for Chloe?"

Who was she?

Chloe's father stood up. "You've came to the right place, Charlotte."

He heard a gasp that he assumed came from Jo or Michelle. Noticing his hands were clenched, he uncurled them, sliding them down his thighs. Chloe would flip if she found out her mother was here.

She nodded but refused to meet Mr. Davenport's gaze. "How is she?"

"She just went back." Chloe's father folded his arms across his chest. "How did you know?"

Darryl arched an eyebrow. Mr. Davenport hadn't called her mother? He thought for sure he was the one who spilled the beans. He turned to catch Jo and Michelle's gaze. Jo looked down, not meeting his gaze.

"JoJo, you didn't?"

He almost laughed at the not so discreet whisper Michelle let out. Jo nodded but refused to meet anyone's eyes.

Davenport sat back down between JJ and Charlotte—the *other* Charlotte. She eyed her namesake warily.

Darryl ran a hand down his face. The tension in the room grew thicker. He was surprised it wasn't visible to the eye. What had JoJo been thinking? He would have never imagined she'd be the one to include an absentee mother, not with the mother she had.

Chloe's mom sat in the middle of the waiting room, a seat separated him from her.

Lord, am I supposed to make small talk? Ignore her?

His mouth dried out as question after question flitted through his brain. He felt his face heat up under someone's gaze. Turning, he stared into Chloe's mother's face. He inhaled as the similarities between the two women branded his brain.

"Hello. I'm Darryl, it's a pleasure meeting you." He held out a hand, thankful it was steady. Somehow he felt like a traitor by welcoming the woman, but what other choice did he have?

"Nice to meet you."

Her handshake was limp and brief as if she was afraid he had cooties or something. He tried to school his facial features and suppress the angst going through him. He wanted to ask why she abandoned her child. Wanted to ask what gave her the right to sit here as if she was a concerned parent.

Too bad his conscience...or the Spirit...told him to be quiet. He was sure it could lead to an enlightened conversation.

"Have you ever had surgery before?" He wanted to roll his eyes at the stupid question, but at least he obeyed the still, small voice.

"No, I haven't. You?"

"No, thank God."

Her mouth quirked up.

Her facial expression hit him right between the eyes.

There was no denying she was Chloe's mother. Chloe had been branded by her parents' DNA in a way that needed no explanation. Funny how you wished you had something of your parents but when it showed up, the mind shouted in horror. He ran a hand through his hair. *Lord, please hurry the time. This is unbearable.*

He glanced over at Jo and motioned with his head. If she was the one who called, she needed to deal with this. He was done talking. All he wanted to do was be by himself as he waited for the love of his life to enter recovery.

Chapter Twenty-Nine

*I*ntense pain radiated from her abdomen. Chloe wanted to curl into a ball. A moan slipped free as she tried to shift to get comfortable. A shock wave of pain halted her movements. Her stomach felt like it was on fire. She took a shallow breath as her body tensed against the pain.

"Ms. Smith, it's me, Nurse Helen. How are you feeling?"

"Hurt," she rasped out.

"Okay, I'll get you some more pain meds."

Chloe tried to nod, but she was so lethargic. It was like there was a weight on her chest pressing her into the mattress. Holding her breath captive. She had read countless forums about what kidney donation felt like. Evidently the words were inadequate. There was no describing this type of pain.

A wonderful first surgery experience.

A chill went through her, goosebumps popping up in response. "Cold," she rasped again.

"Okay, sweetie. I'll get you another blanket."

Warmth enveloped her, and she let out a sigh. She tried to open her eyes but found the light too bright. A wave of euphoria drifted over her. Was it the meds? She had no clue, but welcomed the darkness.

When her eyes opened again, the light was low. The brightness had faded but so had the warmth. She shivered as a chill racked her body. She turned her head and stopped. The figure was blurry and facing the window. She blinked, trying to clear her sight.

"Mama?" The words tumbled from her lips in surprise and confusion. She had never put a label on Charlotte Smith other than 'mother.' It seemed cold and distant…just the way she felt. But waking from a major surgery dropped her defenses.

"How you feeling, Chloe Anne?"

She swallowed. "I hurt."

Her mother nodded and leaned over to press the nurse call button.

"Yes?" The nurse's voice was melodic and soothing.

"My daughter's awake and in pain." Her mother touched her forehead with the back of her hand. "I think she may have a fever as well."

"I'll be right there."

Chloe snuggled deeper under the covers. The moment seemed surreal. She was sick—or rather recovering from surgery—and her mother was there to take care of her. It was like a dream come true. Funny how her earlier anger had faded at the comfort of her mom's presence. She had always wished their relationship could resemble the ones from TV. Claire Huxtable had been the most amazing mother she had ever known.

Maybe truth wasn't stranger than fiction.

Soon the nurse came in and prodded her mouth open with the thermometer. As the thermometer beeped, lines furrowed the nurse's brow.

"101.5." Helen announced. "Since you have a fever, I can't give you another blanket. Let me notify your doctor."

The nurse left in a hurry and dread filled her heart. Was a fever a sign of something bad? She gasped.

"How's Jamie?"

"I'm not sure," her mother said. "I asked to be the first one to see you. How about I get your friend, Darryl, and I'll go find out how Jamie's doing?"

"Thank you."

Her mother nodded. She stopped at the doorway and looked back. "I love you, Chloe."

Chloe stared at the empty doorway so long, she must have drifted off. Her eyes opened and landed on Darryl. He sat next to the bed in a chair, holding her hand. The warmth of his hand soothed her and chased the chill bumps away.

"Hey, babe. How are you feeling?"

"Disoriented. I thought my mother was here."

Lines around his mouth appeared, dragging his lips downward. "That wasn't an illusion. She's here. She went to find out how Jamie's doing."

Her mouth parted in surprise. "Does that mean I have a fever too?"

"Yeah." It seemed an impossible feat, but the lines deepened, showing concern.

"Are they going to give me Tylenol to break the fever?"

"No, they gave you some antibiotics." He tapped her IV line.

She looked up, noticing a round syringe hooked up to the IV. She shuddered. "I'm so glad that's going into the IV and not my body."

His lips twitched. "It's not a needle, just holding the IV antibiotics."

Darryl laid his head gently on her bed. She maneuvered her hand out from his and ran it through his curls. Feelings filled her heart, came pouring out her soul. How could she let him know how she felt? The power of her emotions scared her. Everyone she had loved or wanted to love left her.

She had been surrounded with friends and a grandmother but felt utterly alone. Seclusion was an enemy she had no desire to keep close, but the alternative was equally frightening. Would he make her regret loving him? Would he rip her heart in two, denying her or her love for him?

As much as she hated how her mother abandoned her, she understood it was more about rejected love. Her mother's life had turned upside down as words of rejection hurled straight into her heart.

Living a life alone wasn't so bad. You would never be disappointed. But the power of love would never touch you either.

∽∾

A fever.

It was amazing how a five-letter word could send a chill through his spine like he was in a scene of a horror flick. He had tried to keep the worry from his face, but judging from the look in Chloe's eyes, he hadn't been successful. That's why he found himself leaning against the bed as she ran her fingers through his hair.

It was blissful, comforting, and…maddening.

He should be the one comforting her, not the other way around. The fear that gripped his heart rendered him useless. What was the use of being a doctor if he couldn't heal someone? Slowly he raised his head, keeping his eyes lowered to avoid her penetrating gaze.

He stared at his hands, wrapped around one of hers. Feelings of ineptness besieged him. He wanted to find her doctor and demand access to her chart. But nephrology wasn't his specialty. He'd have to trust the Lord to take care of her, and trust the doctor to do his job.

Lord, heal her. I can't do anything but pray and it's driving me crazy.

The words of James 5:16 scrolled through his mind, "Pray for one another, that you may be healed. The effective, fervent prayer of a righteous man avails much."

It had been his verse of the day on the Bible app, downloaded to his cell. He had no idea if he was a righteous man, but he knew without a doubt that Chloe was a righteous woman. *Lord, if You can't hear my prayer, then hear hers. Heal her and her sister, please. Amen.*

A knock on the door drew his attention. Chloe's mother stood there looking uncertain. At least he hoped that's what her look meant. If anything happened to Jamie, he wasn't sure if Chloe could handle it.

Her hand reached for his, intertwining their fingers. Her hand trembled, and his heart thudded. How he wished he could shield her.

"How is she?" The sound of Chloe's voice was unusually quiet. She had a gentle voice on a good day, but this was lower than the whisper decibel.

"She's not doing so well." Her mother bit her lip as she relayed the news about Jamie.

A tear slid down Chloe's cheek. He squeezed her hand and she squeezed his in return, turning it into a death grip.

"What's wrong with her?"

"The doctors think her body is rejecting the kidney." Chloe's mother licked her lips. "He urged your father and siblings to pray."

Chloe's eyes closed.

At first he thought she was dismayed. Then he noticed her lips moving. He bowed his head and added to her prayer. Once done, he looked up. Chloe's face was streaming with tears.

He grabbed a tissue, gently wiping them away. "God will take care of her, Chloe."

"Are you sure?"

Lord, please give me wisdom and strengthen my faith, so I can have enough for the both of us. Darryl inhaled. "I'm sure He loves her more than we do, so He'll heal her." He begged God to heal Jamie on this side of heaven.

Chapter Thirty

J t had taken two days, but her fever had finally gone. Chloe tapped her fingers against the armrest on the wheelchair. Since she'd been fever free for twenty-four hours, her nurse had been allowed to wheel her to Jamie's room. Well, outside of it. She wasn't permitted to enter her ICU room.

As she peered through the room window, looking at her precious sister, Chloe doubted. The belief that God had called her to donate her kidney seemed questionable now. Now, she doubted herself and her ability to hear or distinguish that still, small voice. How was she supposed to know if it was the Holy Spirit talking to her? Others had to have the same doubts. Wasn't it crazy to believe that God talked to common people? She was no Moses, no Deborah…just Chloe. A girl who had loved God for as long as she could remember, but could no longer say that He heard her cry.

Sure, she could quote scripture and tell anyone who'd listen where they could find them in the Bible, but what did it matter if she didn't believe them? When had she become a hypocrite? She sighed as the nurse slowed and stopped the chair. Her thoughts were going to have to wait. Right now, she needed to pull herself together. To stand strong for Jamie. To fight the fight and believe that God would heal her.

"Can I please go inside?"

Nurse Helen bit her lip. "You had a fever."

"And I'm fever free. I don't have to touch her. But maybe if I could talk to her she'd feel better. Don't ICU patients get visitors?"

"Fine. Five minutes." Helen wheeled her into the room.

All the curtains had been drawn, creating a horrible darkness. It smelled of sickness and...death. Chloe gripped the edge of the bed as she slowly rose to look down into her sister's face.

Her skin had a sallow look, sweat beads lining her forehead and curling her dark hair.

"Hey, Ames. How are you?"

Jamie's eyes blinked and a lazy grin filled her face. "Hey, CeeCee. I heard you had a fever."

"It must have been out of sympathy for you."

Jamie chuckled, then coughed as her body shook.

She swallowed, trying to force the lump of tears back down. *Stay strong, don't fall apart.*

The nurse held a cup of water to her lips, letting Jamie drink from the straw. "Thank you," Jamie rasped out.

"Sure thing. I'm going to wait outside. I'll be in when you're time is up." She looked pointedly at Chloe.

She nodded in acknowledgement.

"You look tired," Jamie said. "Sit down, stop towering over me."

"Jeez even in your sickened state you're still bossy."

Jamie grinned. "I want to hear about your God."

Chloe stared at her hands. Was she asking because she was curious or afraid of death? "What do you want to know?"

"Why do you believe in Him?"

She exhaled. Why did she? She leaned back in her wheelchair, gazing off. "When I was little, I didn't have any kids my age to play with. I'm talking about four or five before I started school."

Jamie nodded.

"I desperately wanted someone to play with. I begged my Grandma but she was always busy at church. One day, she told me that I wasn't lonely because God was always with me." The memory flooded her senses, warming her soul, and stinging her eyes with unshed tears. She blinked.

"From that moment, I talked to Him. I didn't do it aloud, but it was like I was in continual prayer with Him. I told Him when I was happy, sad. I prayed for my friends to know Him and not feel lonely..." Her voice trailed off.

"Did you feel like you were talking to yourself?"

"Not at all. Sure, sometimes I didn't get an immediate response, but I was used to the lulls in the conversation on His end. When I got older I didn't consider them spaces in conversation but a reminder for me to be quiet and listen."

How had she forgotten that?

She met Jamie's gaze, suppressing her own tears as her sister cried. She blinked to keep Jamie from looking blurry.

"I heard Him."

Chloe's pulse quickened. "When?" She leaned forward to make sure she didn't miss a word.

"Yesterday. I hurt. I was cold and miserable. I wanted everyone to leave me alone but not leave me alone. Finally, I cried out for help. I wasn't thinking of

God but I must have subconsciously. I heard or felt…I'm not really sure how to explain it, but I know He spoke to me."

"What did he say?" She gripped her chair in anticipation.

Jamie smiled. "He said you're not alone." ."

∽

The sound of tears propelled him down the hall. He had the eerie feeling it was Chloe. If it was, there couldn't be a good reason for the tears. He jogged down the hall, and then stopped abruptly outside her hospital room.

She *was* crying.

He sent a prayer heavenward and walked into the room. "What's wrong, babe?"

The sound of sobs ceased as she met his gaze. Tears streamed down her face endlessly. "I'm scared," she whispered.

Relief coursed through him. He thought Jamie had died, but if Chloe was scared, then her sister was still alive. "Why are you scared?"

He sat on the edge of her bed and took hold of her hand.

"What if she dies? I don't know if I could handle that."

Softly, he wiped away her tears. "I'll be with you no matter what, as will the Lord. We're praying, the others are praying, even the doctors. God will answer our prayers. You have to believe that."

"And what if He decides to heal her in Heaven?"

He gulped, not sure how to answer her question. It was a valid question. *Help me out, Lord!*

"Does your faith depend on a yes?" He wasn't sure where the words came from. They shocked him to his core and judging by the look on Chloe's face…her's as well.

She bit her lip. "It shouldn't."

"No it shouldn't, but that's not what I asked you. Does your faith depend on a yes from God?"

Her head shook vigorously and then a shout erupted from her. "Yes! I know it shouldn't but it does. How much more does He want me to take? He took my parents then took away the only person who stuck around and loved me. Now He wants to take my sister?"

Sobs erupted from the depths of her soul. He laid down next to her and wrapped his arms around her, taking care not to jostle her. He wanted to say more but his insides urged him to remain silent. Maybe God was at work in her. Or maybe not. All he knew was he'd be there through it all.

Chapter Thirty-One

J amie was dead.

Her mind couldn't comprehend it. Couldn't wrap around those three words. There had to be a mistake. Chloe stared at her sister. She had no idea why her father chose an open casket. It was traumatic. Like a train wreck, she couldn't look away.

The stillness hurt her soul. The sounds of crying and sniffling barely penetrated the haze. All she could think of was the abomination that was the dead body of her beloved sister. Jamie had never been this still in life.

Her skin was pale despite Char's efforts with her arsenal of makeup. Why Char wanted to put makeup on her dead sister was beyond her. No one was reacting the way they should. Instead of Charlotte breaking down in tears, she had vowed to bring life with her makeup. Instead of her father cursing her out for giving a kidney that failed to do its job, he had held her until her tears subsided.

And JJ. JJ broke down in tears. She hadn't seen so much emotion on his face before. He'd always walked the fence of neutrality but in the face of death, God brought forth emotions. She swallowed at the thought of the One she had loved from childhood.

How could He take her sister? Was it because of her response to Darryl's question? She had never thought He'd be a punishing God, but apparently she was wrong. Wrong on so many levels. She didn't know what to do with herself.

Her hand reached out of its own accord and wrapped around Jamie's lifeless hand. The cold didn't concern her, because hers was cold as well. All warmth had left when Jamie drew her last breath. Did she go to heaven? Had her conversation with God led to salvation? Would her sister have felt His presence?

She wished she could ask her. Wished she could have saved her from death.

"Why did He take you from me?"

Jamie's eyes opened. "Because your faith is misplaced. I am not an idol."

Chloe screamed and shot up in bed. She looked around, frantic from the nightmare that had gripped her by the throat. The clock in the hospital wall showed it was four in the morning. Gripping the hand rails, she swung her legs to the side. She needed to see Jamie. Needed to make sure she was alive and well.

"What are you doing, Chloe?"

She paused as her night nurse walked in the room. "I need to see Jamie."

"At this hour?" Kate's brows reached for her hairline.

"I had a horrible dream. I need to know she's still alive."

"Oh, sweetie, calm down. I'll get a chair and take you down."

Chloe shook her head. "No, that will take too long. Just let me walk."

"Fine, but you hold on to me. Don't forget you had surgery."

She grabbed her arm, letting her legs gather strength.

The walk to the ICU seemed endless, but when they entered Jamie's room, she discovered only a couple of minutes had passed. Jamie laid on her side, her face peaceful and free of sweat.

"See the monitors. That's her heartbeat. She's alive."

"Thank God."

Tears came fast and furious, but she welcomed them. Jamie was alive. It was all a horrible dream. The trip back to her room was filled with thanksgiving. The feeling of relief lasted until she snuggled under her covers.

Then her mind began to swirl with questions.

In her dream, Jamie had told her she made her into an idol. What did that mean? She never put anything before God...did she?

What about the desire for friends and family?

Past prayers popped in her mind, reminding her of how often she asked God for friends and family. The friends request had stopped once Jo and Michelle had entered the picture. Her request for a family, however, had never died. She had prayed those words continuously until she tired of hearing it.

What must God have thought?

"You shall have no other gods before Me."

The verse pierced her heart as understanding flooded her being. She had made family an idol. Had desired it above her relationship with God. Had made it the answer to every issue she had. And when God began to give her the desire of her heart she complained, not satisfied with a restored relationship with her sisters and brother. No, she had to bemoan the lack of parental figures in her life.

Never mind the precious years her grandmother had been around. But God had blessed her with time with Michelle's parents, Jo's parents...even Evan's parents had been there for her in some form or capacity. The desire to call flesh and blood her own had consumed her. She had spiraled downward into the pit of her own creation.

"I'm so sorry, Lord. I never meant to put you in any other position but first. I see the error of my ways. I'm so sorry."

Sobs racked her body as she realized the enormity of the situation. She had placed family above God. He was the Father to the fatherless...what made her think she needed anyone but Him?

She hadn't let Him fill the recesses of her heart. Instead, she tried to put people in His place, not realizing they would never feed the need only God was meant to fill.

∼

Chloe was being released from the hospital today. Darryl resisted the urge to hustle down the hallway. He'd offered to take her home...or rather, back to Jamie's place. Miraculously, Jamie had turned a corner the other day. Chloe had informed him how Jamie's body began to accept the kidney and her blood work started showing the results.

His knuckles rapped on Chloe's hospital door.

"Come in."

He smiled at the sight of her in a sundress with a sweater. He was so used to seeing her in dresses that the absence of them had muddied his brain. Now everything seemed right in the world.

"You ready to bounce?"

She giggled. "Who still says that?" She gave a bemused grin. "Yes, I'm ready to go."

He offered his hand, grinning like the Cheshire cat as she placed her hand in his.

As they headed to Jamie's place, silence descended in the car. It wasn't an uncomfortable one but a sign of contentment. Never had he felt so comfortable around another person.

"So, babe, I was thinking of throwing a get together for our families. You know, see how they interact."

"I'm not so sure about that. I still have fences to mend."

He reached over and took her hand. "Then I'll help you mend them. Invite whomever you want. I'll grill. You can make some sides, and together we'll come to grips with the family God gave us."

"Sounds easier than reality."

He sighed. "Trust me, I know it, but we need to take this step. We've let past issues weigh us down for far too long. I want to walk through this life unburdened...knowing I did all I was supposed to do and then some. I can't if I'm withholding forgiveness."

"You're right."

"One for the record books."

The sound of her laughter warmed his soul. When she was happy all seemed right in the world.

Chapter Thirty-Two

*L*ighting the charcoal in his grill, Darryl whispered his entreaty to the Lord. Today *had* to be a good day. He'd threaten anyone bodily harm if they tried to make it a bad one. He smiled at the irony of his thoughts, but it echoed how he felt. He and Chloe were going to attempt to bring their families together this afternoon now that Jamie was out of the hospital.

Somewhere in the recesses of his mind he told himself if their families meshed, then an impending marriage wasn't far from the horizon. He grabbed the kabobs from the fridge and headed outside. Nothing he liked more than to grill in his own backyard.

Of course, his yard wasn't as grand as Evan's or Guy's but that's because he hadn't begged Jo to take pity on it yet. Besides, he was a simple man. All he really needed was a grill and the space to use it.

He glanced at his watch, wondering when everyone would arrive. He knew Chloe would probably be the first to arrive as well as his grandmother, since Chloe had offered to pick her up. She'd been cleared to drive from her surgery.

His mother had driven in from Ohio yesterday with her husband. She promised to come and not make waves.

It was definitely going to be an interesting day.

What would his grandmother say to Chloe's family? He had no idea if they would have any common interests. It was weird how small the gathering would be. He and Chloe got the short end of the stick when it came to family. Her father and mother were coming as well as Char, Jamie, and JJ.

He thought back to the visit with his mother. It had been beyond awkward but hopefully it would soon become comfortable. He'd been praying and praying about his mother and father. That forgiveness would come to him and he'd be able to extend the same grace that God had blessed him with. Yet his stomach still tensed at the memories of his childhood.

The doorbell rang, pulling him from his reverie. He opened the door and sighed with relief.

"Hey, Chloe. Grandmother."

His grandmother offered the side of her face. He leaned forward, placing a kiss on her cheek. "Thanks for coming, Grandmother."

She nodded. "I'm proud of you. Y'all have an interesting mix of company today."

He chuckled. "I do believe you're getting eccentric in your old age."

Her eyebrow raised before 'old' left his lips. "Darryl, a woman of my age is not old, we are merely seasoned with wisdom that the youth so often lack."

She walked away muttering under her breath.

Chloe leaned against him, her arms coming around his waist. "Are we doing the right thing? Maybe we should have done this one on one."

He rubbed her back. "Nah, babe. If we keep on this path, there will be many events that will come and go.

We can't be worried about who we can invite, worried about who will be upset."

Her shoulders rose and breath warmed his chest. "I suppose you're right." Her voice was muffled by his shirt.

As he held her in his arms, he couldn't help but think maybe he should cancel the party. All he wanted to do was sit on the couch with Chloe in his arms. Just be with her. Not to worry about his family. He'd rather start a new family with just her. They could have kids and share the importance of family. Then again, he'd have to have a good relationship with his family in order to cement that fact to their children. He shook his head. *You're getting ahead of yourself.*

He hadn't broached the topic of marriage because he was too scared to hear her thoughts. Plus, he didn't want to move too fast, even though he knew she was the one. She'd always been the one.

Chloe pulled away and looked up at him. "We're going to get through this day."

"Definitely." He leaned forward, brushing his lips against hers.

A sigh greeted him, drawing him in. He slid his hands into her curls, holding her head close as his mouth explored hers.

"Did you invite us over to watch your make out session?"

They flew apart at the sound of Jamie's voice. Darryl felt the heat climb his neck and snake around to his cheeks, heating his face thoroughly with embarrassment. Chloe's father glowered at him.

"Just a little distracted."

"I'll say," Char said with a snort.

"Glad we supplied you with some laughter," Chloe said, though her cheeks were bright read. "Come on in and meet Darryl's grandmother."

He watched as she ushered them inside, guiding them toward the living room where his grandmother waited. It was almost like they were hosting a party as a married couple. He rubbed his hands in anticipation. He went to close the front door, but stopped. His mother had arrived.

"Hello."

"Hi Darryl," she flashed a smile filled with hope and anxiousness.

Some things never changed.

"We're all inside. Almost everyone's here."

He shook Marvin's hand and ushered them into the living room. Introductions were made and the group slowly found their groove.

The sound of the doorbell muted their conversation. He frowned. "Who are we missing?"

Chloe swallowed, meeting his gaze. "That might be my mother."

He exhaled, trying to remember how to breathe. Why had he thought it was a good idea to bring everyone together? What level of awkward would appear at the entrance of her mother? There was only one way to find out.

"I'll get the door, Darryl."

He nodded too petrified to talk. The day was about to make a turn. He could only pray it was for the best and not the worst.

❧

Chloe bit her lip nervously as she stood in front of the door. *Lord, please help me know what to do or say. Please let me be accepting.* When Darryl first suggested the get together, she hadn't intended on inviting her mother. Except God had different plans. She wanted to ignore her mother's presence, but God wouldn't let her.

Now she had to smile and act normal while feeling anything but. Whispering another prayer, she opened the door.

Her mother stood with a bouquet of daisies. "Thank you for the invitation, Chloe Anne."

Her soft-spoken voice reminded Chloe of herself. Her grandmother hadn't been loud, but she had a force behind her voice. Something that skipped her mother and her generation. What were the odds?

"Come on in. We were getting ready to bless the food." In her mind, if they had blessed the food then her mother wouldn't make it. Why couldn't she accept her mother's presence?

"Sorry, I didn't mean to hold you up. I got turned around."

How? It wasn't like Freedom Lake was huge, but maybe her mother had been filled with nerves as well. "No problem. Thank you for the daisies."

Her mother smiled, the look not quite reaching the eyes. "Chloe Anne, I just wanted to say I'm sorry. Sorry I wasn't there when you needed me."

She swallowed, hoping to push down the tears and words she was sure to regret. "Thank you for the apology. I just need a little time to work through all my emotions."

Tears filled her mother's eyes and she nodded. "Understood."

∽

"We survived." Chloe leaned back against the sofa.

"We did." Darryl weaved his fingers through hers. "Let's not do that again anytime soon."

She chuckled. "It was your idea."

"I know. What was I thinking?"

She turned to stare at him. Taking in the curls and chocolate-brown eyes that pulled her in. "You were thinking we needed to stop saying we'd forge relationships with our parents and start doing it."

"I guess we needed to learn to accept our family just as we want them to accept us."

"I accept you, Darryl."

He trailed a finger down her face. "And I accept you. All of you."

She gulped. She needed to tell him before she lost nerve and let her mind talk her heart out of what she already knew. "I love you."

His lips descended in a kiss of acceptance. "And I love you."

Chapter Thirty-Three

*D*arryl strolled slowly down the sidewalk. He lightly gripped Chloe's hand, trying to keep her from sensing how tense he was. Did she have any clue how important their "little" walk was?

Probably not.

He *hoped* not.

He hadn't even told any of his friends to ensure it would be a surprise. If he had, it would have only added to the pressure. His nerves couldn't stand anymore.

"It's so nice out."

Her soft voice washed over him, and he smiled at her. To be able to see her every day. To hold her. To simply do life with her was more than he could ask for. But he was going to ask. *Had* to.

"I'm glad fall is around the corner."

"Why? Football season?" She nudged him softly with her elbow.

He laughed. "Nah, I just like the cooler temps."

They turned the corner, and he tempered his steps as the vacant lot where Chloe's grandmother's house used to sit.

The lot had never been placed for sale, but he was ready to pull strings if necessary.

"Have you ever thought of rebuilding here?"

"I had the option at first, but it seemed overwhelming."

"And now?"

"That house isn't me." She shrugged. "Old Victorians aren't my style. Sure, I like some vintage items, but when it comes to my home and décor. I go for classic yet modern. Something like your place."

She peeked up at him as if hinting.

Or was that his overactive imagination?

"Huh. I would have never guessed you liked my place. It's not like it has yellow in it or anything."

She chuckled. "Jokester, huh?"

He always told himself decorating in yellow and black had been to his appeal, but the longer he was with Chloe the more he wondered if his brain had been trying to help him win points all along.

"Hey, before I forget." He pulled out a necklace box out of his cargo shorts pocket. "I wanted to give you something special. Just because."

Her grin grew wide, showcasing her bright sunny smile. "What is it?" She clasped her hands together in excitement.

He handed it over and watched as she opened it.

Her soft gasp seemed to echo softly. "A locket?" She opened it, and then stood still.

Time stopped. His heart right along with it.

She met his gaze, wonderment shining through. "Is this us?"

"Yeah." He cleared his throat. "My grandmother had it. Apparently, we were toddler sweethearts."

Her hand came up, covering her mouth, shaking with emotion. "I can't believe this. This is probably the best gift I've ever received."

"Then you probably don't want the other one."

Her head snapped up. "You have another one?"

"I do." He nodded, wondering why he had to use those words to reply. "This one comes with strings however."

Her brow wrinkled in confusion. "What are the strings?"

He pulled out the ring box and flipped it open. "Be mine forever."

Her mouth dropped open.

Silence filled the afternoon skies.

And more silence.

"Chloe?" He cleared his throat wondering when puberty had started again. "Chloe, babe, you're kind of killing me here."

A tear slipped down her face. "I'm speechless."

"Good speechless or bad?"

Her shiny eyes met his. "Good."

Relief poured over him in waves. "I can handle good speechless." He swallowed. "I kind of botched the whole thing."

He dropped to one knee. "Chloe Ann Smith, would you do me the honor of marrying me?"

"Yes," she choked out.

He stood up as he slid the ring on her finger. "I love you," he whispered as his lips met hers in affirmation. He pulled away, running a hand down her cheek.

"I love you, too, Darryl. And you didn't botch it. That was the best proposal ever."

The End

ACKNOWLEDGMENTS

To my husband: thank you for walking this life with me. I love you.

To my boys: thank you for naming Chloe's mom and her grandmother. Love you much!

To Andrea Boyd: Thank you so much for your critiques and walking along side me in this writing journey. I can't believe I ever published a book without you.

To my early readers: many thanks to Kara Esslebach, Sally Shupe, Jean Volk, and Debb Hackett. Thank you so much for offering me feedback on how to make this story better. Your encouragement and willingness to read Finally Accepted is a huge blessing.

To Roderick Wiggins: thank you for answering my fire questions. Any mistakes are my own.

To Peri Bever: thank you for naming Chloe's dog and for always encouraging me in my writing.

ABOUT THE AUTHOR

Toni Shiloh is a wife, mom, and Christian fiction writer. Once she understood the powerful saving grace thanks to the love of Christ, she was moved to honor her Savior. She writes to bring Him glory and to learn more about His goodness.

She spends her days hanging out with her husband and their two boys. She is a member of the American Christian Fiction Writers (ACFW) and president of the Virginia Chapter.

You can find her on her website at http://tonishiloh.wordpress.com and signup for her Book News newsletter at http://eepurl.com/cmNFKD.

CPSIA information can be obtained
at www.ICGtesting.com
Printed in the USA
LVHW050007030622
720385LV00002B/210